Logan rose and stepped through the kitchen door of the tavern, took in the scene beyond. A mustachioed man in white was at a gas range to his left, shaking a skillet full of something that sizzled on the heat. The waiter who had brought his wine was arranging slices of crusty bread in a basket at a granite-topped table in the center of the room. He looked up, startled, as Logan came through the door.

"Signor," he said, "you cannot come here. It is not for the customers."

Logan ignored the protest, ignored the bartender in the public room behind him, who was also saying, "Signor, Signor," his voice getting closer. He let his mind go, let the sight and, most of all, the smell of the kitchen just come to him, without trying to focus on any one detail. And again, it happened: *The stove, that's different. The counter, that's the same. And the door leading outside, it's been painted but I know it.*

As he looked at the door that led to the tavern's backyard, it opened. Through it came an old woman in a black dress, her face lined but full of dignity, her dark eyes meeting his with a challenge that left Logan in no doubt that she was the authority here.

The bartender was tugging fitfully at his elbow from behind, the waiter was advancing toward him with a worried look and making shooing motions with both hands, and the chef had turned from his cooking but the expression of outrage that had begun to appear on his face was rapidly dying. Logan did not see any of them.

His eyes were fixed on the old woman. The look of resentment at the intruder in her domain had given way to astonishment, tinged by something that had crept into her own kitchen.

She stood, her dark eyes wide and mouth open. Then she brought one pale hand to her lips and her voice came in a whisper. "Patch!"

Also available from Pocket Books

*Wolverine: Weapon X* by Marc Cerasini
*Wolverine: Road of Bones* by David Alan Mack

# WOLVERINE®

# LIFEBLOOD

a novel by
Hugh Matthews

based on the
Marvel Comic Book

POCKET STAR BOOKS
NEW YORK   LONDON   TORONTO   SYDNEY

An *Original* Publication of POCKET BOOKS

A Pocket Star Book published by POCKET BOOKS, a division of Simon & Schuster, Inc. 1230 Avenue of the Americas, New York, NY 10020

This book is a work of fiction. Names, characters, places and incidents are products of the author's imagination or are used fictitiously. Any resemblance to actual events or locales or persons, living or dead, is entirely coincidental.

MARVEL, Wolverine and all related characters names and likeness thereof are trademarks of Marvel Characters, Inc. and are used with permission. Copyright © 2007 by Marvel Characters, Inc. All rights reserved. www.marvel.com This novelization is produced under license from Marvel Characters, Inc.

ISBN-13: 978-1-4165-1073-4
ISBN-10:     1-4165-1073-7

This Pocket Star Books paperback edition March 2007

10 9 8 7 6 5 4 3 2 1

POCKET STAR BOOKS and colophon are registered trademarks of Simon & Schuster, Inc.

Cover design by John Vairo Jr.; Art by David Mack

Manufactured in the United States of America

For information regarding special discounts for bulk purchases, please contact Simon & Schuster Special Sales at 1-800-456-6798 or business@simonandschuster.com.

To Richard Pedersen, who clued me in.

## Ottawa, Canada, the present

COLD.

Just as the gray day slid toward evening, the north wind brisked up, bringing rain so cold it turned to ice that stuck to whatever it touched. The bare branches of the trees along Elgin Street were sheathed in a glistening armor that dragged them down and froze them to the ground. The smallest twigs had snapped but the chill coating held them in place, would not let them fall.

The small man in the plaid wool jacket and black knitted cap walked into the wind, broad shoulders hunched, scarred hands deep in the pockets of his tattered jeans. But his face met the icy blast straight on, let the frozen crystals sting his skin and make the bones beneath the flesh ache, as if they were being scraped by knives.

Pain was good. Pain was real. It cut through the fog inside him, slashed through the roiling, colorless nothingness that stuffed his head. With pain came memory—or what passed for recollection in a mind that could not connect faces to names nor places to events, a mind that did not know if the pictures it conjured to fill its inner screen came from true recall or false, maybe just from dreams, or stories he'd heard.

Or from the nightmares that chased him, screaming in rage and horror, back into wakefulness, back into the fog.

*Heya, heya, heya.* At first he thought the chant was coming from inside his head. Sometimes he heard voices, random scraps of speech, mostly in English, sometimes in other languages that he understood. *Heya, heya, heya* it came again, louder now as his steps took him past Confederation Park. Off to his right, unseen behind the white rain, someone was beating a drum, a simple double-beat rhythm to accompany the voice.

*I've heard that before,* the man thought. He stopped and let the sound pass through him, held his mind back when it tried to get a grip on the memory. He'd learned that grasping didn't work, would make the recollection disappear, like trying to grab smoke.

*Heya, heya, heya* with the drum beating underneath—*bom-bom, bom-bom, bom-bom*—like somebody had cut open the world to show its living heart, he thought. And that brought up an image: a man split from gullet to groin, lying on his back, looking up, his eyes clouding in death.

*Who is that man?* He couldn't help reaching for the memory, but even as he grasped for it, the picture faded, the dead eyes the last to go. Still, the drum and the chant continued. The small man turned toward them and went into the park, not following the concrete path that was slick with ice but walking through short winter grass that crackled and broke beneath his heavy boots.

*Something big ahead,* he thought. Through the rain he saw a block of gray surmounted by dark shapes—people, animals, a great bird with wings spread wide. Now he came close enough to see that it was a monument. On a massive granite base stood four figures, three men and a woman, cast in dark bronze. Around them were four animals—grizzly, wolf, bison, and caribou—and above their heads a giant eagle soared. On the front of the plinth, a plaque announced in English and French that the monument commemorated the sacrifices of the First Nations, Métis and Inuit men and women who had worn Canadian uniforms in wars and peacekeeping missions.

The drumming and chanting were coming from the far side, but the small man's eyes had dropped from the heroic figures to the two rows of flowered wreaths, standing on wire tripods, that were ranged along the steps leading up to the monument. He had a vague sense that the presence of the wreaths meant that it must be not long since the Remembrance Day observances of November 11. The date brought a flash of memory—a soundless image of men with weary faces and mud-spattered uniforms throwing helmets shaped like soup bowls into the air, some with mouths set in bitter smiles, some weeping openly—then the picture was gone.

One of the wreaths drew his gaze. It stood apart

from the others, a small circle of dark red flowers woven through evergreen boughs. At its center, encased in plastic, was a framed photograph of a man with strongly aboriginal features, the cheeks flat-planed, the narrow eyes almost asiatic. He wore a beret with a parachute badge. Beneath the picture, a wide ribbon bore the legend SGT. THOMAS GEORGE PRINCE, 1915–1977.

The chant and drum grew louder, but the small man did not move. He stared at the black-and-white image and the man in the photo looked back at him with the confident half smile of the consummate warrior, a smile that said, *I know who I am and I know what I can do.*

But it wasn't the smile that held the man motionless in the freezing rain, staring at the image while the ice built on his shoulders and covered his wool cap like a helmet. He stared at the picture of the aboriginal sergeant in the old-fashioned, British-style Canadian Army uniform and more images came: bright sunlight on dry earth, small trees with dark leaves and clumps of green fruit—*olive trees,* said his own voice in his head—a dusty road and soldiers marching in puttees and canvas webbing, bolt-action rifles slung from their shoulders.

"I know you," he said, his voice a grating whisper. And as he spoke the drum ceased, the chant ended on one last *heya.* The small man stooped and reached for the photograph. It came free of the wreath. He pulled the ribbon loose and wrapped it tightly around the plastic-covered cardboard, then he opened his coat and stuffed both prizes inside, against the worn checked shirt that covered his hard-muscled torso.

He buttoned the coat back up. Now he stood in the falling sleet that whispered as it struck the ground, no longer noticing the bite of the wind that made the ice-covered trees rattle like dead men's bones. He put his hand to his chest, pressed the cardboard against the beat of his heart, and said again, "I know you."

When he stepped around the monument to find the drummer and chanter, no one was there.

## The Empty Quarter, Saudi Arabia, the present

HEAT.

Outside the camouflaged hangar, disguised to look like a low-rise in the barren landscape, the air rippled with desert heat under a sun so fierce it seemed to turn the sky white. The lean man with close-cropped iron-gray hair stood within the open doors, the toes of his polished black boots just behind the line of light and darkness that separated the hidden building's shade from the searing blast of the sun. His ice-blue eyes followed the progress of the VTOL jet as it came in low and slow to hover in a cloud of grit a short distance beyond the open hangar. The plane, mottled with desert camouflage paint, settled onto its three wheels. Its whining thrusters throttled down, then turned aft to roll the jet slowly into the hangar.

Wolfgang Freiherr von Strucker turned on his heel with parade-ground precision and accompanied the aircraft into the darkness. Behind him, swarthy men in loose, long-sleeved robes of white cotton, their heads bound in flowing white scarves secured by a doubled black cord, rushed to roll the outer doors closed. The jet's engines cycled down and its double canopy levered up as the Arabs pushed a wheeled staircase into position. The pilot remained in his place, making notations in the airlog, while the man in the rear seat left the plane and descended to the hangar floor.

"*Salaam aleikum,*" said von Strucker, the traditional Arabic greeting accompanied by a curt dip of the head and a click of heels brought sharply together, which the baron had learned as a cadet in a Prussian military academy long, long ago.

"*Aleikum salaam,*" said the visitor, in the accents of Yemen, adding only the smallest gesture of one hand. He wore a Savile Row suit with an understated pin-stripe, but his olive-skinned face had the stark grim-ness of a desert warrior and his liquid brown eyes were lit from within by a gleam of fanaticism that had made him the chief of operations for the shadowy Is-lamist cabal known as the Foundation.

"We will go below," the Prussian said, leading his

visitor toward an elevator at the rear of the hangar. A moment later they were descending deep into the living rock of the desert, the elevator door opening on to a subterranean corridor walled, floored, and roofed in reinforced concrete. Boot heels clacking on the polished surface, von Strucker led the way to a heavy metal door guarded by an Arab man in combat fatigues, who snapped to attention as the two men approached.

Von Strucker acknowledged the salute with a fractional nod, then reached behind the guard to tap a code into a numbered keypad beside the door. The barrier slid silently into the wall, revealing an unlit room beyond. The two men advanced into the room, the door sliding closed behind them. The Prussian indicated a low square table, ten feet by ten, that dominated the center of the space. Its top held sixteen square blocks of a city in miniature: houses in the classic Arab style, with windowless outer walls enclosing courtyards and gardens. The models were faithful replicas, von Strucker knew, of a particular neighborhood in the city of Amman, capital of the Hashemite Kingdom of Jordan. The walls surrounding the table were covered with huge blown-up photographs of the city and large-scale, detailed maps, marked in places with broad red arrows and concentric black circles that represented lines of fire and calculated gradations of blast damage.

The Yemeni cast his eye over the table and the wall displays, his face impassive.

"The plan is complete," von Strucker said. "We

have run simulations based on all likely scenarios and several that are barely possible. The outcome in each case is certain: neither the Jordanian foreign minister nor the American ambassador will survive their encounter with the Green Fist."

The visitor leaned over the table, reached into a representation of a street, and touched a manicured fingernail to the rear of a toy limousine whose fender bore a miniature Stars and Stripes. He flicked the little car, sending it careering down the avenue to strike the curb outside the model of the foreign minister's house. It flipped over, its tiny wheels spinning.

The Yemeni's dark eyes looked up at von Strucker. "The plan," he said, "is changed."

The Prussian stiffened. "The plan," he said, "is perfect."

The visitor picked up the overturned car and set it aright again. "Yes," he said, "*this* plan is. But a new opportunity has arisen. We are calling it Operation Severed Head."

The baron was used to sudden changes of strategy from the Foundation. "Who is the target?" he said. "And where will we strike?"

The Yemeni smiled a cruel smile. "The Green Zone," he said, "in Baghdad."

"And who is the target?"

The Yemeni's thin lips framed their heartless smile again as he savored the thought. Then he told the baron the name of the man who was marked for death.

# Ottawa, Canada, the present

## "I WANT TO FIND OUT ABOUT THIS MAN."

The librarian hadn't heard the man's approach. She looked at the photo of an aboriginal soldier that had appeared on her desk, then at the hand that had placed it before her. There were strange scars between the knuckles, scars on top of scars, as if sharp knives had been thrust into the flesh more than once. She looked up and a cold shock went through her when her eyes met his. She'd seen plenty of crazies—the public library was where the street-dwelling insane passed some of their tortured days—but this one was different. She saw a hunger in his gaze, and behind that hunger she sensed a savagery that was barely contained. He was like something from a bygone age, a time when disputes were settled with spilled blood and torn flesh.

"I want to know who he was," the man said, the voice more like an animal's growl than human speech. And now he flung something else onto the woman's desk, a small bundle of wadded cloth. She pulled at an edge and it became a crumpled ribbon of black satin stitched with letters of gold. She read the name and the dates and a great wash of relief went through her. She could be rid of him.

"Come with me," she said, rising. Her desk was on the edge of the open area that welcomed visitors to the main branch of the Ottawa Public Library. She now set off across the foyer toward a free-standing set of six shelves that displayed several books beneath a computer-printed banner, decorated with stylized red poppies, that read LEST WE FORGET. On a middle shelf stood a small hardcover book, its title *Tommy Prince, Hero*. She took it and handed it to him and as his scarred hand closed on the small volume, she saw a light come into his eyes. It put her in mind of a scene she'd seen in a nature documentary, when the camera had caught a close-up of a timber wolf just as it came out of a stand of pines and saw a yearling moose calf stranded in deep snow.

She shivered, but the man didn't notice. He was already turning away, carrying the book toward a table and chairs. She watched him as he sat and spread its pages open before him, hunched over it as if he were starving and the book was food. Melting ice dripped from his knit cap onto the paper and he carefully wiped the droplet away with his sleeve, then took off the hat and set it down beside him.

The woman backed away, then turned and went swiftly back to her desk. She got her purse out of the bottom drawer and went quickly to an inner door, using a card slung from a lanyard around her neck to swipe open the security lock. The library would be closing in another hour and she had decided to spend that time downstairs in the quiet of the stacks. If the man needed any more help, let someone else provide it.

• • •

His name was Logan. He was pretty sure of that much, because the envelopes with cash in them that were slipped under the door of his apartment once a month had that name printed on them, and nobody had ever showed up to say, "I'm Logan, where's my money?"

The apartment was a nondescript condo in a converted warehouse in Bytown, the oldest part of Ottawa, named for the colonel of Queen Victoria's Royal Engineers who had laid out the original town next to the fork where the Rideau and Ottawa rivers met. Logan was also sure he didn't own the space he lived in—he never got tax notices—and he figured that whoever was sending him the money was also taking care of the rent.

He'd tried waiting at his door, ready to yank it open the moment the envelope was slid under. But all he had achieved was that he got no money that day. Loitering in the hallway or keeping a watch on the building from across the street brought the same result. So when money day came, he went out and walked the streets, peering into faces that always found a reason to look away fast, wanting to see just one person he recognized—one body he could grab and hold immobile in front of him while he said, "I *know* you. Do you know me?"

And now, at last, he had found a face that rang his bell. Tommy Prince—the name meant nothing. But about the face he was sure. When he stared at the photograph, he could see that same face wearing other expressions, could see it from other angles.

Now, hunched over the book at the library, he wanted to tear through the pages, rip the information out of it, satisfy the craving. Instead, he carefully wiped away a drop of water that fell from his hair. He turned to the first page and began to read.

## The Empty Quarter, Saudi Arabia, the present

"IT CANNOT BE DONE," VON STRUCKER SAID.

"It must be done," the Yemeni said, adding, "*Inshalla.*" If God wills it.

The Prussian passed his hand over the stubble of his hair and said, "The security is too tight."

"There is always a way," said the visitor. "Find it."

"Why there? Why not somewhere else?"

The Arab's eyes shone. "Because it is Baghdad, the city of the Caliphs, the successors of the Prophet, blessings and peace be upon him." He paused, then said, "And the timing is most propitious."

"What is special about the timing?"

The Yemeni clasped his dry palms together and touched his crossed thumbs to his lips. "It is a time," he said, "when the enemy is at his most . . . sentimental."

## Ottawa, Canada, the present

SERGEANT TOMMY PRINCE WAS AN OJIBWAY from the Brokenhead band on the Canadian prairies. A descendant of the great Salteaux chief Peguis, he grew up to be an expert hunter in the wild lands around southwest Lake Winnipeg. When World War II began, he volunteered for the Canadian Army, where his skills as a marksman and tracker made him a natural for the first combined special forces unit, the Devil's Brigade, that brought together the cream of Canadian and U.S. fighting men for behind-the-lines operations in the Italian and Normandy campaigns. He became the most highly decorated aboriginal soldier in Canadian history, receiving the Military Medal from King George VI and the Silver Star from President Franklin Delano Roosevelt of the United States. He later returned to uniform and fought in Korea, where he was wounded and was decorated again for valor, then came home to be treated as "just another Indian," in a time when it was illegal for Native Canadians to vote or buy a bottle of whiskey.

It took Logan less than an hour to go through the slim volume. He read about the time Prince had repaired a field telephone cable in full sight of German infantry by pretending to be a cantankerous Italian farmer stooping to tie his shoe. He read about the time Prince led his special forces comrades deep behind enemy lines to capture more than a thousand German soldiers who thought they were safely bivouacked far from the front. He read about how the aging veteran, forgotten and sunk into poverty, had to pawn his ten hard-won medals to buy groceries.

"They use you, then they throw you away," he said to himself, but his voice carried and people looking for books on nearby shelves decided that what they were searching for must be in some other part of the library. The Ojibway soldier's story rang echoes from the deeper cellars of Logan's mind. Some of the incidents itched at the edge of his consciousness, like the remnants of the dreams that clung to him when he awoke in the mornings, but always wisped away when he tried to examine them.

"But it can't be," he said to the sergeant looking out at him from the picture in the book, the same image he had torn from the commemorative wreath. "You were too long ago."

The Canadian Army's Italian campaign had been waged in 1943 and 1944, more than sixty years ago. Tommy Prince himself had grown old and died, had been dead now for thirty years. If Logan had known the man—and some part of his mind insisted he had—then Logan himself could not be much less than a hundred years old.

He looked at his hands. They were hard and scarred, but they were the hands of a man still in his prime. He ran one of those hands over his face, his fingertips rasping on the coarse black stubble that grew back almost as fast as he could shave it. His touch told him that his face was seamed with harsh lines around the mouth and at the corners of the eyes, but it was not an old man's face.

He realized that his other hand was gripping the book so tightly that he was bending its cardboard cover. He set the book down and ground his teeth in frustration, jaw muscles bunching under his thick sideburns. *A false lead,* he thought. *Somebody yanking my chain.*

There were times when he sensed that what had happened to his mind was no accident. He had no bumps or concave depressions on his skull that argued for a head injury. *Somebody messed with me. Somebody wants me like this.* He thought again about the words that had sprung out of him when he read about the Ojibway hero sliding into neglect and poverty: *They use you, then they throw you away.*

There was truth in that. He knew it, if he knew nothing else. But then a second thought hit him: *They haven't thrown me away. Like a valuable piece of equipment, they've scrubbed me clean and put me in storage—against the day they need me again.* Either way, somebody had done this to him, stolen his memories—stolen his *life*—and somebody was going to pay.

He looked again at the picture in the book. It was the first page in a section of black-and-white photographs. He'd already flipped through them once, the images of soldiers and shattered buildings tugging at things buried too deep in him to come out into the light. Then he noticed a detail: a roadside sign, black letters on white paint. It read "Ortona."

*I've seen that sign. I know that word.* The book didn't have much to say about what Ortona was. Maybe Tommy Prince hadn't spent much time there. Logan got up and went back to the display with the poppies and the banner whose words—"lest we forget"—were an unwitting mockery of his situation. Another volume on the top shelf caught his eye, this one a big, coffee-table book, full of pictures. Its title: *Canadians at War: The Italian Campaign.* He took it back to the table and spread it open, flipped through the pages—and fell into the past.

## The Empty Quarter, Saudi Arabia, the present

**THE VTOL JET HAD BEEN REFUELED AND** rolled out onto the apron, the hawk-nosed Yemeni back in the jump seat. Von Strucker watched it lift off vertically, then rotate at fifty feet and move off across the uninhabited desert, an area as large as France, that covered southern Saudi Arabia and the coastal nations of Yemen and Oman. The aircraft would fly under radar height for most of the journey south, then appear on air traffic controllers' screens as a private jet owned by a minor sheik whose ancestral lands were in Yemen's rugged western mountains. No air traffic controller would question its identity—at least not twice.

The hangar doors rolled closed and the Prussian descended again, this time to a deeper level than the planning room where he had conferred with his visitor from the south. As he stepped from the elevator, he heard the voices of men raised in Muslim prayer—it was one of those five times of the day—and when he entered the training room, the sixteen mujahideen were kneeling on the prayer mats, their foreheads pressed to the floor. Then, as one, they sat back and each turned left and right, saying, *"As-salaamu aleikum wa rahmatullah,"* to wish each other peace and the blessings of Allah.

Then they rose and rolled up their prayer mats and formed two lines facing each other, shaking out their arms and flexing their knees. The baron watched approvingly. This afternoon's training was in unarmed combat, and these men were not just as good as any special forces cadre in the world; they were better. They were the best. He had seen to that.

Their leader was a tall, sinewy Pashtun from Helmand province in Afghanistan. His parents had named him Batoor, but the men of the Green Fist had given him the Arabic nickname Al Borak—the Lightning. That had been the name of the Prophet Muhammad's favorite horse, but Batoor's change of name had had nothing to do with horses.

He sent von Strucker an inquiring look across the

sprung wooden floor of the training room, but the Prussian moved the fingers of one hand in a way that told Al Borak to carry on with the exercises. The baron wanted to think about the challenge the Yemeni had brought him, and he thought best when the front of his mind was kept busy watching the skills of his crack mujahideen on display. They were orphans or otherwise unwanted outcasts from several Islamic countries who owed their allegiance to none but each other and to the man who had rescued them from poverty and disgrace—a man who, though an infidel himself, had had them thoroughly schooled in the Holy Q'ran. Especially the suras that explained the rightness of jihad.

Now, as the sixteen men positioned themselves in the wide-legged fighting stance and drew their iron-muscled arms and legs into preliminary positions, von Strucker knew again the same fierce pride he had felt, so many years ago now, when he had presented his troop of Iron Eagles to the bespectacled gaze of Heinrich Himmler.

"The *Eisenadler* are the finest soldiers in the world, Herr Reichsführer," he had said. "Stronger, faster, smarter, braver than the legionaries of Rome, the hoplites of Alexander the Great, the Teutonic knights of old."

Himmler had watched the blond young men go through their paces, completing an obstacle course in half the time it would have taken the best squad of Hermann Goering's elite parachute division. He oversaw a demonstration of close-quarter fighting with trench knives and bare hands, with strikes and counterstrikes too fast for the untutored eye to follow.

Then the diminutive man with a neck so scrawny his uniform collars had to be specially fitted yawned and said, "Yes, yes, Herr Baron, but how do you make them last?"

For there was the problem. The baron had chosen the fittest of the fit from the Wehrmacht and the SS, the most fanatically motivated young men the Reich had to offer. He had trained them to their peak, then he had augmented their superb physical condition with a concoction of his own: a mixture of amphetamines, vitamins, and a few rare substances culled from von Strucker's encyclopedic knowledge of what the medical profession called "nontraditional pharmacology"—everything from the curare of the Amazon jungle to the most subtle potions of ancient Chinese herbology.

"How," Himmler said, "do you keep them from burning out?"

The Iron Eagles would only be useful for short-term missions. The baron's stimulants would keep them functioning far beyond their physical limits, giving them speed and power that would swiftly overrun even the most elite troops of the Americans or British. But after two days, at the most three, the Reich's supersoldiers began to shake uncontrollably. They saw horrors at the edge of their vision, started at sounds only they could hear, until they collapsed—sometimes into psychoses from which they could not be redeemed.

"I will find a way," he had told the SS chief, "to make the effects permanent. Then you will have invincible legions with which to conquer the world."

"You mean the Führer will have invincible legions," Himmler said.

The baron had clicked his heels and struck a rigid pose. "Of course, Herr Reichsführer."

But Hitler had never gotten his legions of *übermenn*, though von Strucker could have delivered them. *That is*, he now thought as he watched the Green Fist leap and strike with inhuman speed, *I could have delivered them if only those fools in the concentration camp had kept their hands on that strange little Canadian.*

He sighed. *But at least I got enough out of him to keep me alive*, he thought. *And if I'm alive, then so is he. And one day I will catch him again.*

Al Borak clapped his hands and the sparring instantly stopped, the sixteen mujahideen forming up in two ranks of eight before coming to attention. Their leader had been working them hard, but von Strucker was pleased to see that not one of them was breathing at more than a normal rate. He knew that if he took the pulse of any man in the squad, it would register as lower than forty beats per minute.

Al Borak again sent a look of inquiry toward the baron, and von Strucker signaled his assent. The tall

Pashtun went to a door at the far end of the training room and opened it, then gestured to whoever was beyond. Two men clad in desert fatigues and armed with Kalashnikov rifles entered, walking backward, their weapons trained on three men who now came through the doorway, their hands bound behind them. The escorted men were followed by two more guards whose AK-47s were leveled at the prisoners' backs.

Two of the three men were clad in the black combat fatigues of the U.S. Navy SEALs. The third man was in desert camouflage, with a sand-colored beret that bore the winged dagger and motto "Who Dares Wins" of the British Special Air Services. The escorts brought them out into the center of the wooden floor and stepped back. Another guard followed, carrying a small roll of canvas. At Al Borak's unspoken direction, he laid the cloth on the floor before the prisoners and unrolled it. The bundle's contents clanked together, then were revealed as two SEALs combat knives and the black dagger that was traditional for UK special forces.

Al Borak waved the armed guards away and they departed by the door through which they had entered. He bent and took up the dagger, hefted it to feel the balance, then stepped behind the British trooper. A flick of his hand and the man's bonds were severed. The soldier brought them forward, rubbing at the wrists.

Al Borak had come back around to face the SAS man, giving the prisoner the full benefit of his strange eyes. For though his features were pure Pashtun, the skin dark and the brows heavy and black above a prominent nose, the Green Fist's leader's eyes were as gray as a winter sky—undoubtedly the legacy of one of the many European armies—Russian, British, even Alexander's ancient Macedonians—that had left their traces, and usually their blood and bones, on the unforgiving plains and mountain passes of Afghanistan. It was the eyes that had caught von Strucker's attention when he had called the youthful Al Borak out of the crowd at the orphanage in Kandahar. But it had been the youngster's more unusual, and quite deadly, talent that had led the Prussian to bring the boy into his Arabian establishment.

Now von Strucker stepped forward and the three prisoners watched his approach with wary suspicion. The Prussian knew he must make an unusual impression, for he was clad in the clothes that he still found most comfortable: a high-collared tunic and riding breeches, both of field gray, and calf-high boots of gleaming black leather, such as he had worn when he had been Oberführer von Strucker of the Red Skull SS in Hitler's Third Reich. This uniform, however, was without insignia or campaign ribbons; the days when the baron's cap and collar had born the red skull of Heinrich Himmler's Special Projects Office were long gone.

He lifted the monocle that hung from a black cord secured to a silver button on his tunic and positioned it before his right eye. He hadn't needed the lens for sixty years—his eyesight had become perfect after he had extracted the elixir from the mysterious man who had then disappeared from the concentration camp—but he liked to use the monocle for effect.

"You are wondering why he has freed your hands?" he said in accented English to the SAS trooper, halting a few feet away and standing with legs apart, hands behind his back, in parade rest. "Because you are going to have a chance to win your freedom."

The soldier looked from the Prussian to the Pashtun, then his gaze came back to von Strucker. His mouth twisted in disbelief.

"I see you don't believe me," the baron said. "I give you my word as a German officer. Here is what you must do: pick one of those twenty men to be your opponent. Al Borak here will give you your stiletto. Our man will be unarmed. You have only to kill him, and you will go free."

The prisoner looked to the squad of mujahideen standing immobile, eyes front and unblinking. The baron saw the man's eyes narrow as he examined his enemies. They were a mixed group, most of them Arabs but with a sprinkling of Afghans and Pakistanis, as well as a Filipino and a Malaysian. Each was in his twenties, superbly fit, though none was overly large in stature.

"Go ahead," von Strucker said. "Choose."

The soldier rolled his shoulders and rotated his

neck to loosen tense muscles, then approached the squad cautiously. When none of them reacted to his presence, he examined the men closely, then finally shrugged and indicated a man in the middle of the second rank. "Him," he said.

He had chosen Ismail Khan, a Pakistani who was second-in-command to Al Borak. Khan was a little shorter than the SAS man and not quite as wide in the shoulders. At Al Borak's command, the mujahideen slid smoothly between the two men in front of him and crossed the open space to stand before his leader. Al Borak handed the man two gray pills and a canteen of water to wash them down.

The Pakistani swallowed the pills and turned to face the SAS soldier.

"Here," said Al Borak, casually tossing the dagger so that it spun lazily in the air. The SAS man looked surprised but caught the weapon with easy skill.

Al Borak stepped back, as did von Strucker. "Whenever you are ready," the baron said.

The soldier's demeanor had changed the moment he caught the knife. *A good fighting man,* von Strucker thought. He watched with interest as the Briton moved forward in a slight crouch, the weapon held low before him.

Khan stood at ease, arms at his sides, his body loose. His brown eyes dispassionately regarded the oncoming man with the knife. For a moment, confusion registered on the SAS trooper's face as his opponent gave no sign of being ready for what was about to happen. Then the soldier lunged forward, the hand that held the dagger making a short upward thrust toward the place where the mujahideen's ribs joined his breast-bone—a killing blow that should have driven the seven inches of razor-sharp black steel into Khan's heart.

But the Pakistani was not there to receive the fatal strike. With eye-blurring speed, he had pivoted on his right heel, turning sideways to present the SAS trooper with a target made of empty air. At the same time, the heel of his left hand came around and caught the Briton at the base of his skull, propelling him down and forward, stumbling and off balance. A burst of laughter came from the squad.

The SAS man rolled and came up smoothly, the fighting knife ready. But Khan was already beside him, a hard-edged hand striking down at the Briton's wrist like an ax. The black dagger flew from the man's deadened grasp, but as it spun away the Pakistani's other hand flicked out like a striking cobra and caught the weapon in midair.

He turned the black metal over, laid it on an index finger to test its balance, then flipped it end over end to catch it by the blade. Now he spun, the knife hand raised to shoulder height, and his arm flashed down with inhuman speed. Almost instantly the dagger was buried in a scarred target hung on a wall thirty feet distant, its quivering hilt and quillions quivering from the force of the impact.

Khan turned back to the British soldier, whose face was now slack with fear. The Pakistani beckoned with two fingers, while a small smile lifted the corners of his mouth. When the trembling SAS man did not come forward, the mujahideen moved, striking with a series of blows so fast that von Strucker could not see them land, but could register only the effects: the eyes popped free on the cheeks, the blood spurting from ruptured eardrums, the sudden slump of the shoulders under the desert camouflage that meant both collarbones had been fractured, the way the Briton's head shot forward that meant Khan's knuckles had crushed his larynx in a killing blow.

Now the Pakistani stood back, looking down at the choking, gargling mess that had, moments before, been a first-class fighting man. Al Borak snapped a command and Khan came to attention, about-faced, and marched back to his grinning squad mates. The front rank parted to admit him.

The leader of the Green Fist turned to the two Navy SEALs, but the prolonged and noisy death throes of the soldier distracted him. He went to where the man lay and knelt on one knee beside him, then placed his hands on the Briton's chest. For a moment Al Borak's face went blank, his eyes looking inward, then suddenly the thick black thatch of hair on his head rose straight up, as did the fine dark hairs on his bare arms and the backs of his hands. Bright flashes of intense electrical energy, like a cascading series of miniature lightning bolts, burst from his palms as they lay upon the SAS man's camouflage blouse. The air filled with the acrid reek of ozone, then came the stench of charring flesh as smoke rose from beneath Al Borak's hands. The dying man's entire body spasmed, his spine arcing so that only his head and bootheels touched the floor, the latter drumming an involuntary death tattoo on the polished wood.

The Green Fist leader drew his hands away. The lightning ceased and the rigid body slumped, lifeless, wisps of gray smoke rising from the corpse's chest, where the cloth of the SAS uniform was marked by two carbonized handprints.

Al Borak turned back to the Navy SEALs. He looked them up and down, then picked up their fighting knives from where they lay on the canvas. He went behind the Americans and cut their bonds, pushing them roughly toward the mujahideen. "Let us even the odds," he said. "This time, we'll make it both of you against just one of ours. Now go and choose."

The prisoners looked at each other and at the smoldering wreck that had been the captured Briton. "Well," said one to the other, "nobody ever said this had to be a long career."

Von Strucker did not stay to watch the inevitable outcome. While he had been watching the mismatched combat, he had felt the first stirrings of an ache in one shoulder. That meant it was time for a visit to the room that only he was allowed to enter.

# Ottawa, Canada, the present

"**THE LIBRARY WILL BE CLOSING IN TEN MIN-**utes." The halting voice came from a speaker set into the ceiling above Logan's head. It was only when the message was repeated that it registered. He looked up from the book about the Canadian Army in Italy and saw that the place was almost empty. The nervous woman who had helped him was back where he had found her, a microphone in her trembling hand, and from the way her eyes moved away when he glanced at her, he knew she had been watching him.

He turned his gaze back to the pictures in the coffee-table book. Many of them were frustratingly familiar: a narrow street of brick houses, all with second-story balconies of ornamental metal; a wide, cobbled square with a smashed fountain at its center and dead bodies in German uniforms strewn about in the ungainly postures of battlefield deaths; a lightweight, open-topped tracked vehicle—his mind supplied the words "bren carrier" and a strong impression that it was a good thing to stay out of—and a group of men in Canadian battle dress, wine bottles and glasses in hand, sitting around tables in an outdoor café or tavern, behind them a wall whose whitewash was pockmarked by bullets and shrapnel. A pretty girl, her hair covered by a scarf knotted under her chin, smiled into the camera.

The last photo held his gaze. The faces were familiar, especially the square-jawed sergeant who was looking not at the camera but up at the girl. So was the wall. At the far right of the picture some words painted on the wall had been cut off. One word was "Oster—" and just below it was "Gambrel—" Below that was Orto—" His mind supplied the rest. *Osteria* was the Italian word for tavern, and the line below meant "of Ortona."

And he had been there. He had walked those streets. He had known some of those men. Unless somebody had somehow managed to plant a false memory of that time and place. But why would anyone want to make him think he had been in Ortona in 1943? Just to drive him insane?

He looked again at the girl and her smile stirred some emotion in him. Wistful. Sad. A sense of something once held precious, now lost forever.

"Five minutes," said the voice above his head. "We will be closing in five minutes. Patrons who wish to check out materials should please bring them to the desk now."

Logan stared at the pictures, willing his clouded mind to pull the scattered memories and impressions into some kind of pattern that made sense. He looked again at the wide shot of the square with the dead Germans in it. The white wall out of focus in the far distance looked as if it could be the tavern where the soldiers had stood drinking wine and saying the kinds of things soldiers always said to pretty girls in between the times that bullets were flying.

But now Logan noticed a detail that he had missed before. At the left side of the photograph was a Canadian soldier in paratrooper gear, a sten gun held loosely in the crook of his arm, his face turned partly toward the camera.

Logan came to his feet so fast that the chair he'd been sitting on shot backward and tipped over. He strode toward the desk, the book in his hand, one finger marking the page with the photo that had sent a shock through him.

"A magnifying glass," he said to the librarian, who had jumped to her feet and looked ready to run away. "All I need's a magnifying glass."

She had large upper teeth that were now biting into her lower lip, but she pulled open a drawer in the desk and fumbled within, coming up with a big lens in a square frame of black plastic. "Here," she said.

He snatched it from her and spread the book on the desk and peered at the man with the sten gun standing at the edge of the photo. The face was in shadow. Both he and the cameraman must have been covered by the shade of a building behind them, looking out into the brightness of the square with the destroyed fountain.

But the image was clear enough. The strong nose, the ridge of bone from which the thick, dark brows sprang, the black hair, swept back but unruly under the paratrooper's beret, the stubble-darkened jaw.

He looked up at the librarian, saw her recoil from whatever his eyes were showing. "I need this book," he said.

"You can check it out," she said, though it took her three tries to get out the third word in the sentence. "Do you . . . do you have a card?"

"I don't think so," he said. "But I'll bring it back."

She looked at the book as if she were telling it, *Good-bye and good luck,* then said to Logan, "Fine, yes, that'll be fine. You can take it right now."

"And the glass."

"We've got plenty of them."

He turned and moved toward the door, slipping the magnifying glass into his pocket and pressing the book against his chest to button his coat over it against the freezing rain that was still coating the city in a shroud of ice.

But as he hurried through the slick streets all he saw was that harsh face beneath the paratrooper's beret. He recognized that face, even in a dark and grainy photo from sixty years ago.

There wasn't a face in all the world that he knew better. It was the face that looked back at Logan every morning when he shaved.

# The Empty Quarter,
# Saudi Arabia, the present

VON STRUCKER BURST THROUGH THE DOOR of his private quarters, deep within the bowels of the facility he had had built here in the wasteland of the Arabian desert. Far above, the midday temperature was nearing fifty degrees on the Celsius scale, heat that would kill a man in a matter of hours. Down here, the temperature was always a comfortable twenty-one—about seventy degrees Fahrenheit—but the Prussian's brow was beaded in sweat as he made his way across the spartan sitting room and into the bed chamber with its simple narrow cot.

He parted a set of double doors in the far wall to reveal a rack on which hung spare tunics and breeches, two pairs of boots beneath. Wincing at the pain in his shoulder, the baron swept aside the clothing. The wall behind was bare rock, the hard granite that underlay the desert sands, rough hewn with un-smoothed bumps and still showing the scars of a power chisel.

The baron set his palm on a rounded projection in the top-right corner of the wall. He pressed, and the bump sank into the granite. At the same time, a harsh grating sound came from within the stone and the entire rear of the closet moved back a foot, then slid sideways on hydraulic pistons. Beyond lay a small chamber, lit by a simple overhead light and containing only a laboratory bench. Atop the bench's sterile surface was a sealed cylinder of transparent glass, of a size to hold four liters. Into one side of the container ran lengths of surgical tubing whose other ends were connected to a small machine that whirred and hummed beside the flask. A single hollow filament exited from the other side of the cylinder and disappeared into a hole in the countertop.

Von Strucker entered the room and palmed the control on the inner wall that closed the massive granite door. Only when he was sealed in did he go to the bench and undertake once again the process that had kept him alive and vigorous all these years. First he checked the readings on the whirring machine and saw that appropriate levels of nutrients were entering the cylinder, and that waste products were being cycled out. The small fragment of human tissue that floated on a net of gold mesh suspended within the saline solution that filled the container remained in good health.

Now the Prussian bent, feeling as he did so a twinge of pain in his lower back. *Just in time,* he thought, as he took a compact centrifuge from a shelf beneath the bench. He lifted it to the countertop, then connected it to a power source.

The bench concealed a secure box, made of the strongest steel, its thick heavy door equipped with a touch pad that recognized only von Strucker's fingerprints. He placed his fingertips against the sensors and the door opened. Had anyone else touched the pad, alarms would now be sounding throughout the underground complex and the secret room would be filling with a toxic gas. Within the safe, held in a foam-cushioned armature, was a solitary Pyrex test tube half-filled with a colorless liquid. The filament that led from the cylinder on the bench's top passed through the rubber stopper that sealed the tube.

Carefully, the baron removed the tube from its holder and withdrew the stopper, replacing it with another that had no hole through it. He rose and opened the centrifuge, placed the tube in a groove designed to hold it, and snugged it down. Then he sealed the machine, set its speed control, and pushed a button. A whirring noise rose through several frequencies of sound until the device was spinning so rapidly that its whine was almost at the edge of human hearing.

Von Strucker leaned against the bench, his elegantly tended fingernails tapping fitfully on the polished top. He noticed a tiny discoloration on the back of one hand and even as he focused on it, the liver mark spread and was joined by another. The skin appeared dry and he could see blue veins beneath it. He was aging rapidly.

A chime sounded from the centrifuge. Its high-pitched whirring cycled down through the frequencies and slowed to nothing as the machine stopped. The baron withdrew the tube and held it up to the light to examine the contents. Most of the tube was still filled with the colorless fluid, but in the bottom were a few cubic centimeters of a cloudy liquid.

He placed the tube in a rack and reached below the bench for a flat plastic box that contained a hypodermic syringe with a needle longer than the test tube. He removed the tube's stopper and used the hypodermic to draw off the substance that the centrifuge had concentrated in the bottom. When the reservoir was full, he removed the long needle and replaced it with another that was less than an inch long. He noticed that his hands were now shaking.

Swiftly, von Strucker removed his tunic and found the length of rubber tubing that he used to bind his arm just below the left bicep. He depressed the hypodermic's plunger to evacuate the air from the needle and when a droplet of fluid appeared at its tip, he put the needle to the now distended vein in the crook of his elbow and slid the steel into his flesh.

He unknotted the tube that constricted his arm and let the fluid flow into his system. He put out his hand and watched as the tremor disappeared and the dark-spotted skin regained its youthful elasticity. The aches in his shoulder and lower back faded like distant trumpets.

The Prussian took a deep breath, let it out slowly. He felt renewed strength flowing through him, the power of distilled life force energizing his limbs, filling his being with unstoppable vigor. Quickly, he disposed of the equipment, then knelt on now uncomplaining knees to place a new tube in the secure box and connect it to the filament that came from the cylinder above. He locked the safe's door, then rose and regarded the small fragment of human bone marrow that was contained in the flask and nurtured by the small machine.

*Safe again,* he said within the privacy of his mind. The injection would repair his tissues and preserve them against the ravages of age. He would remain, physically and mentally, a man in his prime, never aging beyond the day when he had first extracted the elixir from the nameless Canadian. The dark-haired wild man who had growled at him in the office of the concentration camp's commandant, after they had nailed him to the tabletop to keep him still while they investigated why he wouldn't stay dead.

## Ottawa, Canada, the present

WHEN LOGAN GOT BACK TO THE CONDO, A cardboard carton rested outside the door. *I guess it's about that time,* he thought as he unlocked the door and stooped to pick up the box, hearing a *clunk* of liquid-filled glass as its contents shifted. He placed the library book on top of the carton, covering the printed letters that read *Seagram's Seven Crown Blended Whiskey,* and carried them both in, then set the box, as always, on the built-in table in the galley kitchen.

Like the money, a case of Canadian whiskey arrived once a month. Logan didn't know where he had picked up a taste for Seven Crown, but nowadays the thought of drinking any other kind of liquor actually repelled him. It felt natural to sit with a glass in his hand, the smell of the liquor in his nostrils and the sweet aftertaste hardly fading from his mouth before he took another slug.

Normally, he would have opened the case and cracked a bottle. But not tonight. Instead, he left the carton still sealed on the table and carried the book into the living room. He set it on the coffee table in front of the couch, both of them of that characterless breed of furniture often found in midpriced chain hotel rooms and government offices.

He threw his coat and hat into a corner of the couch, then remembered the magnifying glass. He dug it out of the pocket and sat hunched again over *Canadians at War: The Italian Campaign*. He started at the first page and proceeded page by page through the book, examining every photograph through the lens. He noticed that he had a tendency to snap the pages, then let his eyes dart from image to image. *Okay,* he thought, *so I'm not the patient type. But this needs to be done right.* He forced himself to slow down, to go at it methodically. *I don't want to miss anything.*

He found it on page 156. It was another picture of

Tommy Prince, walking toward the camera on some cobblestoned street. In the background were three other Canadian paratroopers. The cameraman had used some kind of deep-focus lens that didn't obscure the details of the middle ground. When Logan pored over the image with the magnifying glass there was no doubt: one of the three men coming up behind Prince was either Logan himself or some uncanny double. Same mouth, same nose, same heavy stubble on his cheeks, same widow's peak of dark hair dipping down into his forehead.

He stared at the image for a long time, wishing he could reach into that flat, black-and-white world and grab the front of that paratrooper's woolen blouse, pull him out of the book and into this anonymous living room in Ottawa and ask him, "Who the hell are you? And who the hell am I?"

Instead, he rose and went to the kitchen, came back with a glass and fresh bottle of Seven Crown. He spun off the screw-top lid with an expert flick of thumb and two fingers. *Done that a few times,* he observed to himself, as he half filled the glass.

He took a good mouthful of the sweet liquor, rolling it around on his tongue. He knew he'd done that a lot, too. *The body remembers even if the mind can't.* But another impression came with the burn of the whiskey passing down his throat. He reckoned he must have sat here enough times, drinking a bottle dry, drinking his way into another kind of oblivion than the fog that filled his head. And too many times those sessions with the bottle had given the whiskey an aftertaste of defeat.

*But not this time.* He screwed the cap back on the bottle. And somehow that small action felt like victory.

And then he wondered how he could get himself to Italy.

## The Empty Quarter, Saudi Arabia, the present

SAFE AGAIN. BUT SAFE FOR HOW LONG?

The thought kept circling in the baron's mind as he returned to the room where Green Fist operations were planned. The morning training session would be over by now, so he summoned Al Borak. While he waited, he mentally ran over the problem of the tissue in the cylinder. When it had been freshly harvested, more than sixty years ago, its output of white blood cells had been enough to sustain von Strucker in perfect health for thirty days. But today he had needed an injection, and today was only twenty-seven days since his last use of the needle.

It was a problem of diminishing returns. The tissue was living marrow taken from the mysterious man's femur and kept in a special nutrient solution that von Strucker's hand-picked team of scientists had developed in the Reich's most secret experimental medical facility, located in a heavily guarded bunker beneath a Berlin hospital that had catered to senior members of the Nazi regime. The solution had been originally developed to preserve limbs severed on the battlefields of the Eastern Front, in the hope that doctors in Wehrmacht field hospitals could reattach them. But as soon as von Strucker heard of its existence, he convinced Reichsführer-SS Himmler to let him use the precious substance for his *übermenn* program.

At that time, von Strucker had been seeking to stimulate artificial mutations in human test subjects. His teams sought out healthy young men and women from the trainloads delivered daily to the camps, but tending to hundreds of breeders would have required a massive establishments of cooks, guards, and head counters, any of whom might be spies planted by the baron's rivals within the Nazi state apparatus. It was so much easier to excise the few parts needed to create embryos, keep them alive in the solution, and send the unneeded tissue—that is, the rest of the test subject—to the crematorium.

While the effort to create mutations was given first priority, the Prussian also had teams of investigators combing the Reich and its conquered territories seeking mutants who had appeared spontaneously. Most of them, of course, were of no use—there is no particular advantage to having six fingers on a hand or an eye that sees ultraviolet—but much was learned from dissecting such subjects.

Rarely, however, a potentially useful mutation appeared. There was a Czech boy whose skin—when he was frightened or excited—was able to divert light. At such times, the outer layer of his epidermis neither absorbed nor reflected light. Instead, it passed the photons "hand to hand," as von Strucker explained it to Himmler, so that it bent around him and made him effectively invisible. But the mutated gene that caused the invisibility effect also suppressed some important factors in the brain's development. As a result, the boy was not much smarter than a chimpanzee.

There was also a Dutch girl who could project her consciousness backward in time, seeing and hearing events that had happened far away and even before she was born. Von Strucker had been working with her to increase her range and improve her targeting ability by meditation and by a diet rich in certain vitamins and plant extracts. Then Himmler insisted on forcing her to attempt to see the future. The girl was still in a coma when the Russians took Berlin and the baron fled.

His mind came back to the problem of the marrow in the vat. It produced the mutated white blood cells that kept von Strucker untroubled by germs, aging, injuries, and systemic breakdowns. But the small piece of stolen flesh was not itself immortal; the nutrient solution in which it lay required a regular infusion of the marrow's own product or it would start to decline. So for more than sixty years, the Prussian had shared its output of life-preserving white blood cells with the tissue that produced them. Shared them, but not equally. In order to have enough for himself, he had short-changed their source, causing the marrow to gradually lose some of its potency.

And now he could look ahead to a time—perhaps decades away still, yet mathematically certain to arrive—when he would need an injection a week. Then it would become an injection a day, then twice a day, until ultimately the fragment of stolen flesh would not be able to produce enough of the elixir to keep the breath of life moving in and out of von Strucker's lungs.

Before that day arrived, the baron needed to find the Canadian again—or one of his descendants, if the mutation bred true. He had no doubt the man was still alive somewhere—he had never met anyone more unkillable—but when his inquiries had yielded no results, he came to the only logical conclusion: the mutant's gift had been recognized, most likely by a government security apparatus, that had done exactly what the baron would have done—yanked him out of his normal life and put him to work.

The door to the planning room slid open. The tall Pashtun stepped through the doorway and the door slid closed behind him. "So," he said, speaking Arabic but with the softer accent of southern Afghanistan, "did our friend from Yemen approve the plan?"

"No," von Strucker said.

Al Borak's gray eyes widened. "Is there a problem?"

The Prussian's thin lips took a wry twist. "More of an opportunity." In a few words he explained the change of target, then said, "We will need a good model of the target area and its approaches."

The Green Fist leader stroked his lean jaw. "It is a hard target. We will lose some men," he said. "Maybe a lot of them."

"That is what they are for," von Strucker said.

"Still . . ."

"We can always get more."

Al Borak pressed his palms together, then flexed his hands so that only the fingertips still touched. "True," he said. "And their deaths will be glorious."

When he separated his hands completely, the air crackled and blue-white sparks leaped from one palm to the other. He smiled at the baron and said, "Or at least that's what we'll tell them."

## Ottawa, Canada, the present

*I MAY NOT KNOW WHO I AM,* LOGAN WAS THINK-ing to himself, *but I'm pretty sure I haven't led a straight-arrow life.* It wasn't just the frequent dreams full of blood and screaming, of crunching bone and the crackle of automatic weapons fire, dreams that always faded when he tried to examine them. It wasn't just the scars on his hands and whatever it was that people saw in his face that made them decide to cross streets or seat themselves at a table on the other side of a restaurant from him.

It was the fact that he knew exactly the kind of place to seek out if he wanted to get a passport he wasn't entitled to—even knew how much it ought to cost. So when the man sitting at a light table in the back room of the print shop had told him the forged document would cost him six hundred dollars, he had not hesitated.

"It'll cost me three," he'd said, leaning over the table. And the man had looked up into Logan's eyes and said, "Right you are. Come back tomorrow night at six."

"I'll wait right here while you do it."

The man hadn't looked too happy about it, but he got out his camera and got to work, and Logan was satisfied with the results. The passport wouldn't stand up to serious scrutiny—its number was not connected to any file—but it looked real enough. The man had said it was one of a batch of pristine blanks stolen from the Queen's Printer so recently that the passport office didn't yet know they were gone.

Now Logan put the document back in an inner pocket of his plaid coat and collected the ticket from the clerk at the Air Canada counter in the departures area of Ottawa International Airport. He'd paid for the ticket with cash—the monthly envelopes contained more than he needed for food and since his liquor was supplied free, he had accumulated a healthy wad of surplus fifties and hundreds.

The security checkpoint brought a surprise. He emptied his pockets of metal objects and took off his shoes, but the metal detector went crazy when he stepped through. A plump woman with a hand-held wand detector and a Punjabi accent asked him to hold his arms out, then showed him a startled face when the instrument seemed to suffer the same kind of overexcitement as the walk-through gate.

When it was eventually established that the wand was reacting to metal that was not in his clothes but *inside him,* she called over her supervisor. This was a skinny, balding man with an Adam's apple that couldn't keep still.

He repeated the woman's wand motions with the same loud results, then said, "Do you have metal pins in your arms and legs, maybe a plate in your skull?"

"I don't know," Logan said. "My memory is pretty bad."

In the end they shrugged and let him board the plane. He settled into a window seat in coach. Nobody sat beside him and once they were at cruising altitude, the flight attendants came around with their cart full of little plastic bottles.

"Seven Crown," he said. "Give me five of them. No ice."

The badge on the attendant's shirt pocket said his

name was Randy. "It's our policy to only sell them one at a time," he said.

Logan looked at him. "It's my policy to buy them by the handful."

Randy decided that Air Canada's policy could stand a minor and temporary change. "But don't tell anybody I did this," he said.

Logan emptied all five of the little bottles into the plastic tumbler and took a mouthful. Outside, it was a late November night and the airbus was thousands of feet above the clouds covering eastern Canada. He looked out at the blackness between the indifferent stars above and the gray blanket below. It could have been anytime out there.

## Ortona, Italy, December 1943

"HEY, PATCH! THERE'S A MAJOR FROM HEAD-quarters looking for you again. He was snooping around the mess wagon."

"But you told him you haven't seen me."

"I did, but I don't think he believed it."

Corporal James "Patch" Howlett, late of the First Special Service Force and currently unofficially attached to the Loyal Edmonton Regiment, accepted the steaming mess tin that Sergeant Rob Roy MacLeish had brought back to the basement of the half-ruined house where MacLeish's squad was bivouacked. The red-haired sergeant had gone to collect the rations for both of them because it would have been difficult for Patch to explain to any passing officer what he was doing a couple of hundred miles from where his unit was stationed.

"What's he want with you?" the sergeant asked his old friend. The two of them had come down from the lumber camps in northern Alberta in the first week of the war and joined up together, only to be separated when a colonel had come through the basic training camp looking for volunteers for a newly forming parachute regiment. Both had put their hands up, but only Patch Howlett had been accepted.

"You know officers," Patch said, sniffing the contents of the mess tin appreciatively before dipping in a steel spoon. "They're always wanting you to do things you don't feel like doing."

He changed the subject. "So, Rob Roy," he said, "tell me about the girl."

MacLeish's green eyes narrowed in wary suspicion. In the old days, he'd lost more than a couple of sweethearts to Howlett. Something about Patch's dark, brooding nature pulled them like moths to a black flame. "What girl?" he said in the most innocent tone he could muster.

Patch squinted at an inch-thick cube of grayish meat on his spoon. "Horse?" he said.

"Our artillery caught some Jerry horse-drawn transport in one of those gullies west of town," MacLeish said. "Cookie said it seemed a shame to waste it."

Patch chewed the meat, then dug into the stew for a chunk of potato. "I've eaten worse," he said. "But back to the question—there's always a girl."

The sergeant's face softened. "Her name's Lucia," he said. "Lucia Gambrelli. Her family ran a tavern down by the harbor, until her father was shot by the Germans in a reprisal for a raid by partisans. That made her brother, Giovanni, decide to join the partisans and get revenge. Now he's disappeared."

"Sounds like she brings out your knight in shining armor."

MacLeish blushed. "Maybe a little. She's a sweet kid. Before her brother went missing we were talking about, you know, after the war's over . . ."

"You've changed," Patch said. "You used to say no girl would ever get you to tie the knot."

"It's the war. It makes you do things you never thought you'd do."

"You don't know the half of it," Patch said.

The rest of the squad trickled in and squatted with their backs against the basement walls to eat their evening meal, casting sidelong looks at the newcomer. If they thought it strange that their sergeant's AWOL friend had attached himself to their squad, they didn't mention it. Besides, the new man's shoulder patch—a red stone spearhead stitched with "USA" and "Canada" in white thread—identified him as a member of the elite fighting unit the Germans had begun calling *Die Schwarzen Teufels*—the Black Devils—for the shoe polish with which they blackened their faces when going out at night to cut throats and take prisoners.

The First Special Services Force, now becoming known as the Devil's Brigade, was a combined unit formed when the battalion of Canadian paratroops in which Patch served had been merged with a unit of U.S. volunteers who had backgrounds as forest rangers, hunters, and lumberjacks. Trained to operate behind enemy lines and as elite assault troops, the FSSF had already achieved legendary status for their successful assault on Monte la Defensa south of Cassino. American and British forces had suffered heavy casualties in repeated attacks that had failed to dislodge German forces dug in atop a mountain that was mostly sheer cliffs hundreds of feet high. The Devil's Brigade had silently scaled the cliffs and attacked the Germans from the rear, taking the supposedly impregnable position in a matter of hours.

"We're going out at twenty-one hundred," MacLeish said.

"Mind if I tag along?" Patch said.

"I was hoping you might."

The corporal scraped a final spoonful of stew out of the tin and wiped out the last traces of gravy with a cob of bread. "What kind of fun will we be having?" he said.

His friend smiled. "We call it mouse holing."

• • •

Ortona was a fishing port and prewar vacation spot on the Adriatic Sea, about midway up Italy's east coast. The Allies' theater commander, Field Marshal Montgomery, had assigned the Canadian First Division to take it. The German Army's high command had decided that the elite troops of the Wehrmacht's Third Paratroop Regiment—Hitler's fire brigade in southern Europe—were the perfect force to defend the place. Rushed into the line to reinforce a battered Panzergrenadier regiment already falling back in the face of strong Canadian and British attacks, the *fallschirmjägers* turned the town into a death trap.

With the civilian population mostly fled or carried off to be slave laborers in Germany, the defenders blocked access by demolishing the empty houses at key intersections. They set up machine gun and anti-tank gun positions in nearby buildings, creating overlapping fields of fire trained on the rubble and the streets along which the Canadians would advance, and spread mines around like confetti. The plan was to lead the assault toward the wide Piazza Municipiale at the center of town, turning it into an escape-proof killing zone.

The Germans had rigged the game, so the Canadians declined to play. Instead of moving through the deadly streets and alleyways, they took to burrowing through the common walls that connected one house to the next, using pickaxes or shaped demolition charges or the PIAT shoulder-fired antitank weapon to blow man-size holes, then leaping through with grenades and small arms fire. It was house-to-house, room-to-room fighting, with both sides rigging explosive booby traps as they withdrew from unholdable positions. It was a mini-Stalingrad of a battle, fought in third- and fourth-floor rooms, the air choking with the dust of shattered masonry and the stink of TNT— a succession of sudden, desperate struggles, fought face-to-face and hand-to-hand.

At 2045, MacLeish's officer, a tired-looking lieutenant, came through the blackout curtain and down into the basement, bringing two canvas satchels of grenades. He saw the stranger sitting in the shadows beside his sergeant and said, "Who's this?"

MacLeish stood. "Old friend of mine, come for a visit. Thought he could come along tonight."

The lieutenant, "Can he fight?"

"Used to be the best bare-knuckle boxer north of Edmonton."

The officer lifted the oil lamp from a rickety table and brought it over to where the special forces corporal squatted on his heels against the wall. He took in the spearhead on the man's shoulder and the VK-42 fighting knife in a scabbard on his hip. "Is that your only weapon?" he said.

Patch rose smoothly to his feet. "I've got this," he said and showed the lieutenant a sten gun equipped with silencer. "All you'll hear is the bolt clicking."

"All right," the officer said. "Just make sure you do what Sergeant MacLeish says."

"I always did."

MacLeish smothered a laugh as the lieutenant gathered them around the table and spread out a hand-drawn map of a street that ran south to north and had six multistory houses along its east side. A house in the middle of the west side had been blown up and tumbled into the street, effectively blocking it. The officer pointed to the house on the northeast corner and said, "The Jerries have a machine gun on the second floor. There are also snipers in at least two of the other houses, but they keep moving around.

"We'll go in through the ground floor of this first house here"—he pointed to the street's southeast corner—"climb to the fourth floor, then mouse hole our way along the row until we've cleaned them out. Grenades down the stairwells, then sweep each room. Watch out for trip wires."

He distributed the grenades, every man taking a few. Two of the soldiers slung their rifles and hoisted pickaxes. Another man hefted a long crowbar, then the lieutenant blew out the lamp and they exited silently into the December darkness.

They went single file along the rubble-strewn streets, Patch falling into place just behind MacLeish. The street they were heading for was four blocks west and they felt their way through the blackness until they came to the final corner, where another squad of

Loyal Eddies represented the farthest forward line of the Canadians' advance.

MacLeish's officer spoke to the sergeant of the other squad. "Anything?"

"All quiet, sir," said the man.

MacLeish whispered to Patch, "That means they've either pulled out so they can blow it up once we're well in, or they're waiting in one of the houses so they can jump us as we come through a wall."

"Then we'll just have to get them before they get us," Patch said. "Hell of a lot of fights get won on the first punch."

They went across the street to the back of the first house, one man at a time, at a dead run and crouching low, in case a German sniper with a nightscope was covering the open space. When the last man was across, the riflemen on the other squad opened fire up the street, making a noise to cover the *crack* that came when the long crowbar pried open the house's back door.

"Let me go in first," Patch said.

"As you like," the officer said.

The door led into a kitchen. The air in the room was stale with the odor of moldering food and the ashes in the open hearth where the cooking was done. Patch moved silently across the stone floor, one hand outstretched in the lightless space, found a wall and then a doorway that led to a hallway. The only other room on this floor was the front parlor, the hallway running from the front door to a staircase that rose to the upper floors.

The place was empty. He could tell. In night operations against the Germans, slipping around behind their lines, he'd found that he could sniff them out by the lingering odor of sausage and cabbage that seemed to be such an important part of their diet. He had used to think that everybody could smell faint scent traces the way he could, just as he'd thought that other people could see in the dark, but now he knew different.

He went back to the kitchen and whispered to the men outside, "Ground floor clear. I'm going upstairs."

He heard them coming in, as he crept up the stairs, placing his feet carefully on the outsides of the risers so the old wood would not creak as it took his weight. The floor above held bedrooms: one across the front of the house, with two tall louvered doors leading to a railed balcony; and a pair of smaller chambers probably meant for children. All were empty.

He went back to the stairs. MacLeish was waiting at the bottom. "Second floor clear," Patch said. "Going up."

He quickly checked the third-story rooms and the servants' cubicles in the attic. "Nothing," he told the Loyal Eddies coming up the stairs.

"Right," said the officer. "Picks and pry bar."

The soldiers set to work in the glow of the lieutenant's flashlight, breaking a hole in the wall separating a windowless third-floor room from its counterpart in the house next door. The picks dug through plaster into old brick beneath, chips flying and dust beginning to billow.

Patch spoke to MacLeish. "I can get onto the roof from the attic. I'm going to go scout farther up the block."

"Watch yourself," his friend said. "They like their booby traps, the Jerries do."

Patch went up to the top of the house. A small window opened just below the eaves above the back alley. He put his head out, listening, sniffing the night air. Then he swung himself up and out and in a moment he was crouched atop the roof. He went north, his boots scritching on the terra-cotta tiles. Two doors up, he found a hole in the roof—when they'd blown up the building across the street, a chunk of it had come flying over and punched right through the tiles and rafters.

Patch lowered himself through the opening into another attic, its floor littered with bricks that smelled of smoke. *The chimney,* he thought. *Must've got lobbed over like a mortar bomb.* He found the open trapdoor that led downstairs and made his way through the floors below. Empty. He came back to the third floor and put his ear to the wall that connected the house with its neighbor to the south and heard faint sounds—MacLeish and his squad were already into the second house and would soon be coming through into this one.

He thought he should go back onto the roof and

farther up the street, to see if he could locate the German positions. But something was tugging at the edge of his awareness. There was an odd smell about this house, very faint. He went out into the hall and sniffed the air, trying to separate the strange odor from the mixed reek of rotten food and the mold that had taken hold of everything after the hole in the roof let in the winter rains.

*Find the Jerries,* his training said. *Know where your enemy is before he knows where you are.* He went up to the roof and made his way to the last house on the street, the one that the lieutenant had said concealed a machine gun nest. He found no convenient hole in the roof, but there was an attic window in the same place as in the first house, and taking a grip on the eaves trough, he agilely swung out and down, kicking his way through the thin slats of the wooden shutters.

Sten gun at the ready, he crouched over the trapdoor, listening, his nostrils flared. He heard nothing, but the scent of German rations came to him, along with the sharp smell of gunsmoke produced by the MG-42—the 7.92-millimeter machine gun known as "Hitler's buzzsaw" for its twenty-rounds-per-second rate of fire.

Silently, Patch went down the ladder that led to the third floor, checked the rooms, then descended the stairs to the second floor. Here was where the machine gun would be, in the front bedroom that would be laid out just like that of the first house, with double doors leading out on to a balcony. He slid back the bolt on the sten gun and eased along the hallway to the bedroom door.

The scent of a much-fired German machine gun was strong. Patch stepped into the doorway and sprayed the room with two long bursts of nine-millimeter parabellum. The sten's silencer was so effective he heard only the clicking of its action and the sounds of the bullets smacking into walls and furniture, while its muzzle flash lit up the space.

The empty space. There was no machine gun, no dead and dying German soldiers. He went into the room, saw where a table and chairs had been piled against the doors to the balcony, doors that were opened just wide enough for an MG-42 barrel to poke out. And, in fact, there was a machine gun barrel lying against a wall—the high-speed weapon overheated barrels so often, German machine gun crews always carried a few spares. That was where the smell of gunsmoke came from. But the Jerries were gone.

It took him only a moment to put it all together. This room had been occupied by the Germans earlier today. They had fired their machine gun to let the Eddies know that they were here, but then they had pulled out without being seen. Patch's muzzle flashes would have told German observers that Canadians were mouse holing through the houses. And his animal-sharp sense of smell had picked up that odd odor in the third house.

He swore, then turned and raced for the stairs, rushed up into the attic. He was out the window and onto the roof in seconds. Careless now of making noise, he raced across the terra-cotta tiles to the hole that led down into the third house. He dropped through onto the shattered chimney below, bellowing, "Get out! Get out! The place is booby-trapped!"

He heard a shout from below, recognized Rob Roy MacLeish's voice giving orders, a rush of boots, and men swearing. Then the world exploded.

"Corporal Howlett," said a man's voice he didn't recognize. "Can you hear me?"

Patch came out of darkness into more darkness. He tried to put his hand to his eyes, but found that he could not move his arms from where they lay at his sides. He seemed to be in a narrow bed whose covers were snugged down tight.

"He can't talk to you," said another man. "Half his face was torn off."

"Go away," said the first voice, a man's voice speaking in the slightly British tone of an educated Canadian. "And make sure we are not disturbed."

"Look," said the second voice, "I had him moved to the VIP ward, as you asked. But this man is under my care. I have a professional responsi—"

The first voice interrupted, its tone purely matter-of-fact. "If you don't leave, Doctor, I will have you shot."

"Are you insane? This is a Royal Canadian Army field hospital, not some Nazi—"

"I assure you, Doctor, I can indeed have you shot. I could have you disappeared to a place where much, much worse things would be done to you, things that would make you beg for somebody to put a merciful bullet in your brain. And no one would say one bloody word about it."

Patch heard a swish of canvas as the doctor departed and knew he must be in a field hospital of the Army Medical Corps. And from the nature of the conversation, he was in a private section, the kind of ward where they put wounded generals, a place with no witnesses.

"So, Corporal Howlett," said the cultured voice again, "let's have a chat."

Patch said nothing. He heard a sigh followed by a rustle of clothing as the man moved. A moment later, sudden agony lanced through the sole of his left foot. He tried to pull his leg away but found that his lower limbs were as immobilized as his arms. He was strapped tight to the cot at chest, hips, and knees.

"I've just made a two-inch-long incision in your foot," the voice said. "It's bleeding freely, as it ought to. But, what's this? The bleeding has stopped."

Patch struggled but the bonds were too tight. The pain in his foot was already fading, but it wasn't the fear of pain that made him desperate to get free.

"And now the cut is closing," the voice said. "I

wouldn't believe it if I wasn't seeing it with my own eyes."

The bound man felt a tingling in his hands but fought to suppress the instinct that the sensation foretold. It was bad enough that someone knew of his recuperative powers. But if he could keep the secret of his hands until his arms were free . . .

Now the voice was saying, "Sergeant Ken Cashman told me something strange. You remember the sergeant? He's your section leader in the FSSF. He was with you when you made the assault on Monte la Defensa last week.

"He said just as you came over the lip of the cliff a German machine gun opened up on you. He saw you fall, saw the spurts of blood the rounds made coming out of your back. He went on with the attack, but when he came back to collect your identity disks, he couldn't find your body."

Patch lay silently. Nothing he could say was going to help this situation.

"Then," the voice said, in a patient tone, "he saw you walking around, sound as a dollar. Though you weren't wearing a shirt, even though it was early December on top of a mountain.

"Do you know what Sergeant Cashman decided? He decided that he had seen somebody else get shot and, in the confusion of battle, had mistaken that unfortunate soldier for you.

"And that," the voice continued, "would have been

the end of it. Except that he talked about it to a couple of people, and one of them talked about it to me. And I remembered hearing something similar when I was attached to the Parachute Regiment."

Patch's mind was racing now. He remembered an intelligence officer who'd joined the regiment shortly before its first battalion had been merged with the U.S. soldiers into the combined special force unit. The man had been there when Patch's company had been conducting an exercise, a night jump in full combat gear, and things had gone terribly wrong.

He remembered the jump. He'd come out of the Dakota's side door all right, and the static line attached to the overhead cable inside the cabin had opened his chute for him. He'd drifted down toward a farmer's field and was coming in for a perfect landing when a sudden gust of wind threw him sideways and into a heap of rocks that generations of plowmen had piled up in one corner of the field.

The impact snapped his right shin, the splintered bone tearing through flesh and the cloth of his jump trousers. He'd screamed in pain as the wind-filled chute tried to drag him across the rocks. A medic had come running and got him out of his harness, shouting for stretcher bearers. They'd strapped him down and hauled him off to an ambulance that had been standing by in case anyone came down wrong, and minutes after he had jumped out of the Dakota he was rolling along a country road headed for the base hospital.

The officer's voice picked up the story. "But when they got to the hospital, the man's leg was fine. He said he'd only banged it on the rocks and that a stick of wood had ripped his uniform. So they sent him back to barracks, and no report was filed.

"The medic was accused of being drunk on duty. He swore that that was no stick he had seen poking out of the man's flesh. It was naked bone. And even after everybody forgot all about it, he used to tell the story when he'd had a drink or two. Everybody got tired of hearing it. They gave him a nickname, used to call him Old Naked Bone."

But not everyone forgot about it. The intelligence officer hadn't. He'd bought the medic a drink or two and gotten the story out of him. Even got the name of the man who'd been carried off the field on a stretcher. Then the officer had a friend at the Loyal Edmonton Regiment back home do some research. His contact had sent him a letter full of tall tales about a man called Patch Howlett who'd been a legendary bare-knuckle cage fighter in the lumber camps of northern Alberta. They'd called him indestructible.

"And then I found myself assigned to the intelligence staff of the First Canadian Division, not a hundred miles from where the FSSF is operating. So I asked your outfit's G-Two to let me know if he heard any strange stories about a Corporal Howlett. And just the other day, he told me about the strange incident in Sergeant Prince's section—and your name came up.

So I went up on La Defensa and poked around—and found a corporal's blouse that had matching bullet holes in the chest and back, and plenty of blood in between. Someone had stuffed it in a crack between two boulders.

"I thought I should pay a visit to your outfit," the officer continued, and now Patch could hear his voice moving toward the head of the cot. "But the moment I arrived and began asking questions, the legendary corporal went AWOL. Of course, the place you'd run to is where your old friend Sergeant MacLeish was serving. That was your mistake, you know. If you'd just sat still and played dumb, you might have gotten away with it."

"Wanted to see my friend," Patch said through the layers of gauze that swathed his head. "How is Sergeant MacLeish?"

"Ah, now we're getting somewhere," the voice said. Patch heard a flipping of pages. "And here's another funny thing. Your chart says that your lower jaw and part of your tongue were blown off when the Jerries blew up that booby-trapped house. Yet, here you are talking to me. I think we should take a look at what's under there."

Howlett felt a tug near his jaw, then another as a ribbon of gauze was pulled out from beneath the back of his head where it lay against the pillow. The tugging continued as the officer unwound the bandages. He felt cool air on his revealed flesh.

"Ahah," said the voice. It was meant to be said with quiet satisfaction, but Patch could hear the excitement the officer was trying to suppress. Finally, a thick pad of gauze was lifted from Patch's eyes and he blinked against the light.

The face looking down at him was narrow, the eyes a little close-set behind wire-rimmed military-issue spectacles, but sharp with intelligence, the weakness of the chin offset by a certain cruelty about the mouth. He had a pencil-thin mustache that he now stroked with one finger as he regarded what had been under the gauze.

"I don't have a mirror, but I'm guessing I don't need to show you, do I?" he said. His eyes widened theatrically. "Why, it's a miracle, my boy."

"What happened to Rob Roy?" Patch said.

"Your friend, the Loyal Eddie? The basement of that house was packed with demolition explosives. He and all of his men were blown to pieces, just like you. Except in their case, the effects were permanent." The officer sat on the edge of the cot. "But he was nobody, and now he's a dead nobody. Let's talk about you. About the special contribution you're going to make to the war effort. And, even more important, to my career."

"I need a drink."

"In a minute."

"Now, or I don't say anything."

"Sir," the officer said.

"Or I don't say anything, sir."

He watched the man pick up a scalpel from a nightstand up near the head of the cot on the right-hand side. That must have been what he'd used to cut his foot. "You heal," the officer said, "but first you hurt."

Patch looked the man in the eye and saw what he expected to see: behind the cool confidence was fear. He had fought enough cage fights to know how to use an opponent's fear against him. He said, "Yes, I heal. But I don't always run away when people find out about me. Sometimes I quiet them down another way."

"You're threatening me?"

"Call it setting some ground rules. If we're going to work together."

The officer put the scalpel back on the nightstand. "All right," he said. "We'll play nice."

"Why don't you start by telling me what you want?"

The major sat on the edge of the cot again, stroked his little mustache, then said, "What I want is a career. I want to be on the inside where the big decisions get made, to be the one who makes those decisions, and the bigger the better."

Patch shifted under the restraints but they were too tight. "What's that got to do with me?" he said.

"This war's going to end," the officer said. "We'll roll up the Germans in Italy in another year or so. Then there'll be a second front in France and we'll kick them right back to Germany, until we meet the Russkies coming the other way.

"And when that happens, there'll be a new war, a long war. But not a tanks and bombers war. Everybody will be too worn-out to go right into more of what we've all been getting. No, this will be a struggle waged in the shadows. A war of assassins."

"I'm a soldier," Patch said, "not a murderer."

The major went on as if he hadn't heard him. "There's a place back home," he said, "called Camp X. It's where they train spies and agents before they drop them into occupied Europe. I know some people there. They're developing new programs, already preparing for the next war. One program is called Weapon X."

He broke off and looked at Howlett. "Do you know what a mutant is?" he said.

"No."

"Never mind. A wolf doesn't need to know what a wolf is. He just needs to be a wolf."

"What's your point?"

"Let's just say they're looking for a certain kind of recruit. And an officer who walks in with just what they're looking for can write his own ticket."

Patch looked away, as if giving the matter some thought. "What's in it for me?" he said.

The major chuckled. "Glory, three square meals a day, an opportunity to travel, 'The Maple Leaf Forever'—whatever floats your boat."

"Huh," Patch said. "So I could write my own ticket, too?"

"Within reason. Better than being a corporal."

"Huh."

The major's voice hardened. "And better than spending twenty years in a military prison. You are a deserter, after all."

"Well, then, they can just shoot me," Patch said. "Then we'll shake hands, say we're square, and all go our separate ways."

"Ha ha," said the major. "If that were to happen, some general would scoop you up and deliver you to the same people I would."

"Doesn't sound like I have much of a choice."

"Sure you do. Think about it. Just don't think too hard. Leave the thinking to me and this could be an ideal partnership."

"I'd still like that drink."

"Sir."

"Sir," Patch said. "This healing thing, it makes me thirsty."

The staff officer's eyes grew bright behind the lenses of his spectacles. "Yes, tell me about that. How does it work? How long does it take? What does it feel like?"

"If I could have a drink, sir."

The major got up, went over to a carafe and tumbler on the nightstand. He poured water and held it to the corporal's lips.

"If you would just untie this strap across my chest, I could sit up and do it myself."

Suspicion seemed to draw the major's close-set eyes closer together. Patch said, "I'd still be strapped in from the waist down. Being able to heal fast doesn't make me Superman."

The man put the glass on the nightstand, then squatted down to do something beneath the bed, out of Patch's line of sight. The strap across his chest loosened and the major stood back.

Howlett slowly eased himself up until he was resting on his elbows. He rolled his shoulders to loosen them. "That's better," he said, then reached with one hand for the glass of water, gulping it down. He set the glass back on the nightstand and put the hand that had held it under the covers again.

"Would you mind pouring me another, sir? Can't reach the jug. You know, the healing thing always dries me out."

Another thing Patch had learned from bare-knuckled fighting was that sometimes it helped to show the other man the opportunity he was looking for. You could draw him in close, where the real damage gets done. The major wanted to know about the mystery, because to him that was the door that could open on all of his dreams. He had his eyes on that prize as he moved in closer to pour another glass. And as the man was paying attention to the pouring, Patch flexed his forearms under the covers, felt the pain rip through the scarred flesh between his knuckles, the hot blood running down his fingers.

The officer moved to put the glass down on the nightstand, saying, "When did it start? Were you always like this, or did it come on—"

As the man's hand withdrew almost out of range, the corporal's left hand came out from beneath the covers, so fast it was a blur. Before the major could react, Patch swung toward him and three razor-edged claws punched down, piercing the hand that had held the glass and pinning it to the officer's thigh. Patch felt the shock of impact as his middle claw dug into the heavy leg bone.

The officer's body convulsed in agony, his knees buckling and his head coming forward, mouth open as he sucked in air for the scream that had to come. But the gasp was the last sound the major ever made, for as his face came within range, the corporal drove the claws of his right hand up and under the lenses of the wire-rimmed spectacles, through the eyeballs they covered, and all the way through the brain behind.

The officer twitched and jumped like a gigged frog, a noise like a dry cough issuing from his still-open mouth as his lungs deflated. Patch yanked free both sets of claws and the dead man slumped to the floor in an ungainly heap.

The corporal paid him no heed. He was already slashing with his bloody razors at the canvas straps that bound him to the cot. They parted like tissue paper

and moments later he was on his feet, if a little unsteady from being doped up and comatose. He flexed
his arms again and the weapons disappeared, leaving
the major's blood smeared on his knuckles.

Patch was naked except for a bandage across his
chest that he now tore free. A tall cupboard on the
other side of the tent yielded no clothing. His own
uniform must have been shredded in the blast that
killed MacLeish. He turned to the dead man and
pulled him by the armpits to straighten him out. He
was about the right height, though narrower in the
chest and shoulders.

Patch sniffed and said, "Good thing you didn't crap
your pants." As he began to unbutton the jacket, he
added, "Sir."

The major's Jeep had been easy enough to spot,
thanks to a division HQ tag on the hood. Now Patch
steered the vehicle along the waterfront road that led
north into Ortona. He hadn't bothered to turn on the
Jeep's slitted blackout headlights—his night vision
was good enough to guide him around piles of rubble
and craters that were gifts from the Germans. They
had rained down 88-millimeter shells on the road in
a vain attempt to stop the Canadians from breaking
through a few days before.

He had to put distance between himself and the
hospital. Eventually, the intimidated doctor would
want to know what had happened in the VIP ward.

He would find the cot empty, its restraints slashed, and a man-size scalpel slit in the outer wall. And when someone thought to look in the cupboard, they would find the staff officer, eyeless and naked as Samson.

Between now and then, Corporal Howlett needed a better-developed plan than a stolen Jeep and an ill-fitting officer's uniform. A mile or so ahead was the town and the harbor. There might be a few fishing boats tied up. Even a dinghy would do. He could row up the coast and go ashore behind the German lines, use his commando training and his old bush skills as a hunter to live off the land and evade capture. He'd heard the hills inland had caves that had been used by shepherds since before Caesar's legions had marched along this same road he was driving.

Ultimately, of course, somebody would want to know how the major had been killed. But at this point, the only people in Ortona who had known Patch's identity were probably still being dug out of the rubble of a row of houses or waiting to be discovered in a field hospital cupboard. If he stayed out of sight for a while, he could come back, tell a tale of being captured by a Jerry patrol and having escaped, then go back to being just another corporal.

He saw a military police checkpoint up the road and pulled the Jeep over beneath a stand of poplars. Nobody would mistake him for a staff officer and he had no papers. He proceeded up the road on foot, then went down onto his belly for the last hundred yards, wriggling his way silently through a grove of olive trees. Past the MPs, he moved stealthily through the darkness until he came to the edge of the town.

He eased himself through the shadows between two little buildings and found himself looking across the road to a seawall, with the masts of ships beyond. He crossed the open space and crouched at the top of the wall. The tide was out, the exposed shore reeking of kelp and harbor sludge. Several fishing boats were tied up below him in a rectangular basin between two stone jetties, but none were small enough for him to get out of the harbor without starting up an engine. He needed something more basic—a rowboat pulled up on a beach.

He recrossed the road and continued north, slipping between houses and shacks, keeping to the darkest spots, and looking seaward between the buildings for the kind of craft that could take him away. A couple of blocks farther on, he came to a broad street that led inland. That was not the direction he needed to take, but he looked up the street and saw that it opened on to a square.

Across the open space he could see the corner of a building, a whitewashed wall with black lettering painted on it: OSTERIA GAMBRELLI. He could see a chink of light through a shuttered window.

A wave of regret washed over him. He remembered Rob Roy MacLeish's face as he'd talked about the girl from the tavern, about the plans they were

starting to make for after the war. He wondered if anyone had told her what had happened to her sergeant,
or whether she was in there right now, pouring wine
and grappa for soldiers and wondering when her Loyal
Eddie would come rolling in, twinkling those green
eyes.

He hadn't been able to save his friend, but he could
do something for Rob Roy's girl—at least tell her gently what had happened, before she overheard it in the
kind of language soldiers used when they were in a
tavern talking about the newly dead. He could just
imagine Lucia Gambrelli's heart lifting when someone
mentioned that Rob Roy MacLeish had bought a
farm, and he could picture how her face would look
when someone explained what those pleasant words
really meant.

He turned toward the tavern, sidling along the
street on its darkest side. The square was empty when
he reached it. He straightened his shoulders and
marched across the open space like an officer who had
every right to do what he was doing. He angled his approach to bring him to the alley that ran along the side
of the *osteria* and worked his way to where a board
fence enclosed the yard at the back of the building. He
put his hands on the top of the boards and vaulted
silently over.

The rear door was unlatched. He stepped through
into a kitchen full of warmth and good smells but
empty of people. In the center was a long wooden

counter, topped in gray stone, beneath a frame from which hung pots and utensils. A black iron range, wood-burning, stood against the outer wall to his right, steam coming from a couple of big lidless pots. He sniffed at one of them, thinking Rob Roy would have got himself a fine cook, would have grown comfortably fat on pasta and cheese sauce. On the inner wall, a pair of double doors painted dark brown led to the tavern's main room. They were still swinging—someone must have gone through them just before he'd come in through the back door.

Patch moved to stand beside the doors and waited. He heard a clatter of crockery, then the doors swung inward and a young woman with lustrous black hair and the kind of perfect face Howlett had seen on statues in Italian churches came through bearing an armload of plates and salvers. She crossed the room to pile them on a counter by the sink and he moved silently behind her. When he put his hand over her mouth she started and struggled, but he held firmly while he whispered in her ear, "I'm a friend of Rob Roy MacLeish."

He had to say it twice before she stopped struggling. He released her and she turned to him. "He not come tonight," she said. "You bring message?"

He saw her big dark eyes moving as she searched his face. Before he could speak, she read what was there and her eyes filled with tears. "Oh, no," she said.

"It was very quick," he said. It was probably true,

and it was better than telling her her man had died an agonizing death, crushed by shattered masonry or ripped open by splintered floorboards.

Her shoulders sagged. She clasped her hands in front of her and looked down at them. "First, my father," she said. "Then my brother. Now the man I love." A tear fell onto the back of her hand and trickled toward her wrist.

"Maybe your brother is just hiding from the Germans," Patch said. "Maybe he got stranded behind their lines when the front moved north."

She looked up at him, a little hope fighting its way through the sorrow. "It is what Rob Roy say. But I think it is just to make me not sad. He say he look for him when they push the *Tedeschi* more north."

"A good plan. We're pushing them back every day."

She sighed and another tear came. "Now nobody look."

"Do you know where he would be?"

"There is a *caverna* we play in when we are *bambini*."

"*Caverna*? You mean a cave?"

"*Si*. A few *chilometri* past my uncle Enzo's olive trees. Giovanni would go there. It has water from the rock."

A cave with a spring. It sounded perfect. Patch said, "I will go and take a look. Tonight. Tell me how to get there."

She stepped back and took a good look at him now. "You?" she said. "The *Tedeschi* will shoot you. They have very good *soldati*—*soldati dei paracaduti*. You know what that is?" Her hands sketched a parachute in the air over her head.

"I know," he said. "But I am a very good *paraca*-whatsit soldier, too."

She looked at the officer's insignia on his epaulets, the uniform blouse that didn't quite fit. He saw a spark of suspicion in her eyes. "Who are you?" she said.

"My name is Patch."

The name meant something to her, but the doubt was still there. "Show me your hands," she said, "like this." She held up two small fists.

He showed her his knuckles. She touched their scars, the old ones and the fresh pink ones, with one small finger. "He tell me of you. Before the war, you fight, he win money on you. Every time."

"That's true."

"You look for Giovanni? Help him?"

"I will go to the cave. If he's there, I will help him, keep him safe until the *Tedeschi* are all gone."

The suspicion came back. "Why? What is Giovanni to you? What am I to you?"

"It is because of what you were to Rob Roy MacLeish. Because he was my friend, and I don't have too many friends."

He asked her if she had a photograph. She went out of the kitchen and came back in a couple of minutes with a black-and-white photo that had been taken right outside the tavern. The man had posed very formally, in the Italian way, one hand tucked inside his buttoned jacket. But his handsome face was broken by a wide smile.

"I make him laugh," she said, "just before Poppi make the *foto*."

Patch studied the image for a moment, then handed it back.

"That is enough?" she said. "You don't forget?"

"I never forget a face," he told her.

## Ortona, Italy, the present

AT ROME'S LEONARDO DA VINCI AIRPORT, Logan had changed his Canadian dollars for euros at the currency exchange booth, the pretty Italian girl behind the glass wicket showing a little surprise as he pulled handfuls of paper money from different pockets. "I packed in kind of a hurry," he said.

He had taken a taxi to Stationi Termini, the city's main railroad station, and learned that if he wanted to get to Ortona he first had to take a train east to the city of Ancona on the Adriatic Sea, then transfer to a southbound line. By midafternoon he was in a coach heading down Italy's east coast. He had chosen a seat on the inland side and now he watched the hills and fields roll by, interrupted by fishing villages and ancient towns whose modern inhabitants made most of their living off tourists.

All of it had looked familiar, and yet none of it had. It was a landscape he had seen before, but none of the landmarks leaped out at him and said, *you were here.* After a while he leaned his head against the window and closed his eyes. Images came to him in flashes, mostly of anonymous places—a row of houses, a wooden door in a whitewashed wall, a rooftop seen at night. None of the pictures connected, but he sensed that there was a thread linking them—or that there had been until somebody had carefully and systematically gone through his brain, snipping the linkages away. Leaving him what he was, a man who didn't even know his name.

The train came into Ortona in the evening. He stepped onto the platform and knew right away that all of what he was seeing was too new to be of use to him. Everything must have been rebuilt since the war. He walked into town, turning corners at random, looking at the buildings lit by the modern streetlights. Waiting for some scene to speak to him, but getting nothing.

Then he came around another corner and found himself at the edge of a small square. On one side of the piazza, a short street ran down to an enclosed harbor where fishing boats mixed with pleasure craft. On the other was a small square building with bright yellow walls, light spilling from its windows and music sounding from behind a pair of doors painted red. From an iron bracket that projected above the door

hung a wooden sign, on which were carved in curva-
ceous letters the words OSTERIA GAMBRELLI.

*That's wrong,* he thought. He couldn't make out
what it was about the scene that was wrong, and the
harder he tried to nail it down the more elusive it became. Then he forced himself not to try. He stood and
just looked at the tavern, even letting his eyes unfocus.
And now it came. The walls should be white. The
backyard should have a wooden fence, not waist-high
iron railings and tables and chairs. The sign shouldn't
be over the door but painted on the wall. But the
name called up a faint touch of a feeling that fled when
he tried to catch it.

He could hear his pulse beating faster in his ears. *I've
been here. Not in a dream. Not just somebody telling me about
it. Nobody implanted this memory in me. I've* been *here.*

He crossed the square, pulled open the tavern door,
stood there letting his eyes roam over what was in the
big public room: tables and chairs, tourists and locals
eating and drinking, a pair of musicians weaving notes
from a mandolin and violin into some happy tune over
a buzz of conversation and laughter. Some of them
looked up as he stood in the doorway, but quickly
looked away again. The full-bellied man in shirtsleeves
behind the bar gave him a more searching inspection,
then put on a professional smile and reached for a
plastic-covered menu.

"Signor?" he said and when Logan made no answer,
"you want a table, some wine?"

Logan just wanted to look, to find out if the inside of the place would call up the same certainty as the outside had. So far nothing was coming and he flicked his eyes toward this man who was distracting him, irritating him. The fellow took a half step backward, then Logan got hold of himself and said, "Yes, a table. No wine. Do you have Seven Crown whiskey?"

"*Non,* signor," the bartender said and led him to a table with two chairs near a pair of swinging doors in the inner wall. Logan glanced at the menu. The whole thing was in Italian, but he recognized some of the items. That didn't mean anything, he told himself— he'd find the same dishes offered in restaurants on Ottawa's Sparks Street mall.

He tried the same technique he'd used outside. It was harder here, with the distractions of the chattering crowd and the musicians, but he let his gaze wander at random around the room, seeing but not focusing on the paintings on the walls—ships on the sea and a big stone church on a hill—and the shapes of the windows.

None of it rang that inner bell that he'd heard when he'd been outside. Not until his eyes came all the way around the room to the two swinging doors. They were of dark old wood, slotted lathes with gaps in between, in a simple frame that had been painted more than once. And now the feeling came again, and with it the urge to see what was behind.

He rose and stepped through the door, took in the scene beyond. A mustachioed man in white was at a natural gas range to his left, shaking a skillet full of something that sizzled on the heat. The waiter who had brought his wine was arranging slices of crusty bread in a basket at a granite-topped table in the center of the room. He looked up, startled, as Logan came through the door.

"Signor," he said, "you cannot come here. It is not for the customers."

Logan ignored the protest, ignored the voice of the bartender in the public room behind him, who was also saying, "Signor, Signor," the voice getting closer. He let his mind go, let the sight and, most of all, the smell of the kitchen just come to him, without trying to focus on any one detail. And again, it happened: *The stove, that's different. The counter, that's the same. And the door leading outside, it's been painted, but I know it.*

As he looked at the door that led to the tavern's backyard, it opened. Through it came an old woman in a black dress, her face lined but full of dignity, her dark eyes meeting his with a challenge that left Logan in no doubt that she was in authority here.

The bartender was tugging fitfully at his elbow from behind, the waiter was advancing toward him with a worried look but making shooing motions with both hands, and the chef had turned from his cooking but the expression of outrage that had begun to appear on his face was rapidly dying. Logan did not see any of them.

His eyes were locked on the old woman. The look

of resentment that she had first cast at the intruder in her domain had been shattered by an outbreak of astonishment, tinged by superstitious fear—as if she had walked into her own kitchen and come face-to-face with a ghost.

She stood frozen in the doorway, eyes wide and mouth open. Then she brought one pale hand to her lips and whispered, "Patch!"

For all Logan knew, it could have been a word from some obscure Italian dialect, a curse to fend off the evil eye. Yet he could tell right away that it was a name, and that she had called him by it. And he knew that the shock on her face was the shock of recognition.

"My name is Logan," he said.

He saw her react to his voice, saw that its sound only confirmed what she had already decided. She crossed the room, moving briskly despite her age and dismissing the waiter and the bartender with a quick flurry of Italian. She came around the counter and looked up at him. Her eyes on him stirred another memory.

"Your name is Logan?" she said.

He was going to say, "Yes." Instead, he said, "I think so."

"Show me your hands," she said, holding up two closed fists, "like this."

He put up his hands. She touched the knuckles with a slim finger.

"Your name," she said, "is Patch."

## Ortona, Italy, December 1943

IT HELPED THAT THE ROWBOAT HAD BEEN painted black. He'd muffled the oars with rags stuffed into the oarlocks after he'd taken it from the little boathouse where Lucia Gambrelli's father used to keep it. The innkeeper had liked to go out on the sea in good weather, to relax and catch a fish or two.

The boat was now drifting empty on the outgoing tide and Patch Howlett was a couple of miles inland from the big white rock on the shore that she'd told him to look for. He'd skirted a farm abandoned by its owner and which was now the temporary quarters of a German infantry company, crawling and wriggling through the sparse grass of a winter pasture. Then he'd found the goat path that led west and into the hills, well away from the old road that was patrolled by the enemy.

The sky was clouded and the land almost completely dark, but his night vision kept him on track. The higher he rose in these foothills of the Appenines, the clearer he could see the Adriatic flat and gray behind him, where an offshore break in the clouds lit the sea with a pearly light.

There were fewer Germans in the higher country. They must expect the real assault to come on the coastal plain, he reasoned. These steep and grassy hills, cut by narrow ravines that ran east and west, were no place for armor to operate. And tank-supported infantry actions were the mainstay of both sides in this campaign, when they weren't trying to slaughter each other with artillery barrages.

He came to a level area at the top of the goat path, a small plateau planted in neat rows of olive trees. *Uncle Enzo's place,* he told himself. The winter-dry leaves of the trees rustled in a chill wind that rolled down from the higher country, but he didn't mind—the sound would cover any noise he made. He went quickly through the first grove, over a low stone fence and through a second stand that ended where the land began to climb sharply again.

He went up a grassy slope so steep he sometimes had to use his hands. The wind was strengthening so that he didn't smell the wet wool of sheep until he almost stumbled upon a small flock nestled in a hollow. The ewes bleated sleepily and the ram snorted at him, but the animals quieted when he kept on moving higher, glad that there was no dog to make a noisy fuss.

He was pretty sure he was following Lucia's directions, and he became certain when he came to the tall standing rocks with a tree growing sideways out of them. Beyond the rocks, the slope eased and he soon came to the brow of the hill and began to descend the other side. The western slope was even more gradual, and he could make out a stand of poplars down and to his left. He angled toward them and moments later he was among the trees.

It was pitch black here, but he heard the gurgle of water that the woman had told him to listen for. He went toward it, then followed the little stream until he found where it issued from a crack in the hillside. A bush covered the fissure, but he worked his way behind it as Lucia had told him to do, and found that the crack widened a little higher up the slope. He put his nose to the cave entrance, smelled damp earth and blood and something else that he could not quite place.

"Giovanni," he whispered. "Giovanni Gambrelli."

"*Sono qui,*" came a faint voice from within. Patch thought it meant, "I'm here."

He squeezed his way through the gap in the rock, his booted foot coming down on the soft earth floor of the cave. In the complete blackness of the interior, Logan could not see anything, but his animal sense told him that someone was nearby. Hands extended, he felt his way forward, sniffing the air. Now he knew what the unnatural smell was: gun oil.

"*Non spari,*" he said. The combined special force had been taught a few Italian phrases that might come in handy on a battlefield. That one meant "don't shoot."

He took another step into the darkness and his eyes were blasted by the sudden glare of a powerful flashlight. Logan looked away, but his field of vision was filled with a purple ring of afterimage.

"*Non si muova,*" said a hard voice and Logan knew that the words meant "don't move." He also knew that they had not come from Giovanni Gambrelli. The accent was German.

Still half-blinded, he swung toward the light again, flexing his arms and preparing to spring. But whoever held the flashlight was not alone. From the side came a burst of automatic fire and the unmistakable rip of a Schmeisser machine pistol. Logan felt the rounds tear into his legs below the knee, piercing his flesh though missing the bones. Still, the impacts staggered him, and as he toppled forward the brass plate of a rifle butt loomed out of the darkness and smashed into the side of his head.

## Ortona, Italy, the present

"HOW CAN YOU BE HERE, UNCHANGED?" THE old woman said. "It is more than sixty years."

"I don't know," Logan said. "My memory is gone. I'm trying to find out who I am."

They were sitting in a small parlor in the living quarters upstairs. She had poured herself a glass of the fiery Italian brandy called grappa—Logan had declined to join her—and now she regarded him with wonder. But she had the kind of mind that does not stand in awe of mystery for long, the kind that has to grapple with the puzzle and make sense of it. When she said, "How can you be here?" she wanted an answer.

"But you remember this place?" she said. "You came here because you remember?"

So he told her what he knew, produced the pictures he had torn from the library book and brought with him. She touched the photograph of the men sitting outside the tavern, and a tear came to her eyes. "I never saw this picture," she said.

"Is that you?"

"Yes. And that is my Rob Roy."

"Rob Roy?" The name echoed somewhere in the fog behind his mind.

"Rob Roy MacLeish." She touched the image of the fair-haired soldier looking up at her long-ago self. "He was your great friend." She paused, then said, "If you are truly you."

"What happened to him?"

She told him. The words went through him like the melody of a forgotten song. He closed his eyes, listening to her, and saw images: a man's face, smeared in blacking; a small window; a rooftop covered in terracotta tiles.

"Do you have a photo of him?" he said.

She rose and went to an ornate credenza, opened a wide, shallow drawer, and reached into a back corner. "I had to hide this from my husband," she said, "all our years together. He would not have understood."

She handed him an old black-and-white photograph, now faded by the passage of time. Logan looked at the smiling face and there was no question. "I knew him. The memory is real." He closed his eyes and let his mind go loose, and more images came to him: MacLeish grinning at him over a mug of beer; MacLeish on the other end of a two-man saw, sawdust flying as they bucked a big spruce log in a lumber camp.

"How can it be?" she said again. "Look at me in your old photograph. And look at me now. Why are you not old?"

"I don't know."

"Did you fall into a hole in time and come out sixty years later? Or did someone put you in a *congelatore* full of ice to keep you frozen?"

"I don't think so. But how would I know?"

"Who was the first man to land on the moon?" she said.

"Neil Armstrong."

"Who is Michael Jackson?"

"A pop singer, kind of weird."

"9/11."

"Planes flying into the World Trade Center."

Her face said, *that settles it.* He had not been catapulted from the 1940s to the early twenty-first century. Nor had he been cryogenically frozen and recently thawed out. "You have lived the same years I have lived," she said, "but something has stolen away the particular memories of your own story."

"Not something," he said. "Someone."

"Ah," she said. "And you mean to find that some-one, to ask him who you are."

"Yes, and then I'm going to ask him why he did this to me."

"I don't think," she said, "the answers to your questions will please you."

"That's all right. I don't think he'll like the way I ask them."

## Ortona, Italy, December 1943

"WHO ARE YOU? WHAT IS YOUR MISSION?"

Patch Howlett tried to see past the bright light that shone into his eyes when they pulled off the blind-fold, but the figure beyond remained in shadow. He was bound to a sturdy wooden chair, his hands mana-cled behind him. The room had whitewashed walls, but the white was flecked here and there with the red of blood. There were dark stains on the concrete floor.

A hard hand came from behind the glare, moving fast, to connect with his cheek and slap his head side-ways. "Do I have your attention now, Herr Major?" the voice said, giving the last word the German pro-nunciation, *my-or.* "Or do I need to—" The sentence was finished by the same hand striking from the other direction, the pain of the backhanded blow embell-ished by a heavy signet ring.

"Let me acquaint you with your situation," the unseen man continued. "You are not a prisoner of war. You are a captured spy, taken in a trap laid for these Italian pigs who cut the throats of our sentries and blow up troop trains."

The interrogator began pacing the floor behind the light as he spoke, and now Howlett saw that the man's uniform was not that of the Wehrmacht, the regular German army. Instead the black collar tabs showed the double lightning-bolt runes of the SS and the single oak-leaf rank insignia of a Standartenführer—the equivalent of a colonel. The heavy ring on his right hand was inset with a black stone inlaid with the SS symbol in silver.

Before the First Special Service Force was deployed to the Italian front, Howlett and the rest of his unit had been warned that if they were captured, the Germans might not observe the rules of war. British commandos taken in raids on German installations in occupied France had been shot by the SS, even though they were fighting in uniform and with proper identity disks around their necks.

"So there will be none of your name, rank, and number nonsense," the SS man said. "No cozy chat with some oaf of a Wehrmacht intelligence officer, then off to a Stalag to sit out the war drinking tea and opening Red Cross parcels.

"You will tell me everything I want to know, sooner

or later. If it is sooner, I may send you off to a concentration camp. If it is later, you will welcome the firing squad that relieves you of your misery."

Howlett could see his face now. Young but not too young, with the blond hair and blue eyes that the Nazis liked to think were the unmistakable marks of racial superiority. But this one also probably had brains, or he wouldn't have risen so soon to high rank in the highly competitive rat race of the SS intelligence service. It would not be a good idea to fence with him—and besides, it was easier to tell the truth.

"I was looking for Giovanni Gambrelli," he said.

The statement earned him another slap. "We know that. You called his name as you came into the cave."

With a little training, the German would have made a decent bare-knuckle fighter, Patch thought. He had the natural ability to hit hard. His cheek stinging, he said, "I promised his sister, Lucia, that I would look for him. She's worried."

This time it was not a slap. The SS man's fist landed a short but powerful punch to Patch's jaw, the ring ripping his flesh and drawing blood. "If you want to play games," he said, "I know some good ones."

"It's the truth," Howlett said. He shook his head to quiet the ringing, thinking the Jerry really could have been a contender. "She's worried about her brother and I'm in trouble. I punched out an officer and stole his uniform. Lucia told me about the cave above her uncle's olive trees. I could hide out there until my unit moved on, then I could come down and help her run the tavern."

The blue eyes were watching him closely. "You are not a major?"

"No."

The German touched the collar tags on Patch's uniform. "Not a divisional staff officer?"

Howlett's head came up and he looked directly into the man's eyes. "Do I look like a staff officer?"

The German's eyes narrowed. "Then what is your rank? What is your unit?"

"The Loyal Edmonton Regiment," Patch said. "I'm a sergeant. Sergeant Rob Roy MacLeish."

## Berlin, Germany, December 1943

WHEN THE ORDERLY OPENED THE DOOR, Wolfgang Freiherr von Strucker strode into the vast, high-ceilinged room in the SS headquarters on Prinz Albrechtstrasse, marched to the ornate desk against the far wall, and stood to attention. With military precision, he threw out his right arm in the Nazi salute and said, "Heil Hitler!" at the same time bringing the heels of his polished boots together in a resounding *clack*. Then he removed his officer's cap with the red skull insignia, placed it under his arm, and waited for the slight-statured man behind the desk to notice him.

For several seconds, the only sound in the room was the scratching of the gold nib of a fountain pen on a sheet of cream-colored vellum paper. The top of the paper bore a swastika-and-eagle-wings emblem, and beneath it, the title Reichsführer-SS that belonged to the mousy little man in the black uniform.

Heinrich Himmler wrote another line in his spiky, compressed handwriting, then added his jagged signature at the bottom. He recapped the pen and laid it on the desk, took up a rocking blotter, and carefully dried the wet ink before placing the page in a basket at the corner of the desk. Only then did he look up at the Prussian baron standing rigidly before him and say, "Tell me, Herr Oberführer, why are you wasting the Reich's resources and producing no results?"

"I am expecting very good results any day now," von Strucker said. "We are near to isolating the brain chemistry that governs muscular reflexes. When we succeed—"

"If you succeed," said Himmler. His voice was mild, but the baron knew the SS leader could order mass murder in the same tone that he would use to call for a cup of herbal tea.

"We will succeed, Herr Reichsführer. It is but a matter of refining the samples taken from the test subjects' brains. Then we will—"

The little man's round spectacles flashed in the light from the lamps. Now the tone grew sharp. "It is always 'but a matter' of this or that. Yet every time you claim to have overcome one obstacle, I immediately hear that a new one has suddenly appeared in your path."

"The brain is a complex—"

"Yes, yes, very complex. But I am a simple man, Herr Oberführer. I give orders, and I expect results. If I do not get the results I want, the results the Reich needs, I give new orders."

"Yes, Herr Reichsführer," the baron said.

"Will I have to give new orders concerning you?"

"No, Herr Reichsführer."

"See that I don't." Himmler reached for another piece of paper from the stack at this elbow and uncapped his fountain pen. It was a moment before von Strucker realized he had been dismissed.

His Mercedes-Benz staff car was waiting outside. The uniformed SS driver holding the door open for him was almost certainly assigned to report any evidence of disloyalty so the baron kept his face rigidly neutral. He told the man to drive him back to the hospital in what had been a leafy neighborhood of Berlin before the Allied bombers had reduced much of it to rubble. The car drove to a service area at the building's rear and through a segmented door that rolled upward as they neared it. They descended by a spiral ramp to an installation deep below street level, where von Strucker went straight to his office and summoned his team leaders to an emergency meeting.

"Himmler has given us an ultimatum," he told the four men in lab coats. "If we do not produce good results soon, this project will be abandoned. I do not need to spell out the consequences."

The four faces paled. The Reichsführer-SS had personally authorized their project. Their failure would be an embarrassment to him if Herman Goering or Joseph Goebbels, his rivals in the Nazi inner circle, got wind of it. So if von Strucker's team were broken up, the breakage might be literal—Gestapo men in black leather trench coats would come for them and the last sights any of them would see would be the graves they would have to dig for themselves in some isolated woodland, as each waited for the pistol shot to the back of the head.

The most senior of the scientists, Dr. Schlimmer, touched a pale hand to the top of his head to make sure the long hair he combed sideways over his bald crown was still pomaded in place and said, "The Iron Eagles are ready for a demonstration."

"Define 'ready,' " said von Strucker.

"We have delineated the correct dosages for optimum effect."

"And the side effects?"

"Minimal."

"What about the man who became psychotic?"

Schlimmer patted his hair again and swallowed nervously. "An underlying psychological flaw that was not detected in the screening. It was unique to that subject."

"You are sure?" the baron said. "The Reichsführer

will want to inspect them closely. We would not want one of them to try to tear out his throat."

"We will screen them all again. Rigorously."

The other three projects were in no shape to put before Himmler for a demonstration. The "invisible boy" had a tendency to throw his own excrement when he was afraid, and since meeting new people usually frightened him, no one could guarantee he would be out of ammunition if he was trotted out to impress Himmler.

The Dutch teenager who could dream her way back through time was better, but von Strucker did not want to produce her until he could deliver a scientific explanation of the genetic basis for her strange talent, so that he could design a reliable breeding program. A corps of spies who could eavesdrop on any conversation within twenty-four hours of its occurring, or read any document that had ever been composed, would be sure to perk up Himmler's interest. But right now all he had was an inexplicable mutation.

"We must bring in more . . . opportunities for study," he said. "Our people in the camps must examine more prospects." As he spoke, he glared at Bucher, the stocky, pink-skinned man who was responsible for coordinating the search for mutants.

"They do their best," Bucher said, perspiration breaking out on his moon-shaped face. "The camp administrators complain that our examinations slow down their processing of the inmates."

Von Strucker made his decisions. To Schlimmer, he said, "Prepare a demonstration of the Iron Eagles. Give them that unit of captured Red Guards for targets, but make sure the Ivans are well-fed and rested."

He turned to Bucher. "You will personally visit each of the camps. Remind the commandants that we are working under the expressed authority of the Reichsführer-SS." But to himself, he thought, *At least, until that authority is withdrawn.*

He suppressed a shudder as his staff filed out of his office, Bucher carefully closing the door behind him like a schoolboy who has just escaped an expected thrashing from the headmaster. The Prussian sat at his desk and stared at the portrait of Adolf Hitler that hung on the opposite wall.

*I am ruled by a blowhard from Bavaria and a man who used to farm chickens,* he thought, *and I am trying to make miracles for them.* He leaned forward to place his elbows on the desk and lowered his forehead onto his spread fingertips. The Iron Eagles demonstration would buy him time, time to intensify the search for mutants. He knew they were out there. His search teams found prospects and fed them back to him, though most of their talents were militarily useless—people who could digest iron or extract the square root of a ten-digit number in an eyeblink.

Most of them turned out to be demented or otherwise unuseful. Still, just going by the odds, there must be others out there—people with valuable inborn talents who were neither insane nor crippled by degenerative physical conditions. But why was he not finding them? Did they learn early to hide their conditions?

If so, he had a solution. He had dissected enough of the useless varieties to believe that he could eventually home in on a vector that would yield a reliable test. The difference would be revealed in the blood, and von Strucker would devise a blood test that would tell their secrets. His searchers would be able to drip a drop of blood into a tube or onto a piece of treated paper and know within moments if the ordinary-seeming man or woman before them was one of the common herd—or one of the precious few.

In the meantime, he could at least make some members of that herd capable of performing amazing feats. He had made a close study of adrenaline and of the neural structures that governed reflex and reaction time. Combining his own researches with those of the Reich scientists who were developing ever more powerful amphetamines, he had produced a formula that stimulated the brain to hyperspeed while providing the skeletal muscles with the energy required to function at their maximum. The hysterical strength that sometimes allowed mothers to lift automobiles off their pinned offspring could now be artificially instilled in anyone who swallowed one of von Strucker's pills.

But the effects were only temporary. The Iron

Eagles were fine soldiers made even finer for a few hours. Then they fell apart, burned out, and were often unusable again. They were perfect for a short-lived blitzkrieg assault. But two years of fighting in Russia had taught even Hitler that some victories could only be won by playing the long game. Now the Reich required supersoldiers who remained super, year after year—and Wolfgang Freiherr von Strucker had sworn to the Reichsführer-SS that he could deliver them.

"You are going to die," von Strucker's translator told the company of Red Guards standing at attention in the broad courtyard of the former military school that had been turned over to the baron for the development of his *Eisenadler.* The place had been used to train cadets since the days of muzzle-loading cannon and unrifled muskets, long before Chancellor von Bismarck and the first Kaiser Wilhelm had assembled the German state from a collection of squabbling principalities.

Not one of the Russians moved or gave any indication that the translator's words meant anything to them. "You will die," the translator repeated, "but you will have an opportunity to die fighting. Like men. Like soldiers."

The elite rifle company's captain took one pace forward, slamming his right foot to the flagstoned ground as if he was on parade before the Kremlin. He looked straight ahead as he spoke. "You have perhaps mistaken us for Ukrainski," he said, in passable German, referring to the black-uniformed Ukrainian SS troops who guarded many of the concentration camps. "We will not fight for you."

Von Strucker waved the translator away and spoke directly to the Russian officer. "We do not want you to fight *for* us," he said. "We want you to fight *against* us."

The captain's broad Slavic face registered suspicion, but he could not keep a shadow of grim curiosity from creeping into the hard stare he turned toward the baron. He and his men had thought their war was over, that they would be sent to be forced laborers— slaves—in Nazi factories, dying of the diseases that came with overwork and underfeeding. If they weren't beaten to death by guards, many of them with Ukrainian accents, who delighted in dealing out sadistic punishment to Russians. It was not the kind of death that appealed to men of a guards regiment that had twice been awarded the Order of the Red Banner, the second time presented by Marshal Zhukov himself.

The Russian turned his head and regarded the SS soldiers ranged on all sides of the walled courtyard, their submachine guns trained on the prisoners of war. "Bare hands against Schmeissers?" he said. "We might still take a few of you."

"No," said von Strucker. "Here are your weapons." He signaled to an SS sergeant who stood beside a pile of wooden crates marked with Cyrillic lettering. The noncom stooped and upended one of the long boxes, then pulled away its lid. Inside were four Mosin-Nagant bolt-action rifles, slow to fire but as accurate as the Mausers that German troops used. The Prussian gestured again and another crate was opened, revealing two of the sturdy PPSH submachine guns with drum magazines that were standard issue for the Red Army.

"They were taken from your own armories in 1941," von Strucker said. "Still in their factory grease."

"I don't understand," the Russian captain said.

"Two kilometers east of here," the baron said, "is a stretch of woodland. You will be taken there with these weapons. You will find waiting for you an ample supply of ammunition and some entrenching tools.

"You will be left there overnight to make whatever preparations you like. In the morning you will be attacked by a special unit of shock troops. They will give no quarter, nor will they expect any.

"You will die. But you will die as men."

The captain's eyes went to the weapons, then back to von Strucker. "What if we decide to try to fight our way home?"

"Then you will still die. But you will die choking on the poison gas that the Luftwaffe will drop on you the moment you attempt to leave the woods."

The captain's face remained impassive as he received this information. Then a light came into his eyes and he showed the baron a humorless smile. He turned smartly on his heel to face his men. "*Tovarichi!*" he said, then barked a string of Russian.

Von Strucker saw the reactions among the prisoners as they looked to the crated weapons and heard their officer's explanation. The same cold fire came alight within them. Fists clenched and jaws set. When the captain finished by asking them a question, they responded as one man with a harsh cry of "*Da, da!*" *Aye-aye.*

*Good,* the Prussian thought. *They will do their part.*

In the gray light of a late-autumn German dawn, Heinrich Himmler's luxurious staff car entered the courtyard, followed by two other vehicles full of his aides and bodyguards. Flanked by an honor guard, von Strucker met the Reichsführer-SS as he stepped from the car, the little man's pale eyes passing over the men standing at attention with no more interest than if they were the stones beneath his feet.

"I have prepared a briefing, Herr Reichsführer," the baron said, leading the visitors into the school's main hall, where a sand table display of the operation's terrain awaited. But after the briefest overview of the miniature trees, fields, stone walls, and paper flags which represented the four squads of Iron Eagles, the head of the SS yawned and turned away.

"Here are the pertinent figures," von Strucker said, offering a sheaf of papers bound in a leather cover. Himmler flicked one finger in the direction of an aide whose boots, belt, and buttons were burnished to perfection. The hanger-on stepped forward and took the data.

"Well," said the little man, "we are here, so we might as well see it."

Von Strucker brought his heels together and thrust out his elbows. "*Jawohl,* Herr Reichsführer!" Within the privacy of his head he suppressed another set of remarks and gestured for the party to follow him out of the building. A path led them past the obstacle course to a steep hill that overlooked the exercise area. A bunker had been dug into the brow of the hill, its meter-thick walls of reinforced concrete pierced by narrow observation ports. Inside, von Strucker had made sure that a wooden step had been installed below the slot Himmler would look out of—making the Reichsführer-SS stand on tiptoe would not improve his mood.

The baron took two pairs of high-powered binoculars from a wooden compartment next to the observation port. He handed one to Himmler and slung the other around his neck. "If you are ready, Herr Reichsführer," he said.

The little man in the black uniform made a small sound that von Strucker took for a yes. The Prussian picked up the handset of a field telephone affixed to the wall and spun the crank on the instrument's side. He spoke into the receiver—"You may begin"—then lifted the binoculars to his eyes and adjusted the focus.

It had snowed briefly just before dawn, so the open field below and the evergreen woods it led to were lightly dusted with white. The *Eisenadler*, in their field gray, were clearly visible as they came out of the ditch at the near end of the field that was their start position and advanced toward the Russians. They went forward in four squads of eight men each, crouched low and moving fast.

The Red Guards were dug in at the edge of the woods. The ground was not frozen and they had had all night to dig foxholes and rifle pits and to cover them over with branches and small logs. The snow had helped camouflage their positions further. As von Strucker swept his binoculars over them, he could not easily make out where the enemy waited.

The Iron Eagles were halfway across the open ground now, advancing in open order through dead, knee-high grass, zigzagging constantly. A single shot rang out from beneath the trees, followed by a rattle of rifle and submachine gun fire. The advancing Iron Eagles dove face forward into the snow-covered grass. From von Strucker's vantage point they remained visible and he thought they resembled nothing so much as large gray snakes, wriggling toward the Russians at an impossible speed.

Each man also continued to move at a tangent, changing direction every few seconds, yet covering the distance to the edge of the pines faster than any Olympic sprinter could have managed on his feet and running straight and level. Now an *Eisenadler* abruptly lifted his head and upper torso above the tips of the dry grass, an automatic pistol in his hand.

The observers in the bunker heard two small *pops* as the enhanced soldier fired twice, but long before the sound crossed the distance, the man was back down again and wriggling sideways to take up a new firing position. Meanwhile, the Russians poured fire into the place where the shots had originated, even as other *Eisenadler* began to pop up and fire before disappearing from sight.

"Our men are armed with Lugers and fighting knives," von Strucker told Himmler, "and each pistol has only eight rounds. The Russians have good rifles and submachine guns, and plenty of ammunition."

"Hmm" was the Reichsführer's lukewarm reply.

"Although they appear to be shooting all along the line, they are concentrating much of their fire at the ends of the Russian position." He drew Himmler's attention to the far right of the Red Guards' firing line. "There you may notice that three of our men are now going into the woods. They will eliminate any command post and reserves, then come at the enemy's forward positions from behind."

Himmler made the same uninterested sound.

The firing from the edge of the woods had slackened. At the left of the Russian line, four more *Eisenadler* rushed from the field into the trees, moving so fast that they had disappeared beneath the shadow of

the dark pines within a heartbeat of rising up from the
grass. The men left in the grass snaked closer, still lifting up and firing single shots until their weapons were
empty, then abandoning them for the knife as they
slithered into Russian rifle pits and covered foxholes.
Occasional faint screams crossed the distance to the
bunker.

A silence fell on the scene below, broken moments
later by the harsh ring of the field telephone beside
von Strucker. The baron unhooked the receiver and
listened for a few seconds, then reported to his visitor,
"The enemy are all dead. We have sustained no casualties except for one man who was grazed by a rico-
chet."

Himmler lowered his binoculars and stepped
down from the observation port. He handed the
glasses to the baron and brushed a nonexistent spec of
dust from the front of his tunic. "I see," he said. "And
what do you believe this means, Herr Oberführer?"

"It means that the Reich has a potent new weapon,
Herr Reichsführer."

"Perhaps," Himmler said. "But creating potent new
weapons is not your assignment."

"Herr Reichsführer—" von Strucker began, but
had to fall silent as the little man held up one finger,
then wagged it warningly.

"You have taken ordinary men," Himmler said,
"indeed, men who are better than ordinary in strength
and coordination, and you have so enhanced their nat-

ural abilities that thirty-two of them armed with knives and pistols can cross open ground and wipe out a full company of better-armed enemy soldiers dug in under cover."

"Yes, Herr Reichsführer."

"But I do not want to enhance ordinary men. I want to create new men, a new breed of men whose superiority is not added by chemicals injected from the outside, but is to be found built into their very nature, born in them, in their lifeblood."

"Herr Reichsführer," von Strucker said. "These men can help win the war."

The little man gave him a look that, accompanied by a small shake of the head, meant that Himmler was talking to yet another fool who did not see the grand vision that was obvious to the Reichsführer-SS. He clasped his pale hands behind his back and began to pace back and forth in the bunker, head down, as if working out a problem.

"I am not concerned about winning the war," he said as he walked. "The dunderheads with red stripes on their pants who infest the general staff may worry about it, but I do not. We will win the war, probably next year when the new weapons come into production, but certainly by the end of 1945. We will win because it is our destiny to win."

Now he stopped and turned to face the baron, his spectacle lenses reflecting the morning light from outside the bunker. "My vision goes far beyond this year, far beyond this war. We are creating a thousand-year Reich. And that is not work for ordinary men, no matter how many drugs you may inject into them.

"That is work for supermen. And the task I have set you, Herr Oberführer, is to find those supermen. Find them or create them. If you can't do that, what use are you to me?"

## Ortona, Italy, December 1943

OF COURSE, THE INTELLIGENCE STANDARTEN-führer hadn't believed that Patch was a garden-variety sergeant of the Loyal Eddies. Not at first, and not even after a thorough beating that left the prisoner with a shattered kneecap, a fractured collarbone, and most of the small bones in his feet broken or cracked. The two SS men who methodically worked him over were experts. They stayed away from his head—because that was where any useful information would be stored—and concentrated on body parts that could be struck again and again, causing excruciating agony, but creating no risk that the man in the chair might be rendered useless.

"Tell me again about your years in the lumber camps," the officer said. "What kind of trees did you cut?"

"Mostly poplar and spruce, for the pulp mills—" Howlett began, then screamed as the beefy noncom standing behind him brought his oak truncheon down on the broken collarbone.

"And the red Indians," said the officer. "You said they were of the Blackfoot tribe, *ja?*"

This time, a bootheel came down on his ravaged naked feet, grinding the instep, making the ends of broken bones grate against each other. Patch howled.

"Gunter," said the interrogator, "I am trying to have a conversation with this man." The German corporal lifted his heel and the officer continued, "So, the Blackfoot, no?"

"No," said the prisoner, through clenched teeth. "The Blackfoot are in southern Alberta. Up north are mostly Cree and Métis."

The Standartenführer consulted his notes. "That is not what you said the first two times."

"You're wrong. It's the truth."

The end of the truncheon ground into the broken collarbone. Patch screamed and writhed under the agony. They kept rebreaking his bones before they could knit. But he concentrated on fighting the terrible itch in his forearms, handcuffed at the wrists behind the chair back. His claws would be useless, but if he let them show the interrogation would take a whole new direction. And he would not easily escape. Maybe never.

"Let us come back to Giovanni Gambrelli. How long did you say you have known him?"

"I don't know him. I know his sister." Howlett

tensed, waiting for the pain that accompanied each question and response. But the SS were masters of their cruel art and knew that as soon as the subject believed he understood the rhythm of the torture it was time to change the sequence of events.

After a while they took him out of the chair and suspended him by his pinioned arms from a chain strung from a hook set into the ceiling. The noncom and the private would lift him up and then let him drop, so that the full force of his plummeting weight would wrench his arms almost from their sockets. They beat him on the knees, ankles, and shins with their clubs, the bones cracking, until he shrieked and bellowed like a wounded beast.

"What is your name?" the officer screamed into his face as the blows landed.

"MacLeish! Rob Roy MacLeish!"

And then, suddenly, it was over. The officer looked at his watch and said something in German to the corporal. Howlett was unhooked from the chain and dragged from the room, down a damp corridor with brick walls and a concrete floor and thrown into a stinking cell.

For a long time, he lay on his side on the cold floor. At first the pain of the hurt they had done him washed through him like a speeded-up tide set to the pace of his own heartbeat, and he could hardly distinguish the fire of torn ligaments in his shoulders from the ice-sharp ache of his cracked shinbones. Then, gradually, the tide slackened and ebbed, the individual pangs and agonies separating themselves like small islands appearing as the sea went back home. He gritted his teeth as his body exercised its phenomenal power of self-repair. He hated bone breakage worse than when his flesh was cut or crushed—fractures hurt even as they healed.

"Are you all right?" The accent was Italian, not German. Patch took his mind away from his pains and noticed for the first time that he was not alone in the cell. A shadowy figure squatted beside him.

"I've been better," he said. "Who are you?"

"Bruno Tattaglia. You want me to help you? There are some rags over there you can lie on. Better than the floor. I have a little water also."

Patch shifted, drawing himself away from the stranger until he could get a better look at him. The cell was windowless and unlit, but a peephole in the door let in some light from the corridor outside, enough to see that the other man was in his twenties, dressed in a torn and filthy suit, his face discolored by fresh bruises. Patch levered himself to a sitting position, leaning back against the damp cold wall, and the man put a tin cup to his lips. He sniffed, and smelling only well water, drank.

"You are British?" Tattaglia said.

"Canadian."

"How did they catch you?"

"I got lost. What about you?"

"I am the schoolteacher in a village up in the hills. They were rounding up those they accused of being partisans."

He offered more water. Patch took another mouthful. "And are you?" he said.

"Am I what?"

"Are you a partisan?"

The man said, "And did you really just get lost?"

"I was looking for someone."

"Who?"

"Giovanni Gambrelli."

There was enough light for Patch to see the other man shrug. "You will not find him."

"Why not?"

"Because he is gone. First they squeezed what they could get out of him. They are very good at squeezing. Then they put him on a train to Germany. To a camp. They are emptying out places like this, before the Allies get here."

"What camp?"

"Who knows?" Tattaglia said. "Besides, it doesn't matter. Whatever camp you go into, you don't come out."

"How do you know about Gambrelli?"

"Because, until this morning, he was sitting where you are sitting."

The sound of a heavy steel bolt being slammed back came from the other side of the door. An SS man entered and deposited on the floor two tin bowls half-filled with thin liquid, then threw down a couple of husks of stale bread. Before leaving, he spat in the direction of the food.

Tattaglia took up one of the bowls, dipped bread into it, and chewed.

"What is that?" Patch said. "What do they feed us?"

The other man swallowed. "Always the same. Some kind of pumpkin soup and stale bread from their own mess. And always they spit. The *Tedeschi* like to turn everything into a routine." He put down his bowl and picked up Howlett's. "Can you eat?"

"I need to keep my strength up."

Tattaglia dipped Patch's bread in the soup and held it so the Canadian could tear off a chunk. While Howlett chewed and swallowed, finding the soup so thin as to be almost tasteless and the bread moldy, the other man ate from his own bowl. Alternating, they soon finished the meager meal.

"That's it until when?" Patch said.

"Another piece of bread and some water in the morning. Then this again in the evening."

"You've been here long enough to know the routine?"

"Yes. Four days now."

Patch leaned back against the wall. His bones had now knit themselves up and his shoulders felt normal again. The bullet wounds in his legs had been healed before the men who had captured him had turned him over to the interrogation unit. Fortunately for him, the SS saw no point in making inquiries about the physical well-being of those they intended to question.

"So," he said, "how far are the train tracks from here?"

"Not far," Tattaglia said, a note of surprise coming into his voice. "If this cell had a window, you could hear them. Why, do you have somewhere to go?"

"You speak pretty good English for a village school-teacher." As he spoke, Howlett tested the manacles that bound his wrists together, two rings of metal connected by a short chain.

"I had a flair for languages."

Patch pushed against the floor, his knees bent, so that his buttocks came clear of the cold stone. He held his hands as far apart as the chain would let them go, then pulled against the metal bracelets. He groaned as skin and muscle tore, heard as well as felt the small bones in his hands being crushed and snapped like dry twigs, but still he forced them down and down, suppressing a scream that might have brought a guard, until he was sitting on the handcuffs. Then he pulled straight up against the steel rings, blood from his self-inflicted wounds acting as a lubricant, until his hands came free of the restraints.

He sat, his legs stretched straight out before him, hands in his lap, feeling the ache as the bones put themselves back together and the flesh grew whole again.

"What are you doing?" said Tattaglia. "Do you need help?"

It was too dark for his cellmate to see what he was doing, but Patch's night vision showed him a look of genuine worry on the bruised face. "I'll be fine," he said, "in a couple of minutes."

"Listen," said the other man, "Giovanni said someone might come looking for him. I want to know if I can trust you with a message he said to pass on. He said it was important."

"Yeah?" said Howlett. "Well, you can trust me."

"How do I know?"

Patch fought to keep a grim smile from twisting his lips, even though he was pretty sure the other man couldn't see. "You think I might be a German?"

The other sounded uncertain. "Well, you never know. Listen, you tell me how you were connected to Giovanni. And if I think I can believe you, I'll tell you what he said."

"What good would a message from Gambrelli do me?"

"You never know. You might escape, or get a chance to pass it on."

Howlett nodded. "It's true," he said, "you just never know."

As he spoke, he flexed his forearms, felt the sharp pain that always came when his claws ripped through the flesh between his knuckles.

His feet were completely recovered now, his shinbones mended. He was still hungry and a little tired, but he was ready. He bent his knees, leaned forward, and came smoothly and silently into a crouch.

"Tell me," said the man across from him, "what did you have to do with Giovanni?"

"Let me whisper it to you," Patch said. "The guards might be listening."

The man didn't disguise the eagerness on his face as he leaned forward. *He thinks it's too dark for me to see,* Patch thought, but he could see his target perfectly as he brought up his right hand in a brutal uppercut that drove the spikes of his mutation through the undefended flesh of the man's lower jaw, up and through tongue and soft palate, and into the brain of this supposed Italian schoolteacher—this man who claimed to have sat here four days living on pumpkin soup and moldy bread flavored with SS spittle, but whose skin exuded a different odor for Patch's animal-sharp sense of smell to detect, an odor of sauerkraut and fennel-spiced German sausage. The same odor that had clung to the two thugs who had dragged Patch to the cell.

The spy twitched and flopped reflexively, but he had been dead the moment the razor-sharp claws had shredded his neural tissues. Even before he ceased to move, Howlett was pulling the clothes from the corpse. He tore off his stolen uniform and dressed in the filthy suit, then put the staff major's torn khaki on the body. Next he arranged the dead man on the pile of rags, facing away from the door, the arms behind and with the handcuffs positioned more or less as if they were confining the wrists.

Then his plan, made as he had listened to the spy, came up against a sudden barrier. *What the hell's the German word for "help"?* he asked himself. They hadn't taught him that one in the special force training sessions. He'd learned, *hande hoch*—"hands up," and *nicht schiessen*—"don't shoot," and *raus,* the general term for "move your butt." But right now none of those would do him any good in getting the cell door opened.

He squatted on his heels and let his memory work for him. He went back to the assault on Monte la Defensa. There had been a wounded Jerry in a machine gun pit off to his right when they'd gone at the fortified pill box with grenades. What had the man been calling?

And then it came. Patch readied himself, crouching over the corpse with his back toward the cell door, his claws out and ready.

"*Hilfe!*" he shouted, just like the wounded machine gunner. "*Hilfe!*"

Almost instantly, he heard the bolt shoot back. Light spilled across the floor as the door was flung open and then was immediately obscured as two SS troopers crowded into the doorway, one of them saying, "Dieter, *was ist los?*"

Still in his crouch, Patch spun and drove his claws into the throat of the one who was leaning down to examine what he thought was a prisoner in distress.

The SS man gurgled and gasped, dying in a rush of bubbling blood from a severed jugular and windpipe.

The second man had been behind the first. Horror and panic swept across his face and he turned to rush from the cell. But Howlett had already flung the first guard from his claws and now he leapt onto the fleeing man's back, knocking him to his knees in the corridor, hearing at least one kneecap snap from the impact of their combined weight. Patch's left arm went around the man's neck, and iron-hard muscles choked off his attempt to shout the same word that had summoned him and his comrade to their deaths. Then Patch's right arm went down and around the man's torso with a blur of speed, his claws striking inward, driven up beneath the ribs to pierce the frantically beating heart. He'd been trained to do the exact same move with the VK-42 stiletto and now, as the man went limp beneath him, he was pleased to find that it was just as deadly with his natural armament.

He flexed his arms, withdrawing the bloody claws, and looked about him. The corridor was empty, the doors to several more cells standing closed. He went to the nearest one, threw back the bolt, and opened the door. A face looked at him, pale and fearful, from within the gloom.

"Come on out!" Howlett whispered.

The fear turned to hope. The man got to his feet and came into the corridor. When he saw the dead SS man, a grim smile took control of his mouth and he grunted something Patch didn't understand, then knelt and rolled the corpse over. The guard had had a holstered sidearm, but in a moment it was in the released prisoner's head.

The Canadian had already gone to the next cell door, opening it and moving on to the next. The man with the gun joined in the effort, and soon the small space grew crowded with more men, and one woman. All were battered and bruised, some limping on broken feet, squinting through eyes surrounded by swollen flesh, cradling arms that had been wrenched from sockets.

One of them took charge, a big fellow in blue workman's overalls. The man Patch had first freed had acquired another Luger from the dead guard in the cell, and this he handed to the leader. The big man ejected the magazine, checked that it was full, and slipped it back into the pistol's butt with practiced skill. He ratcheted back the weapon's slide to put a round in the chamber. Then he smiled, showing a gap where a tooth had recently been knocked out.

He looked at Howlett and said, "*Grazie,*" then turned to the others and followed with a rapid string of Italian that Patch didn't understand. With the two armed men in the lead, the group headed for the iron-bound door of heavy wood at the end of the corridor.

Patch didn't move. "Wait," he called after them, keeping his voice low. "Does any one of you know where Giovanni Gambrelli is?"

The big man turned. "Gambrelli, he go train. *In Germania.*"

"When?"

"*Ieri.*"

The word meant nothing to Howlett. Seeing his incomprehension, the woman chipped in. "Not this day. Day before."

"Yesterday?"

"*Si.* Ee-esta-day."

So the spy in his cell had told the truth. Gambrelli had been put on a train to Germany a day earlier. So where did that leave Jim Howlett?

It didn't take him long to think it through. He hadn't had many friends in his life, but of the few Rob Roy MacLeish had been the best. They'd worked together, drunk together, fought in saloon brawls together, wenched together. It had been MacLeish's idea to come down from the northern Alberta lumber camp and join the army. Volunteering together for the paratroops but not both being accepted had separated them for a couple of years, but the accidents of war had brought them back together.

But only briefly. Only long enough for them to be separated permanently by a German booby trap. Now his friend was gone. All that was left of him was the girl he'd loved, the girl to whom Howlett had made a promise, in Rob Roy MacLeish's name.

There was nothing that would particularly draw Patch back to the FSSF. He liked the men he served with, respected many of them—like the Ojibway sergeant, Tommy Prince—for their guts and go-at-it attitudes. Their wounds didn't heal in minutes the way his did, but they still stood up and went forward, right into the worst that a skilled and determined enemy could throw at them.

The Devil's Brigade could get along without him. And he couldn't go back to Rob Roy's girl and tell her he had failed, unless he could first tell himself that he had done all he could. Besides, it was probably not all that hard to get into a Nazi concentration camp. The tricky part would be getting out.

"Wait!" he said to the people gathered around the door. He tapped his chest, said, "Commando," and "Me first."

The big man looked at the dead SS man on the floor and his battered face formed one of those eloquent expressions that allow Italians to communicate plenty without speaking a word, an expression that said, "Who am I to argue with an expert?" He moved aside and let the obviously lethal foreigner take the lead.

The door was locked from the inside. Patch eased back the heavy metal bolt that secured it. He gently pushed and it swung silently open on well-oiled hinges. Beyond was a set of stone steps leading upward and curving out of sight. Above the door was a single lightbulb and somewhere up the steps was another.

Patch's feet were still bare and he made no sound as he went up the stairs, his right shoulder almost brushing the curving wall. The others came behind in single file, led by the two with guns.

The steps curved up to an archway. Beyond was a hallway painted in institutional green. When he had crept far enough upward to see that much, Howlett also saw what he had expected. An SS guard stood just beyond and to the side of the arch that led down to the cells, his hands cradling a Schmeisser submachine gun slung from a strap over his shoulder. But the guard was there to prevent people from breaking in to rescue those who were confined downstairs. The man didn't expect death to come at him from behind and below.

Howlett brought out the claws of his right hand. As he came to the top of the stairs, he clamped his left hand over the guard's mouth, pulling him backward into the stairwell and letting the man's own weight drive him down onto the three needle-sharp talons. Patch felt the middle claw briefly grate on bone, then its point slipped into the softer material between the fifth and sixth cervical vertebrae, slicing through the spinal cord and killing the man instantly.

The leader of the escapees took charge of the body, slipping the machine gun from the dead hands and passing it to a man behind him. The big man in the coveralls saw the claws extending from Patch's hand. He looked from their dripping tips to their owner's face. Then his own face said, without words, "How is this any of my business?"

Patch gave him a nod. Then he turned and went without a sound into the corridor, saw that it ran about thirty feet to a door that had the look of an exit to the outside. Above the door hung an electric clock that said it was just going on 5:45. The place had no natural source of light, no windows or skylights, but it had that empty feel that argued for its being early morning rather than late afternoon.

Along the corridor were two doors with glass panels in their upper halves. No light shone from within either. Patch went forward. The place looked to have been the jail of a small town—he'd seen the inside of a couple of such places, northern Alberta style, in his bar-fighting days—that had been taken over by the local SS intelligence unit. So probably he would not find a high wall and guard towers outside. There might be a vehicle yard and some kind of fence, or the door ahead might even lead out onto the street.

Beside the door was a light switch. Patch thumbed it off and, with the corridor behind him in darkness, he cracked the door just wide enough to put an eye to it. A man stood outside, in field gray and a coal-scuttle helmet marked with the SS runes. Moments later he was gasping out his last breath on the tiled floor of the corridor and the freed partisans had acquired another machine gun.

The plaza outside was empty and still night-dark. A shoot-on-sight curfew coupled with the predawn cold of a morning in late December kept the town's residents in their warm beds. Howlett scanned the open space that was lit by only a few dim lamps above doorways, including the one above the door in which he stood. Its glass globe was open at the bottom and he reached up and unscrewed the bulb.

Across the plaza was a large building that must have been the town hall. A red banner with a black swastika in a white circle hung from an upper floor. Two armed soldiers flanked the front door, and Patch saw a brief glow as one of them drew on a cigarette.

He closed the door and spoke to the big man, using sign language to augment the message: "Two guards across the street."

"We go . . ." the leader said, then spread his fingers and moved his hands outward to show that the escapees would scatter in different directions.

"Trains?" Howlett said. "Where?"

It took three of them to come up with enough English to explain that he had to go left then right after two blocks, downhill toward the sea.

"Okay. Let's go."

"*Grazie,*" said the big man, and the woman crossed herself and said, "*Benedicali.*" From the way she said it, Patch was pretty sure it meant "bless you."

They went out, one at a time, giving each an opportunity to clear the area before risking motion that might attract the attention of the sentries across the square. Howlett was the last to go, moving silently on cold bare feet. *At least there's no snow,* he told himself.

He kept to shadows and stepped into doorways to watch for Jerry patrols, but the town was quiet.

He found the downhill street and made his way toward the sea. Soon he could hear a steam engine huffing and the clack of railcars being shunted in a trainyard.

## The Empty Quarter, Saudi Arabia, the present

"IT CANNOT BE DONE, NOT EVEN IF WE THROW them all away."

Al Borak leaned over the tabletop recreation in miniature of the Green Zone, the complex of streets and buildings surrounded by impenetrable layers of security that the American forces had built for themselves in the heart of Baghdad. The accuracy of the model was virtually perfect, the data having been acquired from a Russian military surveillance satellite through a series of black market channels.

"The place has been expertly designed for defense in depth," the Green Fist leader said. "Cracking the gate or going over the blast walls only channels us into these confined routes—" he used a wooden pointer to tap the possible avenues of approach, "—that are covered by overlapping fields of automatic weapons fire. The weapons are computer-aimed and -operated, so even if we suppress the perimeter guards with nerve agents, our men will be cut down before they get beyond the first defensive layer."

"What about aerial assault?" von Strucker said. "A high-altitude, low-opening parachute drop, avoiding the outer rings and bringing them closer to the target zone."

"There is no way to keep their approach from being seen. The closest they would get to the inner core would be when they were deposited in the Green Zone's morgue."

"Underground? Sewers and service tunnels?"

"Blocked, monitored, guarded by automated firing systems."

Von Strucker ground a fist into the palm of his other hand. "Our friends are not going to accept 'impossible' as an answer," he said, staring for the umpteenth time at the uncooperative puzzle of little structures and spaces that covered the table. "Beneath their cold calculations lies a certainty that Allah will deliver them victory, by a miracle if necessary." He had worked under people who had that same uncompromising attitude and knew what it led to when it was applied to difficult military situations.

Al Borak said, "If we trained and conditioned a couple of hundred men like the twenty we have now, one or two might get through and reach the objective."

"We don't have the time. This is a once-only opportunity, and the date is fixed," the baron said. He clasped his hands behind his back and paced up and down the side of the table, his eyes probing the model's details. "We will just have to create that miracle."

He left Al Borak to consider the problem and returned to his quarters. In the secret room behind the closet he checked the level of liquid in the Pyrex tube in the safe. It looked to be no less than it had been at the same point in the production cycle last month. But as he resealed the hidden room and stretched himself on his narrow cot, the Prussian had to fight to keep a chill of apprehension from taking hold.

He did not relish the prospect of having to leave this secure place he had arranged for himself, to start again with some other group. The Foundation had been a good find for him, had allowed him to keep out of the sight of those who had hunted him through the wreckage of the Third Reich, who would gladly kill him now if they could get their hands on him—once those hands had twisted and fretted him into explaining in the most exquisite detail how a man who was more than a century old happened to have the well-tended body of a fit and vigorous forty-year-old.

He had come to the Foundation by a circuitous route. In April 1945, with the Russians pounding their way into Berlin and with the Americans and British rolling back Germany's disintegrating armies in the west and south, von Strucker had sent a message to Himmler, telling him that he was taking the remaining Iron Eagles south to the mountains of the Tyrol to prepare for the coming guerrilla war against the Allied occupation. Instead he ordered the last handful of his men to escort him to the Swiss frontier.

Avoiding contact with the enemy as much as possible, fighting only when absolutely necessary, the stimulants in their veins constantly renewed from the last batch to come out of Schlimmer's lab, the burned-out remnants of the *Eisenadlers* had brought the baron to the shores of Lake Constance where he had long since arranged for a one-man submarine to be waiting in a concealed boat shed. He left the former cream of the German forces shivering and hallucinating on the lakeshore and crossed to freedom.

A passport and ample funds waited for him where he had left them in a safe deposit box in Zürich. He became Señor Hans-Klaus Bauer, a prosperous Argentine citizen stranded in Europe by the war, now eager to make his way home to the city of Córdoba in the foothills of the Sierra Chicas. A month later, he was walking its sunny streets and sitting in its outdoor cafés, sipping the surprisingly good wine from the Mendoza region—and planning his future.

The die-hard Nazis who made their way to Argentina and Paraguay, establishing secret societies where they got together and dreamed beery fantasies about someday returning to power, did not interest him. They were a horse he had ridden as far as it would go, and now he looked about for another steed. But he kept in contact with the former gauleiters and

SS gruppenführers, because they were assiduously forging connections with groups that might suit his purposes.

And so it was that, after the creation of Israel in 1947, von Strucker made contact with the Foundation, an organization that had recently spun off from the Muslim Brotherhood in Egypt. His first impression of them, after a meeting in Cairo, was that they were a curious blend of religious fanaticism and hard-nosed pragmatism. But they had access to substantial funding from the Middle East's new phenomenon: the oil-rich sheik. The Prussian formed a consulting relationship with the group's operational planners, advising on methods to improve the fighting abilities of their volunteers. As the organization grew in wealth and power, the relationship deepened and when von Strucker suggested the creation of a highly secret research and development center in the wasteland of southern Arabia, the results he had already delivered to his clients made them happy to say yes.

Thus Wolfgang Freiherr von Strucker, hereditary lord of a stately old *schloss* in an East Prussian forest that had been seized and disposed of by an enlarged postwar Poland, had spent decades in underground corridors beneath a searing desert. He who had once debated the ideas of Nietzsche and the strategies of von Bismarck in the bustling halls and high-ceilinged lecture rooms of Heidelberg's schools had spent most of the past fifty years exiled among swarthy fanatics who constantly invoked the will of a God he had long since ceased to believe in.

The isolation and cultural dislocation might have driven another man mad, the baron supposed. But he had something that he could cling to, a shining ambition for whose realization he would gladly endure another century of this barren existence. For what did it matter if a man wasted a hundred years of his life, if that century was but a tiny fraction of a span that was effectively endless?

Von Strucker meant to live forever. All he needed was to stay alive long enough to encounter once more the little man he had had nailed to the table—to crack his bones and extract more of his marrow, enough to let him unravel the eternal secrets that would give him eternal life and mastery of the world.

There would be a way to carry out the mission. He would find it. And then he would continue, through his client's resources, the search for mutants. He had convinced the Foundation that Allah had sent the faithful a deliverer, an invincible warrior who did not know that he was the chosen. But could he but find this *mahdi,* this "expected one," von Strucker had the means to show him the sign that would prove who he was—the sign that was in his blood, and no one else's.

So now von Strucker rose from his narrow cot and set off to study once again the tabletop model of the Green Zone. He would find a way to carry out a successful assault. Whatever the cost, he would keep his clients happy. And they would continue to provide the resources that would allow the baron to seek his personal grail: the savage little man whose veins were filled with the precious blood of immortality.

He would find his grail, empty it—and live forever.

## Ortona, Italy, the present

"YOUR BROTHER, WHAT HAPPENED TO HIM?" Logan asked Lucia Gambrelli.

"He must have died. He never came back."

"And I guess neither did I."

"Not until now," she said.

Frustration was building in him. He had followed a trail to this room, but it had not been a clear path, laid out before him. Instead it had been a series of bright spots separated by darkness—the photo of Tommy Prince, this tavern in an Italian town, the face and name of Rob Roy MacLeish, a friend who was dead sixty years, this old woman who had been a girl to whom he had made a promise.

But now there was no new patch of light beckoning beyond the darkness ahead. After finding a hope that had drawn him forward through the past couple days, after feeling a growing sense that he was finally getting somewhere, to come up now against a dead end was unbearable.

As if she could read his thoughts, she again offered

him a glass of grappa. "No more booze," he said. "Not until I find . . . whatever I can find."

She took the glass away. "I wish I could help," she said.

An idea came to him. "Wait," he said, "did anyone ever report seeing Giovanni?"

"We asked the Red Cross. Years later, we got a report that he had been sent to a camp called Höllenfeuer, and that he might have died there of—I don't have the English word. In Italian it is *tifo.*"

She spelled it for him. *Typhus or typhoid fever,* he guessed. They used to call it prison fever, because it was spread by lice and fleas when men were crammed together in squalor. Aloud, he said, "Höllenfeuer? Where was that?"

"In Poland, they said."

*Höllenfeuer.* He repeated the word inside the silence of his mind till it echoed in his head. "It means something to me," he told Lucia. "I think I was there."


## Höllenfeuer Concentration Camp, January 1944

WHEN THE TRAIN OF CATTLE CARS FINALLY arrived at the camp, Giovanni Gambrelli was not in good shape. He had been passing blood in his urine and the pain in his lower back was enough to make him scream every time the shunting of cars threw him against the wooden slats that penned in the prisoners but did nothing to keep out the cold. Patch Howlett figured that SS boots had ruptured both the Italian's kidneys.

He heard the rattle of a chain, then the railcar's door slid open. A hard-faced man in a black SS uniform beat on the floor of the cattle car with a heavy wooden truncheon and said, "*Raus!*"

"Come on," Patch said. He knelt and put one hand in Gambrelli's armpit to help him up. The other hand he put over the man's mouth to keep him silent. This was not a place where it was wise to show weakness. He had listened to the conversations among the prisoners during the long train journey out of Italy and across Germany to what seemed, judging by the unpronounceable names of the last few stations they had passed, to be Poland. He had gathered from those who spoke a little English that they were being sent to a labor camp where the only ticket to survival was the ability to work. The day you couldn't do your job would be your last day on earth.

He pulled Gambrelli's arm over his shoulders and, supporting the sick man, led him to the door where they jumped down to the slush-covered concrete of the platform. The Italian groaned at the impact, but the sound was lost in the noise of shouting guards, the puffing of the train's steam engine, the yipping of dogs, and the amplified voice of a man in a black uniform who was barking at them through a megaphone.

Howlett didn't understand much of the German's harshly accented Italian, but all he needed to do was follow the rest of the shuffling mass of prisoners as they were herded along the platform to a wider area. Here the SS men pushed and shoved them into ranks and files. A pasty-faced man wearing a white lab coat over an SS officer's tunic passed along the rows, giving each man a two-second looking over. Some he tapped on the chest or shoulder with a wooden pointer and these were quickly seized by guards and manhandled down the platform and through a gate in a tall wire fence topped with three strands of barbed wire. Evergreen branches had been woven into the fence so that what was beyond remained invisible.

The men who were being removed were the old, the sick, anyone who looked unfit to work. "Stand up," Patch said out of the side of his mouth as the man in the white coat approached. Gambrelli's jaw muscles bunched, but he stood straight as Howlett withdrew the arm that had been supporting him.

The inspector paused before the Italian and looked him up and down, his stick poised indecisively, his eyes narrowing in suspicion. Patch, next along the rank of men, growled deep in his throat. The sound drew the SS medic's attention.

"*Sagten Sie etwas?*" he said.

Howlett didn't know what the German words meant. He shook his head and said nothing. He had decided days before, after he had worked his way into the crowd of prisoners being herded toward the train-yard back in the town where he had escaped the cells beneath the town hall, that the only way he could pass for one of the captured partisans and slave laborers was to pretend to be mute. Now he pointed to his open mouth with two fingers and shrugged.

"*Stummer*?" the medic said, then when Howlett shrugged again, he said, "*Muto?*"

That sounded like Italian for "mute" and Patch nodded. The German sneered and passed down the line, Gambrelli forgotten as he slapped his stick against the chest of an elderly man. Howlett growled again as the black-uniformed guards dragged the old man to the gate in the wire. A stream of people, men, women, and crying children, were being herded directly to this gate from the three cars at the head of the train. Every one of them wore a six-pointed yellow star sewn to their coats. Gambrelli, as well as the half-dozen cap-tured partisans who had been in his car, each had a red triangle with a black letter *I* on his tattered jacket. Those sent as forced laborers were unmarked.

The inspection over, the man with the megaphone shouted more orders and the guards began driving the men down the length of the platform. A flat-faced SS man, his baton held horizontally in both hands, pushed Howlett to move him along. Patch bit back his anger, did not meet the thug's eyes. It would do no good; even if he killed them all, he couldn't escape with Giovanni Gambrelli in his current condition.

He'd had no trouble finding Lucia's brother once he arrived at the trainyards. His first thought was to silently kill the sentries that guarded the warehouse where the prisoners were gathered and lead an escape, much as he had at the town hall. But Gambrelli was in no shape to run.

Patch couldn't abandon the badly injured man. A promise to Rob Roy's girl was as binding as a promise to Rob Roy. There was nothing to do but to go where the Germans were sending the partisan, until he was well enough to abandon the hospitality of the SS.

Shoving backs and beating legs with their clubs, the guards drove the crowd past the rear of the train, then down and across the railroad tracks. Another section of the camp stood behind more wire fencing, though on this side of the rails no woven green branches hid what the fence enclosed. Row upon row of long, low wooden buildings, made of unpainted boards and roofed in tar paper, stretched for hundreds of yards to the left and right. A double gate yawned, flanked by Schmeisser-toting guards with snarling German shepherd dogs slavering to slip their leashes.

The prisoners were driven through into a broad street that ran the length of the camp. Howlett's bare feet slipped in half-frozen mud but he kept going, supporting the injured Italian. They were hurried along past three of the buildings that seemed to be barracks, then around a corner into a wide mud-floored space that occupied the center of the camp.

On three sides stood open sheds without walls, and they were herded toward one of these.

The shed contained several rough tables, just planks set on saw horses, with wooden bins and barrels set beside them at intervals. With impartial blows and curses, the guards shoved the men inside and got them lined up along the tables. A man who had been sitting on the end of one of the trestles now climbed atop it and called, "*Attenzione!*"

He was a short but heavy-shouldered. The knuckles of his ham-size hands had been broken and healed more than once. One cheek was disfigured by the kind of scar a broken bottle makes. He was dressed in no better clothing than most of the men who had come on the train with Patch, but he looked well-fed. On his jacket was sewn a green triangle.

*A brawler and a thug* was Howlett's assessment. He listened to the man's guttural Italian, delivered in an even thicker accent than that of the man with the megaphone. Patch caught only one or two words, but the gestures that accompanied them told him that they would work in the shed, putting things in the bins and barrels. One bin was labeled *Haar,* another *Kleidung/Frauen,* a barrel was for *Schuhe/Kinder.*

"Well," he whispered to Giovanni, "it beats digging ditches."

But the Italian's face had paled even further as he listened to the man with the green badge. He leaned his hands on the plank table and breathed heavily.

"What is it?" Howlett said.

A canvas-covered truck entered the open space from the street they had come along. It turned and backed toward the shed, stopping just short of the roof. Two men got out of the cab and came around to the vehicle's rear. One of them, the driver, also wore a green triangle and looked fit and healthy. The other wore a blue triangle and looked as if he hadn't eaten or slept well in years.

Later, Patch would learn that red badges were for Communists, social democrats, and anybody else whose politics the Nazis didn't approve of. Blue was for foreign forced laborers. And green badges were worn by *kapos*—German criminals whom the SS put in charge of political prisoners, slave workers, Jews, and Gypsies, encouraging these sweepings of the German underworld to give their brutal natures free rein.

The driver grunted something that was probably an insult and signaled the blue badge to unhook the truck's tailgate. It dropped with a crash and two more forced laborers began pushing the vehicle's load out onto the concrete floor of the shed: suitcases, from elegant leather bags to scuffed pasteboard; clothes of both sexes and all kinds and sizes; shoes and boots; toys and books; and big bags of rough sackcloth whose contents couldn't have weighed much because they hit the concrete with scarcely a sound.

Giovanni Gambrelli was shaking. He looked like a man fighting a need to vomit. The two *kapos* were giving orders, clearly telling the men in the shed to get the piles of stuff onto the tables and to start sorting. One of the sacks landed in front of Patch and the man he had come to save. Gambrelli put his hand in the bag's open mouth and drew out some of its contents.

He looked at what was in his hand, then turned to Howlett with a face gripped by horror. "*È la verità*," he whispered. "*Li assassinano tutti.*" It's true. They kill them all.

What he held in his hand was the freshly shorn hair of a little girl.

"Someone has to live to remember this. Someone has to tell the story."

The words remained in Patch Howlett's mind. They were almost the last words Giovanni Gambrelli ever said, translated from the Italian by a man named Bertolli, a former language teacher who had been sent to Höllenfeuer after getting caught chalking up anti-occupation slogans on walls in Rome. The teacher had not lived much longer than Gambrelli—both had died in one of the epidemics of typhus that swept through the camp, carried by the swarms of fleas and lice that infested the unheated barracks, where prisoners had to huddle together for warmth on wooden shelves. The teacher had also translated the name of the camp—Höllenfeuer meant "hellfire" in German. Shivering with cold and fever, the man had said, "Somebody in Berlin has a sense of humor."

Patch had lost his. But he had found a mission. He observed and remembered. He watched the trains roll in, tracked the greasy black smoke that rose up to dirty the winter clouds, memorized the names and faces of guards and *kapos*. Filed it all away, for the day of vengeance.

But the mute man would not work. He would not sort the last possessions of the dead, adding one last insult to the fate of the innocents who were hustled from the cattle cars and rushed behind the fence with the evergreen boughs woven through the wire. He would stand in the frozen mud with the rest of the prisoners when the loudspeakers mounted on the watchtowers summoned them to roll call. He would line up for his bowl of thin soup and moldy bread. He would go to his hut and lie on the verminous boards when the last whistle blew. He would even report to the sorting shed.

But he would not handle the loot from the dead.

At first Helmut, the scar-faced *kapo* who had been a pimp and enforcer in the mean streets of Munich, beat him with the lead-weighted rubber truncheon that was his staff of office.

But still the mute prisoner would not work.

Then the guards went at him with oak batons and iron-heeled boots. Years in the camp had made them experts in the science of inflicting painful, humiliating death. After evening roll call, while the whole of the

work camp watched, they ringed him in the assembly
area, clubbed him to his knees, then kicked him until
his face was unrecognizable and his ribs caved in.
When he was dead they hung him on a frame of
barbed wire and left him there as a reminder to anyone else who did not want to work.

But when the prisoners turned out for the morning
roll call, his body was not there. Hauptscharführer
Müller, the senior SS noncom in the work camp,
raged at the assembled forced laborers. His face turned
brick red and spittle shot from his mouth as he strode
along the trembling front rank, shoving men at random and bellowing *"Wo ist er?"* Where is he?

"Herr Hauptscharführer," came an uncertain voice
from the rear of the formation. *"Er ist hier."* He is here.

It was Helmut the *kapo* who had spoken. Müller
wheeled and went down the side of the block of men.
He found the ex-pimp standing behind the last row,
his meaty hand gripping the arm of the small man
who wouldn't work. The man who showed no sign of
the murderous beating that had been laid upon him
the evening before.

The SS noncom pulled up short. Confusion struggled with rage in his face but, as it always did, his core
of brutality overruled every other reaction. He un-
snapped the flap on his holstered Luger, withdrew the
weapon, snapped back the slide, and aimed it squarely
at the mute's forehead.

*"Überleben Sie dieses, kleiner mann,"* he said with a

cruel smile—survive this, little man—and pulled the trigger. Blood, bone, and brains flew from the back of the prisoner's head, and the small man fell lifeless to the ground.

Müller rounded on Helmut, the smoking gun still in his hand, and issued curt orders.

"*Jawohl,* Herr Hauptscharführer," said the green badge in a voice that shook with fear. He grabbed two men from the rear rank and sent them for a wheelbarrow and shovels. When they returned, he had them load the body and led them out of the work camp and to the open ditch where those who died of illness or abuse were buried en masse. They threw the corpse on top of three frozen bodies that had lain there since the day before and quickly shoveled earth over all of them. Then they went back to the camp, where Helmut made a point of not letting Müller's eye find him for the rest of the day.

But at the evening roll-call, the count was one more than expected.

When Karl-Heinz Baumann came to Höllenfeuer in February 1944, it was his last hope to rescue his career within the SS. Obersturmbannführer Baumann had once been a key aide to the Schutzstaffel's golden lion: Reinhard Heydrich, Reich Protector of Moravia and Bohemia, and architect of the "final solution to the Jewish problem," whose headquarters were in Prague. Like his mentor, the man Hitler had affectionately dubbed the "Blond Beast," Baumann combined a considerable intelligence with an icy ruthlessness. He had been delighted to be seconded to Heydrich's staff because it was clear that the man would someday emerge as the successor to the charismatic corporal who was leading Germany to its rightful dominance among the nations. And when that day came, Karl-Heinz, who had once won a prize at the University of Graz for an undergraduate essay on symbolism in Goethe's epic tragic play *Faust,* would be a trusted aide to the most powerful man in the world.

Then, on May 27, 1942, all of his plans were plunged into the pit of despair. Czech partisans, working with the British OSE, had waited where Heydrich's open-topped staff car slowed to take a sharp corner. They had killed him by throwing a bomb into his lap. Reichsführer-SS Heinrich Himmler, relieved to see one of his major rivals removed from the game of power, had appointed a far less competent man—an oversize Austrian drunkard named Kaltenbrunner—to take over Heydrich's duties. Karl-Heinz Baumann, having risen through his dead boss's influence to the SS equivalent rank of lieutenant colonel, found himself facing, at best, an assignment to shuffle papers in some pointless office. At worst, he might be moved over to the Waffen-SS and sent off to fight Russians.

Karl-Heinz Baumann did not mind seeing blood spilled, even German blood. He just saw no point in spilling any of his own. Thus, he used every connection and contact he had developed within the SS to wangle, after weeks of treading water in Berlin waiting rooms, a private interview with one of Himmler's closest aides. Somehow he managed to make enough of a case for his administrative abilities that, after more months of paper shuffling, he was recalled to Prinz Albrechtstrasse and ushered into the presence of the Reichsführer-SS himself.

"Klaus tells me that you know how to get things done," Himmler said.

Baumann stood rigidly to attention before the elegant desk. "I do my best, Herr Reichsführer."

"There is a concentration camp in Poland. The closest anyone could come to pronouncing the barbarous Polish name of the nearby town was Höllenfeuer, and the name has stuck."

"Yes, Herr Reichsführer."

Himmler drew a piece of paper toward him, arranged his rimless spectacles more securely on the bridge of his nose, and said, "Productivity and morale there have plummeted lately. The commandant has committed suicide."

Before he could stop himself, Baumann said, "Why, Herr Reichsführer?"

Himmler looked at him without expression. "I don't care why," he said. "I only care that the problem is fixed."

"Yes, Herr Reichsführer."

"If you fix it, we will talk again."

"Yes, Herr Reichsführer."

The little man removed his glasses, breathed on the lens, and polished them with a snowy white handkerchief. "If you do not fix it, we will never talk again."

"I will fix it, Herr Reichsführer."

And then he was dismissed. But as he marched across the Persian carpet to where Klaus held open the door, Himmler said, "Heydrich thought highly of you."

Baumann stopped, about-faced, and said, "Thank you, Herr Reichsführer."

"Don't thank me. I didn't think highly of Heydrich. You have a month."

## Höllenfeuer Concentration Camp, February 1944

THE COMMANDANT'S QUARTERS AT HÖLLEN-feuer had been the home of the local railroad station master until the camp had been built around it. Obersturmbannführer Baumann found it cramped but adequate for a *kommandantur.* A rug had obviously been removed from the office—the floorboards were a lighter color where it had lain—and right next to one edge of the pale oblong was a darker stain.

"Your predecessor's blood," said Hauptsturmführer Otto Schenkel, the plump, damp-eyed SS officer Baumann had inherited as an adjutant. "We have not been able to get all of the stain out. The rug was ruined completely." He had entered carrying a box of books that had been in the baggage compartment of the train that had brought the new commandant. "Shall I put these on the shelves?"

"Yes," said Baumann, sitting at the desk and taking up one of the several files neatly arranged on its top. He opened it and scanned the rows of figures on the first sheet, then methodically made his way through the information as Schenkel supervised the bringing in of his books.

"These are beautiful volumes," the adjutant said, running his hands over the calf-leather binding and gold-embossed spines. "Goethe, Schiller, the poetry of Heine. You must be proud to own such fine books."

"I was, once," the new commandant said. "I prided myself on having absorbed the grand ideals of German civilization, of being able to recite verses and quote long passages."

"And now?" Schenkel said, organizing the Goethe next to the Fichte.

Baumann did not look up from the file. "Now I am proud to have surpassed such folly."

"Yet you keep the books?"

"They are the trophies of my final victory over sentimentality."

An SS guard came in, his arms straining to hold a heavy wooden crate that tinkled musically as he moved. "Careful!" Baumann snapped. "That wine is priceless! It has been in my family for generations. My father handed it to me and someday I will pass it on to my own son."

"The house has a cellar that would do for keeping wine," Schenkel said. He gave orders for the crate and several others to be taken there. Then he said to his new commandant, "Herr Obersturmbannführer, may I sometimes borrow a book? I had only a grammar school education and regret not having been exposed to those 'grand ideals of German civilization.' "

Baumann closed the first file folder and reached for the second. "You would do better to read Nietzsche and, especially, the Führer's *Mein Kampf.* Then you would understand that life is about *will,* not windy idealism and overblown romanticism." He scanned the first page of the new file, then said, "On second thought, you would do better to give more attention to your duties. The organization of this camp is a disgrace to the Reich!"

Schenkel came to an attention with a click of his bootheels. Beads of sweat appeared on his upper lip. "There have been problems, Herr Obersturmbannführer. Unusual circumstances."

Baumann slapped the folder closed. "Circumstances are about to change!" he snapped. "And whatever these 'problems' may be, they will be solved!"

"*Jawohl,* Herr Obersturmbannführer!"

The commandant rose and ordered the adjutant to assemble the senior officers so he could inspect the

camp. As Schenkel made for the door, Baumann called
him back and said, in a milder tone, "Herr Hauptsturmführer, obviously there are problems here. That
is why I have been given this command. Solving those
problems, quickly and efficiently, will bring both of us
recognition and credit. You do not want to be stuck
here forever, do you?"

"No, Herr Obersturmbannführer."

"The war will not last much longer. At your level
you cannot know it, but the Reich will soon have
weapons beyond the dreams of ordinary men. The
world will be Germany's, and men like me—and perhaps you—will be its rulers."

"Yes, Herr Obersturmbannführer," said Schenkel.
He saluted, turned, and left to carry out Baumann's
orders. The new commandant did not chide himself
for encouraging his adjutant to believe a lie. Schenkel
would never be a ruler of men, not even of his own
meager destiny. But truth and lies were words without
meaning, mere empty concepts to be filled by those
who had the will to dominate, the will to shape the
world to their own liking.

Karl-Heinz Baumann was such a man. And this
camp was about to be shaped by his will.

There was an indefinable sloppiness to the place, Baumann decided as he let his senior officers lead him
through a systematic inspection of Höllenfeuer. It was

visible in the details: in the way the guards came to attention, without the quivering rigidity that his rank should have stirred in them; in their frayed cuffs and poorly shined boots, the patches of unshaved stubble on their cheeks. Of course, one couldn't expect too much from the Ukrainian SS guards who made up much of the camp's complement. But even the Germans' tunics showed soup stains and tarnished buttons.

The "special handling" facilities for Jews seemed to be adequately run, he noted. His on-site assessment matched the impression he had gotten from the figures in the files Schenkel had laid out for him. The real problem was in the section of the camp where political prisoners and other social undesirables were organized into work gangs to cut firewood, to grow the crops—mostly turnips—that were mainstay of the inmates' diet, and to sort the materials left over from the processing of the Jews. It was here that productivity had fallen off in recent months, and even before Baumann reached that part of his inspection, he believed he had a good idea as to why.

"They are too well-fed," he said. "I have reviewed the figures and we are giving them too much food."

"*Jawohl,* Herr Obersturmbannführer!" said Untersturmführer Krentz, the junior officer in charge of the commissary. He did not tell the commandant that the figures were unreliable. They did not take into account Krentz's unofficial sideline: a hefty portion of the food listed as going to the prisoners was actually sold to local wholesalers.

The party of SS officers entered the zone of the work camp where the prisoners were sorting the possessions of the dead. Baumann's eyes swept over the scene and again he saw evidence of the slackness that had contaminated the operation.

A noncom at the corner of one of the open sheds spotted him and shouted, *"Achtung!"* as he simultaneously came to attention. The motion lacked a proper SS snap and Baumann approached the man.

"Name," he said, slapping his gloves against the side of his greatcoat.

"Hauptscharführer Müller, Herr Obersturmbannführer."

"Are you in charge of this section?"

"Yes, Herr Obersturmbannführer."

Baumann inspected the man closely, saw the bloodshot eyes, the ruddy tint of skin, the puffiness of the flesh. He leaned in closer and sniffed. "Have you been drinking on duty, Müller?"

"No, Herr Obersturmbannführer."

"Why are you trembling?"

"It must be the cold, Herr Obersturmbannführer."

The commandant stepped back from the man. He smelled something unpleasant. He thought it might be the smell of fear. He looked again at the prisoners working at the long tables, throwing items into the bins labeled in ornate German script: "Hair," "Clothing/ Women," and "Shoes/Children." The men were thin, shivering in their rags. They kept their attention on their work and not one of them met his gaze.

Then Baumann looked farther down the shed and came upon something that made him blink in surprise. Standing beyond the end of the unwalled building was a small man clad in a ragged dark suit, shoulders hunched forward and hands in his pockets. He was staring directly at the commandant, his eyes a hard, dark glitter, his darkly stubbled face grim beneath a shock of unruly black hair.

Baumann turned to Müller. "Hauptscharführer," he said, "who is that man standing with his hands in his pockets?"

"He is just a mute, Herr Obersturmbannführer. We ignore him."

Baumann couldn't believe what he was hearing. "You ignore him? He stands there doing nothing, and you ignore him?"

Müller's mouth moved, but he said nothing. Baumann rounded on his officers, found them looking anywhere but at him. Or at the little man with the stony eyes.

"Schenkel," he called. "What do you know of this?"

The adjutant's Adam's apple went up and down twice and he stammered when he spoke. "It is difficult to explain, Herr Obersturmbannführer."

"Then I will explain it for you," Baumann said.

"You have collectively lost all sense of discipline. You have let this—" he gestured at the small man, "—this *üntermensch,* this inferior subhuman of a mute, place his will above yours."

"Herr Obersturmbannführer—," Schenkel began. "It is complicated. The man—"

"Silence!" the commandant shouted. He turned to Müller. "Bring him. Stand him against the wall of that building."

The noncom looked vaguely ill, but he beckoned two guards. The SS men marched to where the small man stood, seized his arms, and dragged him to the wall. The mute stood where they put him, his hands still in his pockets, his eyes never leaving Baumann.

"Now shoot him!" the commandant ordered.

"*Jawohl,* Herr Obersturmbannführer!" Müller unslung his Schmeisser and aimed at the man's chest. His hands trembled, the muzzle of the submachine gun wavering.

The mute began to whistle, a low tuneless sound that made the hairs rise on the back of Baumann's neck. "Give me that!" he snapped, tearing the weapon from the noncom's sweaty grasp.

"This won't be quick," he told the whistling man. He set the Schmeisser for single-shot action, then carefully aimed at the mute's right knee. The bullet passed right through the joint. Blood and bone splinters sprayed onto the wall behind. The little man groaned and fell over onto his side and the wounded leg shot out from under him.

Then he looked up from the frozen mud, locked his eyes on the commandant's, and pursed his lips. The low whistle came again.

"Swine!" The Obersturmbannführer cursed him as he aimed at the man's left knee. He fired and saw the man's other leg flop against the ground, heard a growl in the mute's throat. Then the eyes came back to his, striking him with the cold stare of a caged beast, and the whistling began again.

Baumann reset the Schmeisser and emptied its magazine into the hateful mute, ripping his torso from groin to throat, putting the final shots into his head. Blood and brains flew, and when the firing stopped, there was no more whistling. The hard black eyes had been obliterated by good German lead and steel.

He thrust the weapon back into the noncom's hands. "Now get rid of him!" he snapped.

"*Jawohl,* Herr Obersturmbannführer," Müller said, but his voice lacked conviction. He gestured to the two guards and they stooped and dragged the ruined corpse away by its bare feet.

Schenkel looked as if he had something to say yet was reluctant to speak. But Baumann had seen and heard enough. "Gentlemen," he said. "you have one week to show me a new camp, an efficient camp. Or I might just shoot one or two of you."

The officers came to attention.

"Dismissed," the commandant said, but he detained Krentz, the commissary officer. "Cut the prisoners' rations by twenty percent," he said. "Tell them they will remain cut until productivity shows a substantial improvement."

"*Zu befehl,*" the Untersturmführer said. At your order. He hurried away. Baumann was momentarily puzzled by the officer's happy grin, then he put it out of his mind and strode from the assembly area. A demonstration of will had been necessary, and he was pleased to have given them one.

## Western Poland, the present

THE MODERN EUROPEAN RAIL SYSTEM WAS efficiently run, Logan thought. He'd caught a train that ran all the way from Ortona to Berlin, crossing the Austrian Alps at night with moonlight shining on the icy peaks. At Berlin's Zoo Bahnhof train station, he'd changed trains for Poland. Not once along the way had he been asked to show his passport.

Lucia had had a book about Höllenfeuer. There were a few pictures, but they were poor quality and grainy, apparently shot by inmates who had bribed guards to smuggle in cameras. But the exposed film, tucked away in hidey-holes, had deteriorated before the rolls could be brought to a lab where the images, some horrific, some just hopelessly sad, were finally printed.

The rural train station that the camp had been built around was gone, along with the village that had stood nearby, destroyed in the fighting that pushed the German armies back to their homeland in early 1945. The nearest town dated from the postwar rebuilding boom and was full of dreary Soviet-era apartment blocks, but in anticipation of Poland's joining the European Union a hopeful town council had established a tourist information center. Logan was directed to it by the owner of the small hotel where he'd found a simple room and bath.

"I'm looking for information about the Höllenfeuer concentration camp," he told the young blonde woman behind a counter on which maps and brochures in several languages were spread for the taking. "I want to go to the site."

Her English was precise but adequate. "There is nothing there. The prisoners revolted and burned it down."

"Still," he said. "I want to see it. Where can I get a guide?"

"Are you sure you wouldn't prefer to visit the sausage-making factory? It has won prizes. They give you free samples."

He leaned over the counter and she stopped talking. "A guide," he said.

It turned out there was a man who tended the site

for some organization in Germany. He was willing to show it to visitors.

"Can you call him?" Logan said. "Tell him I will pay him if he can come now and take me there."

The man arrived within fifteen minutes to find Logan waiting outside the tourist center. He was a fat-bellied, thin-haired Pole of mature years who drove a smoky-engined little box on wheels that was left over from before the 1989 collapse of the Soviet bloc. The gears ground whenever he shifted them, but the car got them out of town and down an unpaved road lined with leafless trees. After a mile or so, they bumped over some old train tracks, then came to a closed wooden gate. Behind it was a muddy track winding into a patch of woodland.

"We have to go by foot," the man said. "Car doesn't enjoy mud."

He led Logan along the track, their feet slipping on patches of ice between the frozen ruts that gouged the earth. They came to a place where the trees abruptly ended. Beyond was open ground, marked by several large, low mounds covered in short grass, with stone-flagged walkways between them. In front of each mound was a man-high stone cairn that bore a dark metal plaque.

He went to the marker. The plaque had Polish, German, English, and Hebrew words on it. The English said, "Mass Grave #1. Estimated to hold the remains of four thousand forced laborers killed between June 1942 and February 1943."

He examined all the other plaques. Each told the same tale of the anonymous dead. He turned to the man who had brought him here and said, "What else is there?"

"No-thing" was the answer. "All fired, long ago. Trees grow up."

*A dead end,* Logan thought. The place evoked nothing. There were no buildings, no watchtowers. The trees were just trees, the grass just grass. All the thousands of dead behind the cairns could tell him nothing.

The fat man had produced a camera. Surprisingly, it was an up-to-date German digital. "I take picture?" he said. "For memory?"

Logan cursed. "No," he said. "This is not the memory I need."

But the man snapped the shutter anyway.

"Back to town," Logan said. "I need to talk to the girl at the tourist center." But when they were in the car, another thought came to him. "Do you keep copies of the pictures you take, pictures of people who come to see the graves?"

"No," the man said. "I not keep."

Logan was grasping at straws. "Who pays you?" he said.

"A German *organizacja*. At Berlin."

"Why? Are they survivors of the camp? What is their interest?"

"I don't know. I cut grass, show visitors."

"What is the organization's name? Where can I find them?"

They had got back onto the unpaved road. The guide lit a strong-smelling cigarette, threw the match out the window, and said, "I have card. I show you."

They drove to his home, a fourth-floor flat in a run-down, faceless apartment block whose concrete façade was crumbling. The elevator in the foyer bore a hand-lettered sign in Polish that must have read OUT OF ORDER because they went up several flights of fire stairs to emerge into a narrow hallway that smelled of old cabbage.

The man's apartment was small and scantily furnished—a tired old couch and a couple of wooden chairs, a battered coffee table covered in empty beer and vodka bottles. In one corner a much-thumbed pile of Dutch and Danish porn magazines looked ready to topple over. "Please to wait," he told Logan and disappeared through a curtained doorway.

Logan looked out of the grimy window at an identical apartment block that stood across an open space paved in cracked asphalt. Anger stirred in him, born of frustration that after coming all this way he had hit a brick wall. He balled his fists and felt the muscles of his forearms bulge. As soon as he did so, a stark and nameless fear took command of his mind, as if the

most terrible thing in the world was about to happen
to him.

It always happened when he clenched his fists and
the fear did not fade until he willed his hands and
arms to relax. He brought up his hands and looked at
the scars on his knuckles and thought, *What have I done
with these, to put such a fear in me?*

The Pole had been gone a long time if all he was
doing was fetching a card with an address on it. Logan
went to the doorway and eased the curtain aside with
the backs of his fingers. Beyond was a bedroom as
small and grungy as the living room, with an unmade
bed and a musty, mud-colored carpet decorated with
unwashed socks and gray underwear.

But against a wall, a small scarred table supported a
modern notebook computer, its top open and its
screen showing a screensaver of two women who
seemed to know each other very well. The guide sat in
a wooden chair before the computer. He must have
been waiting while it went through its start-up cycle
because now he worked the mouse pad, sliding a finger up and down and double-tapping as the image of
the women disappeared and an e-mail program's
prompt came up.

The man did something with the digital camera
that made it click. A moment later the computer
beeped. He tapped the built-in mouse again and a
window appeared on the screen, then a blue bar
rapidly filled its center, moving from left to right.

When the bar had gone all the way, the man double-tapped the mouse again and the program closed. He reached to pull down the top of the notebook.

"What are you doing?" Logan said.

The guide jumped, came up in a half crouch, turned toward the door. "Is my job," he said. "Take *fotografía,* send to Berlin."

Logan came into the room. The pot-bellied man backed away, eyes and mouth wide in a face that had suddenly gone pale, and Lógan realized he must look like a madman about to attack. He stopped, made a conscious effort to calm himself. "I am not going to hurt you," he said. "I just want to know why you sent my picture to Berlin."

"Is my job," the man said again. "I send *fotografía,* they send euros." He rubbed his thumb and two fingertips together. "Is not make bad thing."

"Where is this card?"

It was on the table beside the computer. The man offered it to Logan as if he were offering a dog biscuit to a snarling pit bull.

The card bore the name Höllenfeuer Erinnerunggesellschaft. with an address on a street called Invalidenstrasse and an e-mail address, but no telephone number. Logan pointed to the e-mail address. "Is that where you sent my picture?" he said.

"Yes."

"Who do you send the pictures to? Who lives at that address?"

"No peoples are living there. Is *organizacja* only."

"Did you meet someone from the organization? Did someone come here and give you the job?"

The Pole was growing more nervous. Logan had the sense that the interrogation was reaching a point where the man would begin making up information just to have something to offer a questioner who frightened him. Even as he recognized that he had to reassure the man, he was wondering, *Why do I know that? What have I been, back in that past I don't remember?*

"Listen," he said, putting some warmth into his voice, "let's go sit down in the other room, just talk a little." He remembered what the man had said, and parroted his words back to him, "Is not make bad thing. Just important to me."

The guide looked to be calming down, some color coming back into his face. "Okay," he said.

"Do you have anything to drink? Maybe some vodka?"

"Yes. In *kuchnia*."

"In the kitchen?" Logan said. "Good. Why don't you get it?"

He went back through the doorway and took a seat in the living room. The man was still scared and might run for the door, so Logan reached into his pocket and said, "I want to give you some money."

The Pole was halfway across the living room, at a point where he could go left into the kitchen or straight to the door that led to the hallway. He stopped. "Money?" he said.

Logan made the same gesture with thumb and fingertips. "Euros," he said and produced a hundred-euro note. It showed a bridge crossing a river and a map of Europe on it.

The man went into the kitchen. Logan heard a *clink* of glasses and a refrigerator door opening and closing, then the Pole returned with two tumbler glasses and a half-full bottle of vodka. "Not make bad thing?" he said with a tentative smile.

"Not make bad thing," Logan said. He handed over the hundred euros and the guide's smile grew. Soon they were sitting across the coffee table from each other, the guide perched on one of the wooden chairs. The thought of drinking the vodka brought a taste of bile to Logan's mouth, but he put the glass to his lips and pretended to swallow.

"Now," Logan said, "this word"—he pointed to the long string of letters on the card after the word Höllenfeuer—"how do you say it?"

"*Erinne-rungge-sell-schaft.*"

"What does it mean?"

The Pole took more of the vodka. "It mean 're-membering.' 'Remembering . . .' " He added some Polish words, then said, "people who are together, re-membering together."

"Good," Logan said. "And this is a street address?"

The Pole was happy to help. "Invalidenstrasse," he

said. "*Strasse* is 'street.' *Invaliden* is men who are not soldier, finish being soldier."

"Veterans?" Logan said. "Veterans Street?"

The man nodded encouragingly. "Yes, maybe."

"And this word, *postkasten,* with a number after it?"

"Is for put letters in." He mimed sliding an envelope into a slot.

"Post box."

The guide nodded some more and took another slug of the vodka. It made him smile.

And now that he had the man feeling comfortable, Logan could ask the questions he really wanted answered. "Did people come from Berlin to see you?"

"Man comes, I start work for *organizacja.*"

"Did he bring you the camera and computer?"

"Yes."

Logan took the bottle, poured more vodka for the other man, and pretended again to sip his own drink. "What was the man's name?"

The Pole paused with his glass halfway toward his lips, clearly ransacking his memory. Then his brow cleared. "Holzbauer," he said. "Josef Holzbauer."

"And he's the man you send the photos to?"

"I think it so. Yes."

"So he would have photos of all the people who have come here?"

The Pole shrugged.

Logan stood up, drained his glass, and took out another hundred-euro bill, immediately capturing the man's full attention once more. "Can you give me a ride to my hotel and then to the train station?" he said.

"You are betting on it," the guide said.

When the crazy rich foreigner was safely on the train to Berlin, Taddeusz Czazinsky took out the two hundred-euro notes and regarded them happily. On the way back from the train station he stopped at the store on the corner and bought another bottle of vodka, this time the best on the shelf. Back in his apartment, even before he took off his overcoat, he poured himself a healthy glassful and drained it, then poured another. It was only then that he noticed a discreet beeping sound from the bedroom.

The sound came from the notebook computer. He flipped it open and saw that he had received an e-mail that was marked with the double chevrons that meant its priority was urgent. He opened the message and read it. It was from Josef Holzbauer in formal Polish, without any of the shorthand that Czazinksy and his Internet contacts used when they traded addresses of porn sites.

It said, "What is the name of the man whose photograph you sent today? What is his address? Do you know where he is now or where he is going?"

Czazinsky laboriously typed out a reply. "I do not know his name or where he lives. But I have just put him on the train to Berlin. He is coming to see you."

Holzbauer must have been sitting at his own computer, because Czazinsky's notebook was beeping to tell him that he had received a reply to the message before he had even had time to get back to the vodka in the living room.

"What train?" said the new message. "When did it leave?"

The Pole typed in the information. He waited to see if there would be another response, but when none came after a few minutes sitting before the little computer, he again heard the vodka sweetly calling him from the living room.

## Höllenfeuer Concentration Camp, January 1944

KARL-HEINZ BAUMANN WAS DISAGREEABLY surprised to discover that the station master's house had never been wired for electricity and that the previous commandant—who was starting to look more and more like precisely the kind of romantic idiot that the German school system all too often produced—had actually preferred to work by the inferior light cast by a coal-oil lamp's yellowy flame. He resolved that electrification would be the first improvement he would order, once he had the camp running as it should.

He was at his desk, reviewing through-put figures for the past year. The columns of numbers spoke to him clearly. Höllenfeuer's performance had been consistently on the low end of acceptable until a couple of months ago. Then had come a sharp downturn in the work camp's output. Quotas were not met. Disciplinary infractions had mounted: guards reporting late for duty, failing to turn out in proper uniform, offering insubordinate responses to their superiors' orders. Then the numbers seemed to show that discipline had improved, but Baumann knew better. He knew that standards had fallen even further, so much so that officers and noncommissioned officers had begun to overlook offenses that should have resulted in the offenders being brought up sharp and punished.

A tap on the door drew him out of the web of statistics. "Come!" he barked.

Schenkel entered, closing the door quickly against a gust of ice-laden wind. "You said I might borrow a book, Herr Obersturmbannführer."

"If you must," the commandant said, "but you would be better to study the Führer's book."

"I have of course read it," the adjutant said. "It is a brilliant analysis of Germany's situation."

"Which," Baumann said dryly, "is exactly what is printed on the dust jacket."

"Yes, Herr Obersturmbannführer." Schenkel had taken a thin volume of verse from the shelves.

"You will never get anywhere, Schenkel, until you understand that life is about the exercise of will."

"Yes, Herr Obersturmbannführer."

Baumann leaned back in his chair. "Take this place. It is rife with incompetence and insubordination. Why? Because the officer who was supposed to provide the fundamental strength from which all would draw their energy was a weakling and a coward."

"Yes, Herr Obersturmbannführer."

"He must have been a weakling and a coward because he shot himself right where you are standing."

Schenkel looked down and saw that he was standing on the stained floorboards. He moved a step to one side.

"Will," Baumann said. "It is all about will."

"Yes, Herr—" Schenkel began, but the commandant cut him off, his head cocked to one side, listening.

"What is that noise?" Baumann said.

"I hear nothing," Schenkel said. "Perhaps the wind."

"It sounds like whistling." The Obersturmbannführer rose and strode to the door. "I will not have my men whistling on duty. And I will certainly not have any of those Italian swine . . ." He broke off, standing in the open doorway, peering out past the overhang of the porch as the wind drove sleet into his face.

An SS guard was supposed to be stationed beside the door, but there was no one there. The yard beyond was dark, only half-lit by the electric bulbs strung along the top of the perimeter fence. Something moved out there in the murk and now Baumann heard again the sound that had caught his ear: a low, tuneless whistling.

He turned back to the lighted room, where Schenkel was studiously avoiding looking at him. "Call out the guard!" he ordered. "A prisoner is loose in the yard."

His adjutant turned a pale face toward him, a tic at one corner of his mouth. "Herr Obersturmbannführer," he said, "if I may advise—"

The commandant's eyes bulged and his cheeks grew red. "You will not advise! You will carry out my orders or I will see you on the next train to the eastern front!"

"*Jawohl,* Herr Obersturmbannführer!" The man dropped the volume of poetry and squeezed past his superior. Outside, he made quickly for the nearest guard post, shouting orders in a voice that cracked with strain. He pointedly did not look at the shadowy figure who stood in the yard whistling.

Four SS men in greatcoats and helmets came running, rifles in their hands, led by Hauptscharführer Müller. They slammed to attention in front of their commandant.

"Don't stand there looking at me, *scheisskopf*!" Baumann said, pointing into the yard. "Arrest that swine!"

The squad turned around and Baumann clearly heard, over the whistling, an involuntary groan from the noncom. The men did not move. "I will have you reduced to the lowest rank," the officer said.

"*Kommen Sie,*" Müller said and moved grimly through the ice-crusted snow, the four SS behind him. They marched to where the whistling shadow stood. One of the guards raised his rifle and drove the butt into the small man's face. Bone crunched and the figure toppled over. The others crowded around, their boots and weapons doing more damage. Then, at Müller's order, two of them bent and hauled the bleeding victim to his feet. They dragged him to where the light spilled from the commandant's open door.

Baumann drew his Luger from its holster. "So," he said, "dead and buried will not do for you, *ja?*"

The small man raised his battered face and shook the long black hair from his eyes. His eyes locked onto the officer's in a glare as hard as obsidian. He pursed his split lips and began to whistle.

The nine-millimeter bullet tore through his forehead and blew out the back of his skull. Blood and brains and bone stained the crusted snow behind him.

"Now take him," Baumann said, "to the crematorium."

Müller said, "With respect, Herr Obersturmbannführer, the fires are not lit."

"Then light them!"

Müller snapped to attention, said, "At your order!" Then he turned to the squad and across his face flashed an expression that Baumann knew he was not supposed to have caught. But the commandant had seen that look and the Obersturmbannführer was not a man to let things slide.

"Hauptscharführer! You have something you wish to say about my order?"

Müller snapped to attention again. For a moment it seemed to the commandant that the noncom was wrestling with some inner question. Then his heavy face took on the expressionless cast of an SS trooper and he shouted, "*Nein,* Herr Obersturmbannführer!"

Baumann watched them march off toward the other section of the camp, Müller in the lead, the four SS guards each holding onto an arm or leg of the dead mute.

The commandant turned to find his adjutant standing on the porch, the book of poetry in his pudgy hand, watching the small procession fade into the sleet-blown darkness. "There you see," he said. "It comes down to will."

"Yes, Herr Obersturmbannführer," Schenkel said, "it does."

## Berlin, Germany, January 1944

"THERE IS A RUMOR AT ONE OF THE CAMPS IN Poland," Bucher said.

"There are rumors at every camp in Poland," von Strucker said. "What does one more matter?"

"This one is interesting," the pink-skinned man

said, coming farther into the baron's office and closing the door behind him. "I got it from an SS commissary officer who drinks too much and probably sells half of the inmates' rations on the black market."

"Thieving drunks are not interesting," von Strucker said. He had more important things on his mind, including the tersely worded memorandum on his desk. It was signed by one of Himmler's aides and it demanded an update on the progress of his special projects section. But von Strucker had no progress to report.

"Herr Baron," Bucher said, "you should listen to me."

The Prussian raised his close-cropped head and sighed. "Very well. I'm listening."

"The camp has been in trouble for months. Its last commandant shot himself."

"By accident?"

"Not unless he accidentally pulled the trigger of his sidearm while the muzzle was in his mouth."

"All right. So why did he do it?"

"A prisoner drove him mad. In fact, the man has driven half the SS contingent to drunkenness and desertion."

"Is that also rumor or is there some fact behind it?" von Strucker said.

Bucher leaned in closer, lowering his voice even though the two of them were alone in the office. "I looked around the camp. It was clear there was something wrong. Morale was nonexistent. The new commandant was in a perpetual black rage. And whenever I asked the usual questions about whether there were any 'unusual' prisoners, I kept getting the strangest looks—sideways looks, as if there was a big secret that no one dared talk about."

"But someone did talk about it."

"Krentz, the commissary officer. As crooked as the runes on his collar. But he likes his drink, so I took him to a blind pig in the nearby town and bought him enough slivovitz to refloat the *Tirpitz*. And he talked."

"So what did this alcoholic criminal tell you?"

"That there is a prisoner in the camp who does not die."

The baron sat up straighter. "That is unusual," he said. "Dying is what they are best at."

"This one has been beaten to a pulp, had his brains shot out, been buried alive, burned in the crematorium."

"That sounds like dying to me," von Strucker said.

"But he keeps coming back. Without a mark on him."

"A ghost story? Every camp has its ghost story."

"No ghost," Bucher said. "He comes back alive. They say that he heals. Even from the grossest wounds. That if you throw him into the ovens his flesh heals faster than it can be burned."

The baron put in his monocle. He tapped his fingers on the supercilious memo from Himmler's aide. "What is the name of this camp?"

"Höllenfeuer. Its commandant is Karl-Heinz Baumann. He used to be one of Heydrich's little ducklings, but these days he is swimming for his life."

"Himmler doesn't care for him?"

"If Baumann is a duckling, the Reichsführer-SS is a bad-tempered fox."

Von Strucker made up his mind. "Call the Luftwaffe liaison office," he said. "I want a plane. Now."


## Berlin, Germany, the present

IT WAS PAST MIDNIGHT WHEN THE TRAIN pulled into the Bahnhof Zoo station. Logan didn't think there would be anyone at the Invalidenstrasse address, but he had the taxi driver take him there anyway. *Always scout the objective thoroughly,* a voice said from the back of his mind. *The worst time to find out what you're getting into is when you're neck-deep in it.*

It wasn't his own voice. Somebody, somewhere—some*when*—had drilled strategy and tactics into him. The memory of how he had learned his lessons had been taken from him, but the lessons still remained.

The vodka-loving Pole had been right: no "peoples" were living at the headquarters of the Höllenfeuer *Erinnerunggesellschaft*—"remembrance association," he guessed was a proper translation. The cab stopped in front of a nondescript office building whose windows were all dark. It looked to be the kind of place to house businesses and societies that only required a couple of rooms—import/export firms, insurance brokers, clubs that consisted mainly of mailing lists of like-minded people who got together in hotels for annual conferences at which they reminisced about the good old days.

"Is there a good hotel within walking distance of here?" he asked the cabdriver.

"The Mercure is not far."

"Take me there."

The hotel was clean and not fancy. Logan stretched out on the room's double bed in the dark and stared up at the ceiling. He had no great hopes about what he would find at the Höllenfeuer Remembrance Association's office in the morning. Maybe they would not want to let him look at the photos of those who came to view the grassy mounds and the stone cairns. He intended to insist, and it seemed that whenever he insisted, people became eager to accommodate him. But what were the chances he would recognize a face? And, if he did, anyone he might have known at the camp—assuming he had actually been there—would now be more than sixty years older. Or more likely, dead for sixty years.

He closed his eyes and willed himself toward sleep. That, too, seemed to be an ability he had learned somewhere back in the impenetrable fog that was his past. And as the night wore on, he dreamed. The dreams did not offer him a coherent narrative. Instead, he caught snatches and flashes: a face contorted in pain, voices crying out in agony or shouting harsh words, images of fences and rough wooden walls, of fists and boots coming at him.

The dreams shook him loose from sleep. He awoke with the thin light of a Berlin winter dawn trying to penetrate the hotel room's drawn drapes. He struggled to hold on to the last few images, wanting to make a pattern of them, but they all evaporated from his mind.

## The Empty Quarter, Saudi Arabia, the present

"WHAT IF WE ACQUIRED AMERICAN UNIFORMS and gear?" Al Borak said. "Some of the men could pass for Latinos."

Von Strucker shook his head. "No. The security procedures are tight at the best of times. With the target on the premises, nothing will be left to chance. Not even his own mother could get within shooting distance of him without someone checking her identification."

The tall Pashtun folded his sinewy arms and stared for the umpteenth time at the unhelpful model of Baghdad's Green Zone. "Then we must tell them it cannot be done. It would mean throwing away a fine weapon for no purpose."

"These are the kind of people who are happy to send their children to blow up other people's children, just to make a statement," the baron said. "For them, the fact that an operation is completely futile is not necessarily an argument against carrying it out."

"Well, if we have to smash the Green Fist, then we have to smash the Green Fist. We would only have to start all over again. The madrassas are full of underfed boys that no one wants."

"You don't understand," von Strucker said. "They might not expect an old infidel like me to charge into the muzzles of the Americans' rifles, but they will not want you to miss your chance of being welcomed into Paradise by seventy-two virgins."

Al Borak's pale eyes flickered. "I have never been all that interested in virgins," he said.

"Then we need to think of something."

"If necessary, could we not tip off the Americans?"

A phone on the wall rang. Von Strucker crossed to it, snatched the handset from its cradle, and snapped, "I gave orders I was not to be disturbed!"

The voice of the facility's chief communications officer quavered slightly. "I regret the interruption, sir," he said, "but I am calling pursuant to one of your standing orders."

"Which one?"

"Standing Order Nine."

For a long moment the baron said nothing. He kept the handset at his ear, but his eyes lost focus as if he was staring into the far distance.

"Sir," said the communications officer, "are you still there?"

Von Strucker came back to the here and now. "Yes," he said, "relay me the message."

"It consists of only one word, sir. In German. That word is *kontakt.*"

The Prussian realized he had been holding his breath. Now he let it out and found that the smallest smile had taken control of his narrow lips. "Alert the hangar crew that I may want the Gulfstream V brought to immediate readiness for departure."

He hung up the phone on the communication officer's acknowledgment of the instruction. Ordering the plane had brought up a sudden sense of déjà vu, but it soon faded as he turned to Al Borak and said, "Get your men ready to leave," he said. "They will use the visas and identification that will allow them to enter Europe as a soccer team owned by our friend in the United Arab Emirates. We will refuel at his field in Abu Dhabi and fly direct to Berlin. They will need civilian clothing suitable for a German winter, but you will not be staying long."

The leader of the Green Fist was looking at him curiously. "I do not believe I have ever seen you so excited," he said.

The baron knitted his fingers together and touched

his knuckles to his lips, almost as if he were praying. Then he opened his hands and lifted them as if praising heaven. He said, "The solution to our problem may be about to walk into an office in Berlin. And more than the solution to just this business." He flicked his hand toward the model buildings on the table. "Much, much more. Now get the men ready to leave at a moment's notice."

The Pashtun departed. The baron went through the door right after him, but as Al Borak hurried toward the barracks and training area, von Strucker went swiftly to his private quarters. With the door closed and secured, he opened a notebook computer and turned it on. Alternately tapping the mouse and the keyboard, he sent a deeply encrypted signal that was received without any record of its reception by an official Royal Saudi government telecommunications satellite. The signal was then relayed through a number of facilities in and above the Middle East and southern Europe, until it ended at a secure terminal in an office on Invalidenstrasse in Berlin.

The response from Berlin was almost immediate. Moments after he sent the signal, von Strucker's notebook alerted him that he was receiving a j-peg file. He waited, again holding his breath, as the download's blue bar passed across the window. Then he touched the computer's mouse. The liquid crystal display filled with an image—a stretch of second-growth woodland, some grassy mounds, a tall stone cairn that bore a dark metal plaque—and glowering into the camera, a pair of dark eyes beneath a forehead into which descended a widow's peak of raven black hair.

The baron found that his mouth was dry, that his hand trembled as he reached to send a new signal to Berlin. With a deliberate effort he took control of himself. He typed a single word and tapped the mouse. Up to the Royal Saudi satellite went the message: RAT-TRAP.

Von Strucker let out another inheld breath. Again, he felt that involuntary smile taking over his lips. But this time, staring back at that face on the notebook's screen, he let the smile spread.

## Berlin, Germany, the present

At 8:00 A.M., THE FRONT DOORS TO THE office building on Invalidenstrasse were unlocked. Logan went in and found a lobby that was typical for a building whose owners didn't believe in wasting their money on useless decor. Instead of a reception desk and security guard, they had opted for an easy-to-read directory—white plastic letters on a black background—that told him that the Höllenfeuer *Erinnerunggesellschaft* had an office on the fourth floor.

Both the building's elevators were in use. Logan didn't want to wait anymore, so he went up the fire stairs two at a time. He emerged into a bland hallway paneled in fabric-covered pasteboard with doors of dark-stained wood. He moved along the corridor with rapid steps, almost running, his eyes flicking to the plastic plaques mounted on each door at head height.

Six doors from the fire stairs, he came to the office he sought. Its plaque showed the same words as were printed on the Polish guide's card, but underneath, taped to the wood, was a piece of paper with a hand-printed sign: GESCHLOSSENE HEUTE—KRANKHEIT IN DER FAMILIE.

Logan tried the door. It was locked. He knocked and waited, then knocked again, louder. No one came. He folded his arms and leaned his back against the wall, waiting, thinking. Of the six words on the sign, the only ones that he was confident of translating were *in der Familie,* which almost certainly meant "in the family." And the only reason he could think of for someone to put a sign like that on a door was to tell people that the place was closed up because of death or sickness in the family.

Still he waited. Maybe the sign was put up yesterday or the day before. Any moment, the elevator's chime might herald the arrival of the office's occupant, back after a brief period of mourning or a course of antibiotics, to open up the Höllenfeuer Remembrance Association for another day's business.

The elevator did not come. Instead, the door to another office opened and a middle-aged woman stepped out, carrying an empty carafe from a drip coffeemaker. She started and stopped dead when she saw the strange man push himself away from the wall with a quick flex of his knees and turn toward her. Logan saw the fear on her face and made an effort to sound unthreatening.

"Excuse me, please," he said. "Do you speak English?"

"Of course," she said, holding the carafe in two hands before her as if she might have liked to take shelter behind it. "How may I help you?"

"I am looking for a Mr. Holzbauer. I believe this is his office."

"Yes, it is." Her eyes went to the sign. "But this says he will not be in today. There is illness in the family."

"Ah," Logan said. "So that sign was put up today."

"It was not there yesterday," she confirmed. A new thought changed her expression. "It is strange," she said, "but I know that Herr Holzbauer is a bachelor and I thought he has said he is without family."

"Do you think he will be here tomorrow?"

She shrugged. "*Geschlossene heute* means 'closed today.' Herr Holzbauer is a very precise man. He would not say 'today' if he meant tomorrow also."

Logan sighed. "I will come back tomorrow then."

"He opens the door exactly at nine," she said.

Back outside, Logan had nowhere to go and twenty-four hours to kill. He walked back to the Hotel Mercure, but when he arrived at its front doors he realized he couldn't spend an entire day and night sitting and waiting.

Restless, he crossed Invalidenstrasse at a traffic light and began to walk at random. He could always find his way back by telling a cabbie to take him to the hotel. He came to a street called Lüisenstrasse and turned on to it. He seemed to be in the heart of Berlin, many of the buildings monumental in style and with a governmental look to them. He hadn't walked more than a mile before he saw down a side street something he recognized—the eighteenth-century Brandenburg Gate—and turned toward it.

He reached the old stone monument and stared at it, waiting to see if something would bubble up out of his damaged memory. But nothing came, and he realized that the fact that he could identify the six-pillared gate meant nothing. He'd recognize the Eiffel Tower or the Taj Mahal if he came upon them, but so what?

He walked on, heading south on a street called Ebertstrasse, and after a quarter mile he came to a strange sight. A whole block of the downtown seemed to have been leveled, the buildings replaced by a maze of gray stone blocks—hundreds, maybe thousands of them—as big as old-time tombs, with narrow cobble-stoned lanes laid between them. Some of the blocks were taller than he was, some low enough to sit on. They were not sited randomly but in straight lines, the heights increasing and decreasing so that the whole arrangement looked like billowing waves of granite.

*Some kind of cemetery,* he thought, and went toward it. But when he examined the first block he came to, there was no inscription. Nor was anything written on the next, or the one after that. He went down one of the aisles and found that the sound his bootheels made striking the cobblestones was muted. Soon he was in a stretch where the blocks rose higher than his head. All he could see was a narrow corridor of gray stone stretching before and behind him, and the cold blue sky above. But there was no need to worry about getting turned around and lost among these stones. He wasn't in a maze—the lanes all met at right angles and any straight line would take him out.

Now something was stirring in the back of his mind, some memory that this strange arrangement of faceless gray granite slabs was pulling up out of him. It wasn't a sense that he had been here before, not in this particular place. It was a feeling that he had been in a situation like this—hemmed in, confined to a place where all the options narrowed down to nothing but the basics, with only cold, hard, unyielding stone to push back against.

He couldn't remember the situation, but he could remember the feeling. And he was sure he had pushed back.

## Höllenfeuer Concentration Camp, February 1944

KARL-HEINZ BAUMANN STOOD ON THE PLAT-
form beside the train tracks. He kept his head erect
and his gloved hands clasped behind his back, the
confident posture of a senior officer who awaits the
arrival of his superior. But he knew that when he
unclasped his hands they would tremble and it
occurred to him that he should have breakfasted on
something other than a full bottle of the Montrachet
1878. The vintage was magnificent but the wine had
left his mouth sour, with acid at the back of his
throat. He was sure that the SS Obergruppenführer—a rank equivalent to that of a full general—
who was coming to inspect the camp would smell its
fumes on his breath.

Rumor had it that Ernst Kaltenbrunner, the man
whom Himmler had named to replace Reinhard
Heydrich, also knew his way around a bottle. But
even if Kaltenbrunner was a raging alcoholic, it didn't
mean he was going to forgive an Obersturmbannführer who had failed to straighten out a camp that
was going from bad to worse.

A high-pitched whistle sounded from somewhere
off in the distance and Baumann flinched. But it was
not the low-toned sound that now haunted his
dreams, that had made him open bottle after bottle of

the rare and precious wines. They were supposed to have been a legacy for his eldest son, but the commandant no longer believed he would ever have an heir to leave them to. He no longer believed in the future. For him, there was only now—and now was hell.

The whistle sounded again, closer. The first notes of a shrill laugh escaped the Obersturmbannführer before he could suppress it, causing his plump adjutant to turn toward him in concern. Baumann waved Schenkel away, noticing as he did so that his gloved hand did indeed shake. He disguised the tremor by taking his chin between thumb and forefinger, stroking it as if pondering some weighty thought.

Puffing steam and dark smoke, a polished black engine came into view down the track, already slowing to stop at the station. The engine flew twin swastika flags from its frontwork, as well as a pennant that identified it as pulling the private train of the head of the SS security division, the Sicherheitsdienst, or SD.

Behind the coal tender were two carriages, the second of them luxuriously appointed and adorned with an eagle-and-swastika motif in gold paint over crimson-painted wood. Before the special train had even come to a halt, black-uniformed, white-gloved SS descended from the first car and positioned themselves around the platform, submachine guns at the ready. Even here in the depths of a Polish forest, their commander had no intention of suffering the kind of fate that had befallen his predecessor in Prague.

As the train stopped, a junior officer jumped down from the second carriage and placed a white-painted wooden step beneath its stairs. Then, as Baumann and the senior officers gathered around him came to attention, a man almost seven feet tall in his jackboots, wearing a full-length greatcoat of black leather, stepped from the train. As he looked about him, his face, marked by dueling scars from his student days at the University of Graz, wore an expression that said he did not expect to see much that would please him.

The camp commandant and his officers threw their right arms out in the Nazi salute and Baumann was mortified to see that his limb was visibly shaking. He quickly brought it back down to his side, stepped forward, and offered his hand to the Obergruppenführer. But Kaltenbrunner merely raised his own right arm in a half salute and ignored the proffered handshake.

Baumann's heart sank, but he tried to put the best face on it. "All is in readiness for your inspection, Herr Obergruppenführer," he said.

"I hope it is," said the head of the SD. "For your sake."

The "special handling" operations had been suspended for the day, but Schenkel had prepared a full dossier of statistics on daily and weekly through-puts. Kaltenbrunner glanced at the columns of figures, then handed them without comment to the crisply uniformed Standartenführer who was his principal aide.

He allowed Baumann to lead him and his party behind the fence with its interwoven evergreen branches and along the narrow corridor that led to the extermination chambers that were disguised as shower rooms.

The Ukrainian SS guards who handled most operations in this section of the camp stood in formation for inspection. Baumann was relieved that their turn-out showed no glaring flaws. *Perhaps it will all go well,* he thought.

While the Obergruppenführer walked up and down the rows of Ukrainians, the commandant whispered to Schenkel, "Tell me again."

"Müller took him in chains to the lake," the adjutant said. "It must be twenty kilometers from here. They went out on the ice, broke a hole through it, and let him sink. He is at the bottom."

*Why shouldn't it work?* Baumann asked himself. *All right, so the monster can't die. So let him live on through the years—in cold mud beneath a hundred meters of water. By the time the chains rust away, I'll be an old man sunning myself on the French Riviera.*

Kaltenbrunner was coming back. Baumann scanned his superior's face, saw nothing to alarm him. The tiny hope he had kindled now flickered a little brighter. "Herr Obergruppenführer," he said, "allow me to show you the labor camp. Then we have prepared a light meal for you and your officers."

They crossed the railroad tracks and entered the work camp. The German SS troopers at the guard posts responded to the presence of general officer rank with reasonable snap and precision. The visitors did not go into the prisoners' barracks—they would have been alive with fleas the moment they stepped inside—but Kaltenbrunner looked through the door of one and nodded his head.

They inspected the equipment and mechanical sheds, where inmates who had useful skills maintained and repaired camp fixtures and vehicles. All was in good order in both places and it seemed to the commandant that Kaltenbrunner's expression was now less severe than it had been when he had stepped down from the train.

"I understand that you are an aficionado of fine wine," Baumann said as they left the mechanical shop. "I would be pleased if you would give me your opinion of my Château d'Yquem 1874."

The SD chief's eyebrows went up. "A Château d'Yquem '74?" he said. "I look forward to it, Baumann."

They went down the work camp's main street and turned into the assembly area with the sorting sheds on three sides. Baumann had ordered work stopped early the day before so that there would be plenty of material to be processed during the inspection. As the visitors came into view, Helmut and the other green-badge *kapos* dug their truncheons into ribs and barked at the starved and shabby men behind the trestle tables heaped with pathetic loot.

The prisoners' frost-bitten hands sorted and folded. The barrels filled with shoes and toys and hair. The stack of empty suitcases rose at the end of the plank tables. And the head of the SD, the man at the pinnacle of the organizational pyramid of which these sheds were the bottom-most layer, stood resplendent in his greatcoat of black leather, his oversize hands snug in calfskin gloves, and watched with evident approval.

"Not so bad," he said over his shoulder to Baumann. "Indeed, much better than I had been led to expect, Herr Obersturmbannführer."

Baumann clicked his heels. "Thank you, Herr Obergruppenführer," he said and was relieved to hear that his own tone had regained some of its old force. "Perhaps you would now care to try the Château d'Yquem '74?"

Kaltenbrunner turned with a smile on his face. He laid a companionable hand on the commandant's arm. "I would like that very much, Baumann. A magnificent vintage. And there is no reason why duty should not also include a little pleas—" He broke off as an expression of puzzlement replaced the indulgent smile. He was looking at something behind the commandant, and not liking what he saw.

A silence fell, broken only by a low, tuneless whistling. Baumann felt a cold sensation run all the way through him, as if someone had poured ice water into his skull so that the chill fluid could seep straight down, dissolving his insides and flushing them through his boots into the dirty slush that covered the assembly area.

"Herr Obersturmbannführer," the head of the Reich's Security Service said, all warmth now fled from his tone, "there is an odd-looking little man glaring at us. Can you explain to me why he isn't doing something to justify his existence?"

## Berlin, Germany, the present

THE GULFSTREAM V LANDED AT ONE OF THE private terminals at Templehof Airport and taxied to a waiting hangar. Customs officers met the passengers as they came down the plane's gangway, but the formalities were brief. When the officials had stamped their passports and left, a middle-aged German with a nervous tic in one eye came out of a glassed-in office and approached diffidently.

"Are you Holzbauer?" Al Borak said in rudimentary German.

"Yes," the man answered. "All is in readiness. The van is waiting outside."

"Good. Where are the keys?"

Holzbauer held out a ring and identified the keys that opened the Invalidenstrasse location's front door, the office on the fourth floor, and the loading bay at the back. "The key to the van is in the ignition."

"Very well," said the Pashtun. "You will now go home and stay there all day tomorrow. You will have no contact with anyone. The next day you will go to work as usual. Is that understood?"

It was. Holzbauer left in the direction of a taxi stand. Al Borak waited until he was well out of sight, then made sure that no one else was in the terminal except his own men and the plane crew. Then he went up into the aircraft and knocked twice on the door to the luggage bay.

A panel at the rear of the compartment slid aside and von Strucker stepped out. "All ready?" he said.

"Yes. I will bring the van inside," Al Borak said. He regarded the Prussian curiously, then added, "It must be strange to be back in your homeland after so long away."

The baron returned him a cold look. "I have more important things to think about," he said.

## Höllenfeuer Concentration Camp, January 1944

THEY HAD SHOT THE RAGGED LITTLE MAN, OF course. With the chief of the SD looking on, incredulous that a prisoner was standing around with his hands in his pocket, whistling and doing nothing, there was no choice. Hauptscharführer Müller had shot him and two of his men had dragged the mute away, blood trailing behind them in the gray snow.

Kaltenbrunner's scarred face now wore the same grim scowl that he had showed on arrival. He declined to speak to Baumann again, and left it to his chief aide to announce that the Obergruppenführer would not dine at the camp after all. Baumann could send a bottle of the Château d'Yquem '74 to the Obergruppenführer's private train, which would be departing soon.

But as his party left, Kaltenbrunner could not resist turning back to sneer at the hapless commandant. "You are a disgrace to the SS, to the homeland, to the Führer," he said. "I will see you transferred to a place where you can do less harm—and where your career can come to the miserable end it deserves. You will command a penal company on the eastern front. The Ivans are always laying new minefields to be cleared."

"Yes, Herr Obergruppenführer," Baumann said. His staff had drawn away from him, leaving him isolated before the furious visitor.

"Consider yourself lucky that I do not have you shot out of hand as an example to your officers and men," Kaltenbrunner said. He spun on his heel and strode back to the train tracks, his aides and bodyguards following.

Baumann saw Müller coming back from wherever they had taken the little man. The commandant called him over. "What did you do with him?"

"We put him behind one of the supply sheds," the

noncom said. "There didn't seem much point in—"

"Yes, yes," Baumann cut him off. He sighed, then said, "Go and get him. Take him to my office and tie him securely to a chair. I am going to have a little talk with him."

In the parlor next to the commandant's office, the sideboard was heaped with the buffet that would have been offered to Kaltenbrunner and his entourage. Beside the piles of sausage and sauerbraten, the kugel and *kirschtorte,* were ranked the finest wines of Baumann's collection. A gap in their ranks showed where the Château d'Yquem had been removed by Schenkel and carried off to the Obergruppenführer.

Baumann surveyed the foregone feast for a long moment. Then he swept his arm along the length of the sideboard, sending plates and dishes and all their contents crashing and splattering to the floor. A sausage landed on the instep of his polished jackboot and he flicked it away to splat against the wall. He reached for the nearest bottle—a magnificent Château Haut-Brion 1877—and worked the tip of a corkscrew into its stopper. As he twisted the screw in and pulled the cork free, he heard behind him in his office the sounds of the mute being brought in, then the clank of chains as Müller secured him to a sturdy oak chair.

Baumann did not bother with a glass. He upended the bottle and let one of the most glorious wines of the nineteenth century pour over his tongue and down his throat. He did not even swallow, let alone pause to savor the taste, but just let the priceless liquid fill his belly. He drained half the bottle before he took its mouth from his lips, then belched up the air that had accompanied the wine's descent to his stomach.

"Herr Obersturmbannführer," Müller's voice came from behind him, "your orders have been carried out."

"Dismissed," Baumann said without turning around. He heard the noncom and his men leave, heard the outer door close. He raised the bottle again and drank long and deep, the fumes from the wine rising into the back of his throat and filling his nose. Then he turned and looked at the fate that had befallen him.

The ragged man was slumped in the chair, the chains tight across his chest and arms, his legs and ankles similarly held. His chin was on his chest, his long hair hanging down. The commandant went to the bound man and examined him. He'd never seen what happened after each time the inmate had been taken away dead. Now the commandant counted the bullet holes that had pierced the mute's chest in a burst from Müller's Schmeisser. There were seven.

*Not bad grouping,* he thought. He reached forward with one gloved hand and poked a finger into one of the wounds. The dead man did not react. When he took it out, the fingertip was not stained with blood— the wound had already cauterized itself.

Now as he watched, the wound filled in from within, the steel-jacketed nine-millimeter round pressed out of the body so that it fell to the man's lap, then bounced onto the wooden planks of the floor. The bullet rolled and came to rest beside the stain they had never been able to get out, the mark of the previous commandant's final defeat.

Another bullet appeared on the man's chest and tumbled down, then one more. *The rest must be trapped in his clothing,* Baumann thought, then wondered at how his mind could be so calmly, coolly analytical when his whole world had come to an end.

*Though not quite to an end,* he thought. *It could take them two or three weeks to cut my new orders and deliver them.* And while he waited, he would use the time productively.

The man in the chair gasped, a sudden intake of breath filling the still chest. His head came up, his eyes opened, and he looked at the commandant.

"So you know that they call you 'the man who won't die'?" Baumann said. "Too bad." He drained the last of the Haut-Brion, flipped the empty bottle so that its neck landed in his hand, then swung the container against the mute's head. The bottle shattered, shards of the thin glass slashing and piercing the prisoner's face. Blood flowed and one eye was ruined. The man's scream was satisfying.

Baumann waited until the prisoner's remaining good eye focused on him again. He gestured to the stain on the floor. "My predecessor understood only part of his relationship to you. He grasped that his true situation was not that you were locked in here with him, but that *he was locked in with you*. And so he put his pistol in his mouth and freed himself."

The prisoner's torn eye was healing itself even as he watched, the cuts on his face closing, fading. The hard face looked back at him with undisguised contempt and undiluted hatred.

"Too bad," the commandant said again, examining the jagged remnant of the broken bottle that was left in his gloved hand. "Too bad for my predecessor that he lacked the will to break through his despair and see the truth behind the situation. Because the real, terrible truth is not that you are a man who won't die, but that you are a man who *can't* die.

"But," he continued, "you can certainly suffer."

Baumann drew back the arm that held the bottle and swung and slashed. He gouged and ground the weapon into the screaming man's face and neck. And when the sharp points had snapped off, and the bottle was reduced to just a stub of its neck, he went again to the parlor and got another one.

He waited, drinking, not even noticing what he drank, while the ruined flesh knit itself back together. He was in no hurry. He had all day. And all night. And the day after that.

## Berlin, Germany, the present

THE EFFICIENT YOUNG MAN AT THE FRONT desk of the Hotel Mercure had identified for Logan the strange grid of faceless tombstones south of the Brandenburg Gate.

"It is a national memorial," he said in almost unaccented English. "To remember the Jews killed by Hitler. Underneath, there is an information center."

Logan hadn't seen the stairs that descended to the information center. He had walked through the array of granite blocks and continued on through the streets of Berlin. Eventually, he had decided that its wide streets and imposing buildings had nothing to tell him about his past. He had found a cab and come back to the hotel, eaten dinner, and gone to bed.

But something was working in the back of his mind, because the night brought dreams. He heard voices speaking in German, harsh voices shouting orders. He did not understand the words and phrases, but with them came ghosts of strong emotion—anger, outrage, pity, and a great sadness that drove him out of sleep and left him surprised to find a tear trickling down one cheek.

He had trouble getting back to sleep. The dream fragments left him confused and angry. He kept thinking about how he would like to lay his hands upon whoever had done this harm to his mind. *We live only in the present,* he told himself, *in that thin membrane between what has been and what is to come. But without our past, whatever joys or horrors it may hold, we have nothing but that flimsy tissue. And it is not enough.*

Yet as he lay on a rented bed in an anonymous hotel room in a city that had nothing to do with him, one welcome thought came to him. The images and voices that speckled his dreams, the faces he had recognized—Tommy Prince, Rob Roy MacLeish, Lucia Gambrelli—they must still be stored somewhere inside him. Whoever had savaged his memories had not been able to wipe them clean. Perhaps all they had done was to lock his past away in some sealed room in the back of his mind, or to bury it beneath dead layers of fill.

*But even the strongest locks can be broken,* he told himself. That which is buried can be dug up again and brought back to the light of day. Logan might not know who he was or where he came from, might not even know his true name, but he was becoming increasingly sure of his true nature. *You can lock me away,* he thought, *but I will break free. You can bury me alive, but I will come up out of the earth. And then there will be a reckoning.*

After a while he slept again, without dreams, and awoke to find the room brightly lit by light seeping past the closed drapes. When he threw them back he saw that Berlin had received its first snowfall of the coming winter. The streets and rooftops were coated in pristine white, the sounds of the awakening city muffled.

At five minutes before nine, he stepped out of the hotel and walked the short distance to the building on Invalidenstrasse. In the lobby, two young men were waiting beside the elevator, both olive-skinned and black-haired, bundled up in identical overcoats. As Logan came in from the street, brushing snow from his hair, one of them pushed the button to summon the elevator. Then both separated, as if politely making room for him to be first aboard when the car came.

Logan had no patience this morning. He strode to the fire stairs and went up them two at a time. Behind him he heard one of the men speaking in a language he didn't know, the tone urgent yet controlled. He had heard people speak like that before, he thought—not in that language, but in that way. But when he tried to get a grip on where and when, as always it slipped from his grasp. He let the question go. His business was on the fourth floor.

The hallway was as empty as it had been the day before. When he came to the door of the Höllenfeuer Remembrance Association, the note was gone. He knocked and a voice from inside said, *"Kommen Sie."*

The office was small and blandly furnished: a utilitarian desk and a couple of chairs, a computer and phone, a credenza and file cabinets against one wall. The wall space above the furniture held frameless blowups of black-and-white photographs: a watch-tower above a wire fence, empty train tracks, an aerial view of barrack rooftops and muddy streets, a small house with a swastika flag hanging from a pole that jutted out from the front porch roof.

The last image gave Logan a twinge of memory, but he did not try to reach for more. Instead, he focused on the person behind the desk, a tall man with close-cropped dark hair, a hooked nose, and startlingly gray eyes, who sat with his outsize hands clasped together on the desktop.

"Do you speak English?" Logan said.

"A little."

The accent was odd, like nothing Logan had so far heard on the streets of Berlin. "Are you German?" he said.

"Turk. How I help you?"

"Photographs. Höllenfeuer camp."

The man smiled and rose from behind the desk. "In room," he said, gesturing to a door in the office's inner wall. "Many photo. You open."

Logan crossed to the inner door. When he opened it, there was no light within. He reached inside, feeling for a light switch, but when he found one and pressed, nothing happened.

"The light's out," he said, turning his head to look over his shoulder. Only to find that the gray-eyed man had come silently around the desk and was close behind him.

Then he felt the man's palms on his shoulder blades and he was pushed into the darkness, the door singing shut behind him. He put out his arms to break his fall, but his hands encountered hard, muscular flesh beneath cloth. He couldn't see, but he had an animal sense of people in front of him, around him. He struck out with his fists, tried to get a leg up to swing a kick. But it was as if he were in one of those dreams where he moved in slow motion while everyone around him was fast and unencumbered. Some kind of cord had been slipped around his legs at the ankles and even as it was tightened, another went around his knees.

His arms were seized—it felt as if two or three pairs of hands had hold of each limb—and forced down to his sides. More restraints snaked around him, trussing him snugly from shoulder to wrist. And it was all happening so *fast*!

He growled and struggled against the bonds, surprising himself by the sheer bestiality of the sound that came unbidden from his throat. The muscles of his forearms were bunching and burning, and some part of his mind was telling him that that was a bad, terrifying thing to be letting happen. He felt a searing pain begin in his hands and the pain drove the anxiety to new heights. His pulse was thudding in his ears like the heels of a flamenco dancer on speed. But behind the growing panic he felt an anticipation of impending release, almost sexual in its intensity.

Then another pain registered, a pinprick in his shoulder muscle. He knew that sensation. It was a hypodermic needle going in, and the burning pressure that followed meant that something was being injected into him. A tidal wave of darkness began to rise in his mind, but he fought it down, forced it back. He was thinking, even as he struggled to hold on to consciousness, *I've done this before.*

A voice was speaking near his ear, in a language he didn't know. But Logan could interpret the meaning from the tone: the speaker was complaining that the injection hadn't work. Another voice responded, giving curt instructions, and now he felt a second stab in his shoulder, more of the cold burning sensation, and again the darkness tried to claim him.

But again, he held it at bay. Like a man facing rising floodwaters, he built a dike of will against the pressure of oblivion, a levee of sheer refusal to succumb. Even as he bent all of his concentration to resistance, a part of him was sensing a familiarity. This kind of thing had happened before and he had survived it. *Because of who I am,* he thought. *Because of what I do.*

The complaining voice spoke again. The voice that gave orders snapped back, then shouted something. The door opened and light not only flooded in from the outer office but from overhead lights in this room. Logan saw that he was in a windowless conference room, its long table upended and pushed back against the wall, the chairs stacked in a corner to leave space for the several young men who swarmed around him, keeping him from falling. They were dressed as civilians but each one wore military-issue night-vision goggles, and they had the look of a team that had been trained to work together.

Except that things clearly weren't going according to plan. One of them, slightly older than the others, spoke and Logan recognized the voice as the one who had been giving orders. He was answered by the gray-eyed man who now stood in the doorway. *Sergeant and lieutenant,* Logan thought. It was there in the tone of voice and the body language.

Another wave of darkness tried to claim him, but he fought it down, shaking his head to clear it. One of the men held up a full hypodermic and asked a question. The man in the doorway spoke over his shoulder to someone in the outer office that Logan couldn't see and received an answer that must have been negative, because the man with the needle put it away unused.

Now the gray-eyed man stepped into the conference room-turned-snatch zone and approached Logan. He examined the trussed man, then said something to the others. The hands that supported Logan fell away and he tottered, his legs bound and his head struggling to remain above the dark tide. Then gray eyes reached for him with those outsize hands. He saw strange calluses on the fingertips and palms before they went past his eyes to touch his temples.

He never heard the sharp *crack,* nor saw the flash of bright light, nor smelled the charred flesh. The world went black and rushed away from him as he fell into nowhere.

## Höllenfeuer Concentration Camp, February 1944

AS THE CAMP'S ADJUTANT, HAUPTSTURMFÜHRER Otto Schenkel had always worked in a small room down a hallway from his superior's quarters in the *kommandantur.* But after Baumann moved the man who wouldn't die into his office, it became too difficult. Höllenfeuer had thousands of inmates, hundreds of guards. That made Schenkel the chief administrative officer of an establishment far larger than the midsize manufacturing company that his father operated in Bremen, turning out fountain pens, mechanical pencils, and similar goods. Keeping the camp running involved a great deal of detailed work, and that work required concentration—a quality that the adjutant found difficult to sustain when he was constantly disturbed by the prisoner's screams and Baumann's own loud drunken rants.

So Schenkel had moved his desk and files to a separate building, bumping Untersturmführer Krentz, the commissary officer, out of his space. Krentz was now sharing a smaller room with Weber, a thick-necked SS junior officer who looked after the camp's transport. Today Weber had come to Schenkel and confided that the commissary officer had been selling camp supplies and using the money to buy liquor.

"Krentz no longer makes any attempt to disguise what he is doing, Herr Hauptsturmführer," Weber said. "He is drunk all the time."

Schenkel had other worries, bigger worries. "So is our commandant," he said. "But there is nothing to be done until a new senior officer arrives to replace him." He gestured to the reports that littered his desk. "And while we wait, this place goes to hell and damnation."

Weber ran a finger nervously around the inside of his shirt collar. "That is what concerns me, Herr Hauptsturmführer." He lowered his voice. "Krentz may be selling pistols."

"He deals with Polish black marketeers," Schenkel said. "They like to shoot each other. What's another dead Pole or two?"

"But I think he may be selling them inside the camp."

"Inside the camp?" The words made no sense to the adjutant. "The inmates have no money."

"They find it hidden in suitcases or sewn into clothes. The *kapos* get most of it, though they have to share with the noncommissioned officers."

Schenkel was outraged. "That is the property of the

Reich," he said. "How long has this been going on? We must conduct an investigation."

"With respect, Herr Hauptsturmführer," Weber said, "I think the possibility that the inmates are arming themselves is the more serious problem. There have been revolts at other camps—Sobibor and Treblinka—where the inmates have shot the guards and escaped."

"There have been no revolts. Those are only rumors spread by defeatists."

"Again, with respect, Herr Hauptsturmführer, they are not. I have a cousin who was on furlough from Sobibor when the camp was taken. He returned from leave to find the place a smoldering ruin, the inmates scattered into the forest. He spent weeks rounding them up again."

"Do you think it could happen here?" Schenkel waved away Weber's response. Even as he'd asked the question, he'd known that the answer was a definite "yes"—Höllenfeuer must be the worst-run concentration camp in the Reich.

He rested his elbows on the desk and his damp palms cupped his jowls. What was he to do? The SS worked on the basis of top-down leadership. Decisions came from above and were carried out efficiently by subordinates, each of whom knew the exact extent of his responsibilities. Schenkel's clear duty was to put this matter before the commandant, as Weber had put it before him, so that the superior could decide what action would be taken.

But Baumann had gone mad. He stayed in his quarters, much of the time in a drunken stupor. His waking hours were spent alternately torturing the small man in rags or carrying on one-sided rambling conversations about Nietzsche and the supremacy of will. In doing so, he was depriving his adjutant of the thing a subordinate most needed: a superior officer who would give him orders to carry out. Schenkel envied the men in Berlin who were daily exposed to the clear calm leadership of Adolf Hitler.

"What do you think we should do?" he asked Weber. "I don't know when we'll get another commandant."

"Herr Hauptsturmführer," the transport officer said, "it is not my place—"

"Neither is it mine!" Schenkel yelped, "but someone must do something!"

Weber thought for a moment, then said, "Müller! He's a practical man."

Relief blew through the adjutant like a spring breeze. "Yes, he is. Get him in here!"

But even as Weber opened the door to leave, he found Hauptscharführer Müller just outside, his hand raised to knock for entry.

"What is it?" Schenkel said.

Müller came into the room, deep worry etching

lines into his coarse-featured face. "An Oberführer has arrived unannounced at the camp gate, Herr Hauptsturmführer. He is demanding to see the commandant."

"No one sees the commandant!" was Schenkel's automatic response, then his mind focused on the noncom's first statement. "An Oberführer, did you say?"

"Yes, Herr Hauptsturmführer. And with a red skull on his cap."

"*Ach, mein Gott!*" Schenkel said. A red skull meant that everything had just gotten worse. Immeasurably worse. He needed to think. "Where did you put him?"

"In the visiting officer's quarters," Müller said.

"Good." The adjutant turned to Weber, still hovering at the door. "You go and keep him company. Tell him the commandant is indisposed, but I will join him shortly."

Müller came to attention. "If I may speak freely . . ."

"What?"

"He does not look like a man it would be wise to keep waiting long."

Schenkel waved a hand to shoo the noncom from the room, then buried his face in his fingers. A Red Skull Oberführer, one of Himmler's Special Projects people, and a senior one at that. Oberführer was a political rank, officially equivalent to a colonelcy, but in practice it meant that its holder was outside the rank structure of the SS. He would be the head of a unit, and he would report to no one but Himmler himself. A man who had the ear of the Reichsführer-SS was always a very good man to impress—and always a man it could be lethal to disappoint.

Trembling, Schenkel rose and put on his greatcoat and cap. He went first to the commandant's quarters. Perhaps Baumann had come through his crisis and was clearheaded again. But even before he reached the *kommandantur*'s front steps, he could hear the bellowing. The words were indistinct, slurred by drink and madness, but the commandant seemed to be shouting a single question over and over.

*And if he expects an answer from a mute,* the adjutant thought, *he's crazier today than he was yesterday.* Still, the madman was in command, and Schenkel's duty was to report to him, to try to get him to take responsibility. Perhaps the news that a Red Skull Oberführer had arrived would shock Baumann back to sanity. Holding that faint hope, Schenkel went up the steps and in to the *kommandantur.*

The office looked like a slaughterhouse at the end of a busy day. Blood had pooled on the floor around the man bound to the chair, some of it fresh, much of it dry. More gore stained the walls, in arcs and sprays of red droplets. Baumann himself was drenched, his uniform sleeves crimson to the elbows, his tunic's front sodden. The commandant was striding back and forth in front of the prisoner, his boots crunching shards of broken glass underfoot, a blood-smeared book open in his hand.

"Do you believe that?" he was shouting at the bound man who, though blood-smeared, was unmarked by so much as a bruise. "You do, don't you? You believe it!"

When Schenkel came through the doorway, Baumann's bloodshot eyes struggled to focus on him. The commandant stopped and took a stumbling step backward as though faced with an apparition. He blinked and stared at the adjutant for several seconds before he recognized his subordinate.

"Schenkel!" he said. "Just the man." He slapped the open book with his free hand and said, "I've been debating von Schiller's famous line with our friend here."

Schenkel came cautiously into the room. "Yes, Herr Obersturmbannführer. Fascinating. But there is an urgent matter I must—"

Baumann cut him off, quoting from the book in his hand, his eyes blinking blearily at the page. "'Against stupidity the very gods themselves contend in vain,'" he quoted, then snapped the volume shut and gave Schenkel a drunken, lopsided grin. "What horseshit!"

"As you say, Herr Obersturmbannführer. Now there is a—"

"It is not stupidity the gods struggle against," the

commandant said, overarticulating in the way of drunks who seek to make a point. "It is *will*! Will is everything!"

Baumann threw the book into a corner and leaned toward the other officer, giving Schenkel a gust of foul breath. "This swine here," he gestured at the man in the chair who glared back at him with eyes like black diamonds, "this *üntermensch* thinks he has will. But he has only stupidity. I am showing him, Schenkel. I am showing him will. I am showing him the difference between will and stupidity, but—" and here the drunken madman laughed as if he had just made a wonderful discovery, "—he is too stupid to see it."

"Yes, Herr Obersturmbannführer. But—"

Baumann was paying him no attention. He groped on the floor beside his desk and came up with a half-empty bottle of wine, raised it to his lips, and drained most of its contents in a series of long gurgling swallows.

Schenkel was willing to try one more time, but even as he opened his mouth to speak he heard a thud of boots ascending the outer steps and crossing the porch. Then the doorway was filled by a lean-faced SS officer with close-cropped blond hair and double oak leaves on his collar tab. The adjutant's gaze was drawn to the red skull on his uniform cap as if the symbol had hypnotic power.

The Oberführer's cold blue eyes took in each of the

elements of the scene, then came back to Schenkel. "I am Oberführer von Strucker," he said. "Are you in command here?"

"No," Schenkel said. "I am the camp adjutant. Obersturmbannführer Baumann, here, is in command."

"Clearly," said the newcomer, "he is not even in command of himself." He turned to speak to whoever was behind him in the hallway. "Get some men and escort this drunk to a secure place. He is relieved of command."

Schenkel heard Weber's voice from the hallway, saying, "*Jawohl,* Herr Oberführer!" followed by the clump of the transport officer's footsteps and then his shouting for Müller.

Von Strucker came into the room, his attention fixed on the prisoner in the chair. Behind him, Baumann had drawn himself erect, though he wavered like sea grass moved by strong waves. "I am—" he began.

"You are finished," said von Strucker, without taking his eyes off the prisoner. "I am taking temporary command of this facility, by the authority of the Reichsführer-SS. And if you say one more word in my presence I will have you shot."

Baumann cleared his throat, at which the Red Skull Oberführer turned and put his icy eyes on the commandant. Baumann staggered again, as if he had been physically struck, then his shoulders slumped.

Schenkel, watching from a corner of the office into which he had backed, believed he now finally understood what the madman had meant when he talked of the supremacy of will.

Bucher found a vacant office down the hall from the blood-drenched room. Von Strucker had the fat and nervous adjutant summon a couple of guards, who carried the bound man, chair and all, down to the clean space. When the prisoner was set down in the center of the empty room and the guards dismissed, the baron turned to the perspiring Schenkel and said, "Leave us."

But the man lingered in the doorway. "Herr Oberführer," he stammered, "there is a situation in the camp."

"I would not be surprised," said von Strucker, "to learn that there are several situations."

"But—"

"You are now in command of this establishment. Except for this room. But if you do not leave us, the next thing you will be commanding is your own burial detail."

Höllenfeuer's new commandant left and the Prussian immediately forgot all about him. "Shut the door," he told Bucher, and when the pink-skinned subordinate had done so, the baron said, "Now let us see."

He took off his cap and greatcoat and hung them on a hook behind the door. Then he circled the man in the chair, inspecting him from all sides. The prisoner was lean and underfed but hard-muscled. The long hair and heavy beard growth along his cheeks made it hard to precisely define the shape of his skull, but from the facial features and pale skin, von Strucker judged him to be of Celtic stock. Weber had said the man had come on a train from Italy and that he was a mute.

He came around to the man's front and said, *"Verstehen-Sie mir?"* Do you understand me?

The man gave him the same agate-hard stare he had given the drunk, but the baron saw no flicker of comprehension. He tried the question in Italian, with a similar lack of result, then in French. Nothing.

Then he tried, "Do you understand me?" in English and though the prisoner made no voluntary response, von Strucker was a keen enough observer to know that he had been understood. He continued in English.

"So. You speak English. Are you an Englishman? Or a colonial? Not Australian, though." He watched the man's pupils and the action of the tiny muscles around the eyes. "Perhaps Canadian?"

He saw the faint flicker of expansion and contraction. "Ah," he said, "so it is Canadian.

"What about family? Is someone worrying about you somewhere? A mother, a father? Brothers, sisters?"

*No,* the Prussian saw from the microexpression

that the prisoner could not disguise, *no family*. That was a disappointment. He had hoped for the possibility of breeding this one to a similarly mutated mother or sister.

"Never mind," he said. "But let us see what we have." He drew from the inner pocket of his tunic a small flat case, opened it to reveal a dissecting scalpel and some probes. The man's rags had been torn free from one shoulder by the insane commandant's ministrations, and the baron applied the tip of the scalpel to the deltoid muscle. The prisoner's breath hissed inward and he pulled against his bonds as the blade cut through the skin and underlying tissue, deep into the fiber beneath, until von Strucker could see the white of bone. Blood immediately welled, then just as quickly stopped.

The baron put in his monocle and leaned closer. He had made a cut three inches long and an inch deep at its center, but even as he watched, the tissues drew themselves together. He had seen time-lapse photography of plants emerging from seeds to become full grown, a week's growth in ten seconds. Now he was seeing the equivalent before his very eyes.

"Remarkable," he said. He positioned himself in front of the specimen, squatting so that they were at eye level. "Is it all kinds of tissue? Do your teeth grow back? Do your bones heal?"

The black eyes glittered and he heard a growl deep in the man's chest.

"I doubt you're really a mute," von Strucker said. "The Canadian Army wouldn't have taken a mute. Perhaps you are shell-shocked?" He stroked his chin. "I wonder: If I cut you in half, would each half grow a whole new you?"

The growl deepened.

"Well," said the Prussian, standing up, "we'll have time to explore all of your many mysteries, won't we?"

To Bucher, he said, "Go and find that fat fool. Tell him we'll need some kind of dissecting table. And have him find a generator and rig some decent lighting in here. I want to do a few preliminaries, then we'll take him back to Berlin for a full work-up."

Bucher bustled out. Von Strucker wiped the scalpel clean and put it away. He stared at the bound man and smiled. "How marvelous," he said, "to have found you."

What this situation called for, Schenkel decided, was a damn good report. "If you don't want to be last, get your story in first" was one of the golden rules of bureaucratic systems. After the encounter with the terrifying Red Skull Oberführer, he returned to his office, poured himself a schnapps to fight down his panic, and began to think the situation through. The liquor helped clear his mind, and he realized that the Oberführer's intervention presented a wonderful opportunity.

Everybody knew that Kaltenbrunner and Himmler

did not care for each other, but concentration camps were under Kaltenbrunner's authority. If things went amiss here at Höllenfeuer while one of the Reichs-führer-SS's Red Skulls was in temporary command, it would be a black eye for Himmler. Kaltenbrunner's position in the Reich's highest political circles would be enhanced. As the officer who dutifully brought the situation to the notice of the chief of the SD, Schenkel would be remembered, at least sheltered, and possibly rewarded.

Of course, he could not write officially and directly to Obergruppenführer Kaltenbrunner. But he could send an unofficial note to the man's aide. Despite what the rulebooks said, Schenkel knew that the world was tied together by back-channel communications. He put pen to paper for a preliminary draft. The right phrases came easily: "disruption of the normal chain of command," "a nonmilitary officer arrogating to himself authority over military forces," "protests ignored." In only minutes, he had the perfect instrument to redirect all blame for anything that now went wrong at Höllenfeuer.

He made a few minor alterations, then copied the finished draft onto official camp letterhead, signed at the bottom, and placed it in an addressed envelope that he marked "private and confidential." He tucked the letter into the inner pocket of his tunic and breathed a sigh of relief. An SS motorcycle courier would arrive early tomorrow morning and carry the letter to the nearby Luftwaffe airfield. By nightfall, the report would be in Berlin and by morning it would be in the in-tray of Kaltenbrunner's Standartenführer.

And then, let the heavens fall, for plump little Otto Schenkel of Bremen would have made for himself an island of safety.

He poured himself another schnapps to celebrate. As he put it to his lips, the short, pink-skinned man who had accompanied von Strucker opened the door without knocking and strode into the office.

"The Oberführer requires a generator and some decent lighting in the *kommandantur,*" he said.

"We do not have a spare generator," Schenkel said. "All are in use." They were supposed to have two backups, one in case a regular unit failed and another for emergencies, but the last inventory had found them missing. Krentz's doing, the adjutant assumed.

"Take one out of use and light the Oberführer's room," Bucher said.

"You are giving me an order to do so?"

"Yes."

"Very well," Schenkel said. He would need to revise the report to include this detail.

The man left. Schenkel rose from behind his desk and stood for a moment, studying the map of the camp that hung on one wall. Then he went out and made his way down the hall to the orderly room. The clerk on duty stood to attention.

"Inform the engineering officer that generator

number four is to be disconnected and moved to the *kommandantur,* along with wiring and portable lighting."

"At your order, Herr Hauptsturmführer," the man said.

"Make sure that the engineering officer is aware that the order comes directly from the new commandant."

"*Jawohl.*"

And as the man departed on his errand, Schenkel added, "And tell Untersturmführer Weber to have a staff car brought around. I won't need a driver."

Schenkel went back to his office, a smile on his face. He revised his report, then gathered up a few items he didn't want burned and carried them out to where the staff car waited. A minute later, he passed through the front gate and turned in the direction of the Luftwaffe airfield. Personally delivering his urgent letter gave him a perfect excuse for being away from the camp.

## Berlin, Germany, the present

"HE'S HEAVY," KHAN SAID.

"It must be the chains," Al Borak said. "He's smaller than any of us."

"It's not the chains. It's like he has rocks in his belly."

They were in the freight elevator of the building on Invalidenstrasse, the Pashtun and four members of the Green Fist, descending to the first basement parking level where the van waited. The baron waited there, too, in case they needed someone who spoke German to deal with any curious passersby. Their prisoner was tightly wrapped in chains, his head encased in a bag of heavy cloth, propped upright on a two-wheeled dolly.

As the elevator reached the basement, the small man began to struggle against the restraints. "He came to very fast," Khan said.

"That's why the baron is interested in him," Al Borak said. He directed two of the men to go out among the parked cars and make sure no one was watching. When they returned to report that the area was clear, their leader told Khan and the other man to wheel their burden the short distance to where the van waited behind the loading bay door.

The van's rear doors opened and the baron stepped out. He watched as the Pashtun directed the four men to lift the prisoner feetfirst, dolly and all, into the vehicle. Though they were all fit men, they had to strain to handle the weight.

"He is definitely heavy," Khan said, puffing from the exertion.

The baron peered at the prisoner. "He wasn't abnormally heavy when I first encountered him. I wonder what he has been up to."

Al Borak whistled, and the rest of the team came swiftly from all directions, where they had been stationed to warn if anyone approached the operation area. They crowded into the van on either side of the man lying on his back in chains.

Then, before the doors were closed, the baron said, "Just to be sure, remove the bag."

The Pashtun tugged the cloth away. A hard and angry face looked up at him, then the dark eyes flicked toward the Prussian.

The baron spoke to the man in English. "Remember me?"

## Höllenfeuer Concentration Camp, February 1944

"**What do you think?**" von Strucker asked Bucher, "systemic, or some special gland or organ?"

"Systemic, I'd say. It's not as if some parts of him heal and others don't. And they all heal at the same rate."

"I agree," the baron said, gazing down at the man on the table. "My first inclination is to look at the blood. The mutation could be in the lymphatic system, but blood constantly circulates through every part of the body."

"A unique blood cell?" Bucher suggested.

"Most likely."

The pink-skinned man said, "It's a shame we can't ask him, he being a mute. He may know."

The Prussian sneered. "No. When Socrates said, 'The unexamined life is not worth living,' he was referring to man-shaped beasts like this one."

The man on the table growled and the baron checked the restraints again. Once they had rigged the lights, they had begun by chaining him to a sturdy oak table from the officer's mess. It had taken six burly SS troopers to effect the transfer from the chair. But even chained, the subject had been able to wriggle, making fine work difficult. The baron had summoned the camp's carpenter and had him nail the man to the table, using heavy spikes driven through wrists, elbows, ankles, and above the knees. The heads of the spikes were then hammered sideways, bending them over to guarantee that the subject couldn't tear himself free.

"If it's the blood, then we should be looking at the marrow. That's where blood cells get made," Bucher said.

"Agreed," said von Strucker, picking up a chisel and a heavy mallet that had come from the camp's metalworking shop. "Slice open his right thigh. We'll remove a portion of his femur."

Hauptscharführer Müller didn't like it. With the number four generator taken out of service, a substantial portion of Höllenfeuer was unlit, including the row of two-man huts that were bachelor officers quarters, before one of which he stood guard. The floodlamps that lined the fence along the east side were out, so that the nearby barracks that housed the political and deviate prisoners were black shapes in the darkness. Even the searchlights in the watchtowers were dead. Who knew what the swine were doing out there in the blackness? He thought again about the rumors of pistols being smuggled into the camp.

He would have liked to be out there patrolling with some picked men, but the visiting high mucky-muck had specifically ordered that the camp's senior noncommissioned officer had to guard the drunken former commandant. *You have the most to lose if he gets loose,* the Oberführer had said and Müller had had no doubt that it was a threat to be taken seriously. He had stared straight ahead, but his eyes kept wanting to go to the red skull on the officer's cap. All kinds of strange tales circulated about the ultrasecret Special Projects units: how they reanimated the dead to fight again, heedless of their wounds; how they had recovered the spear with which the Roman legionary had pierced the side of Christ, a sacred relic that guaranteed victory to whoever owned it; how they had found an entrance to a vast subterranean world beneath the Alps, peopled by dragons and golden-eyed folk, that Germany would conquer and rule once the Ivans were crushed.

Now Müller came back from his dreams to the reality of darkness. Someone should be patrolling while

the lights are out, he knew, but no one had ordered it.
Schenkel was nowhere to be seen and the Red Skulls
were closeted with the weird little mute that nobody
liked to think about. Nobody except Baumann, who
now thought about nothing else. Müller resolved to
do the best job he could at guarding the drunken
madman who muttered and raged on the other side of
the door against which the noncom leaned his shoulders in the old sentry's trick to save the feet. Perhaps if
he impressed the Red Skull, it might lead to his being
invited to join those Special Projects teams. Then he
could live in a world of wonders, instead of this *scheis-
sebohrung* full of verminous scum.

*Shitbox, indeed,* he thought, as the icy winter wind
swung his way from the east and he caught the odor
of unwashed bodies and dysentery that always hung
over the barracks. The wind was strengthening. He
could hear it swinging the unlit light fixtures against
the wire fence. He strained to hear over their clicking
and the suffling sound of the wind. Was something
else moving, out there in the dark?

Abruptly the wind died for a few seconds before
gusting up again. In those few moments of dead air, it
seemed to Müller that the stink of rancid sweat and
dried excrement grew stronger. He pushed his shoulders away from the door and stood erect, swinging the
Schmeisser that was slung across his body to point its
muzzle at the darkness. As he did so, a chunk of that
darkness suddenly achieved greater solidity right in

front of him. He felt something hard poke against his greatcoat just over his midriff. Then a giant's fist smashed him back against the door as a nine-millimeter slug from a Luger tore through his upper abdomen and lodged itself in one of his vertebrae. The pistol was wrapped in rags to muffle the sound of the shot.

A hand slipped the submachine gun from the Hauptscharführer's failing grasp, even as he slumped to the steps that led up to the hut's front door, but Müller was already far away. As he slid into death, he was hoping that there would be golden-eyed strangers to greet him, but all that came was a blackness even deeper than what lay over the eastern side of the camp.

The man who had shot him tried the doorlatch of the hut the SS man had been guarding, found it locked, and moved on. There was no time to stand still and nothing to be gained in making too much noise too soon. He handed the Schmeisser to one of the scarecrows in stinking rags who came behind him. The man with the Luger was more warmly dressed, wearing a once-fashionable overcoat that had most recently belonged to Helmut, the green-badge ex-pimp. The *kapo* would not be needing it anymore.

The small piece of marrow floated in a dish of sterile saline solution brought from the camp's infirmary. Bucher poked it with a probe so that one end lifted above the surface of the liquid. "What is it now, two hours? And no sign of necrosis."

The baron examined the specimen closely, one eye closed, the other peering through his monocle. "You're right," he said. "The tissue might have been extricated only seconds ago."

The Prussian turned away from the dish on the table in the visiting officers' quarters and paced the room, head bowed, hands clasped behind his back, thinking out loud. "This reconfirms the importance of the blood. It must be a mutated blood factor. The marrow is producing enough of whatever it is—probably borne by the white blood cells—to keep the tissue alive. Probably indefinitely."

"*Mein Gott,*" whispered the pink-skinned man, "it's immortality!"

The baron said, "I wish I had not been in such a hurry to get here. We should have brought some of the Iron Eagles for security. I don't like having that priceless specimen guarded by the fools that infest this farce of a concentration camp."

"Shall I have them double the guard?"

"Yes. But first go and get that senior noncom. We'll let him guard our prize. That's more important than keeping a drunken lunatic from wandering loose."

Bucher put on his coat and cap and departed. The Prussian looked again at the fragment. Then he unstoppered a sterile flask that stood beside the dish on the bench and carefully poured both specimen and fluid into it. He pushed the stopper in tight and held the flask up to the light. The fragment floated weightlessly in the clear liquid. Alone now, von Strucker permitted himself an unchecked display of the emotion that had been rippling through him for more than an hour, ever since he had first cut into the mute. A wide smile split his grim face, and an almost ecstatic shiver passed through the muscles of his back.

He shook the flask, watching the tissue bob up and down, and let his mind explore what would come his way: greater power and wealth than his forebears among the minor Prussian aristocracy had ever known; and life that would go on for centuries. The Nazis prattled mistily about a thousand-year Reich. He would see every moment of every year of it, and more, much more.

At that moment, shots came from outside—the *snap, snap, snap* of an automatic pistol, followed by the high-speed rattle of a Schmeisser. Then the lights went out.

Patch Howlett growled as he heard the footsteps coming down the hallway. He had been lying in the darkness, straining against the bent spikes that secured his flesh to the heavy wooden table, but had been unable to tear either them or himself loose.

The door opened and the lights came on. He craned his neck to see who was coming into the room, but he already knew by the smell it was neither the drunken commandant nor the ice-blooded man with the scalpel. Four emaciated faces looked down at him, faces he recognized. One of the men shook his head in horror and said, in Italian, *"Gesù Maria."*

Somebody found a pry bar in one corner, where the carpenter had been told to leave his tools. The man put its curved and slotted end to a spike through Patch's right wrist and pulled the nail squeaking from the wood and flesh. A man wearing Helmut's green-badged overcoat said, *"Baumann, dove è?"* gesturing with the Luger in his hand.

Patch shook his head and shrugged. The spike was gone from his right elbow and the man with the pry was working on his left wrist. The wounds in his right arm had already closed and he reached and took the tool from the man to complete the job.

*"Andiamo,"* said the man with the Luger. We're going.

Patch nodded. He sat up and leaned forward to begin work on his ankles and knees as the men went out. Moments later, the putter of the generator outside the building died and the lights went out.

Patch worked on in darkness, feeling for the remaining spikes and fitting the pry's notch to them. Getting them out was not as easy as he would have liked. The spikes straightened well enough, but the carpenter had hammered them deep into the close-grained oak beneath and from a sitting position Howlett could not use his full strength. As he worked, rocking the spikes from his flesh, he listened to the rising gunfire, shouts, and screams from outside the *kommandantur.* The sounds of battle were coming from several directions now. It was time for him to go. He had discharged his duty.

His father had been of the old breed, a yeoman farmer left over from the Victorian age who had transplanted himself to the rangelands of Alberta. To the old man, there was nothing more important than to do his duty—duty to family, duty to friends, duty to king and country, done without fuss or bravado. It was his measure of what it meant to be a man, and he had passed on to his son the same standard.

Patch had owed a duty to Rob Roy MacLeish that could only be discharged by helping his friend's fiancée. In the kitchen of the Osteria Gambrelli, at her request, that duty had been transferred to her brother Giovanni. Then in the flea-infested squalor of Höllenfeuer's barracks number eighteen, that duty had again been passed forward, had become an obligation to endure the unendurable, to see and remember what had happened in this small, frigid corner of hell.

Now this place was winding up, the inmates taking murderous revenge on their tormentors. They would leave nothing but smoking ruins. That meant that Patch Howlett's duty was done and dusted, as his father would have said. He could move on—though first he ought to pay a visit to his old friend the drunken commandant, then find the men with red skulls on their caps.

He unbent the last spike, set the pry beneath its

head, and began rocking it loose. The darkness in which he worked suddenly brightened, though not by much. A yellowy glow came from the corridor outside the open door, accompanied by the sound of approaching, though unsteady, footsteps.

Patch exerted a renewed effort and the last spike came loose from the wood and his flesh. He noiselessly set down the pry bar and slipped off the table, pressing himself against the wall behind the half-opened door. The light brightened as its source neared and then the commandant came through the doorway, his tunic stained and half-unbuttoned, an oil lamp held high before him in one hand. The other held an open bottle of wine.

*"Wo bist du?"* he said, almost crooning, like an indulgent pet owner calling for a strayed lapdog. He peered, bleary eyed, at the empty table, then held the lamp out toward the dark corners of the room. Finally he stooped to look under the table. Patch swept out an arm and slammed shut the door.

Straightening, the German turned as if the slam had been no more than a gentle tap on his shoulder. *"Ach,"* he said, followed by some words that Patch took to mean "there you are." The man put the lamp on the table and took a swig from the bottle, then rocked unsteadily on his feet, bloodshot eyes struggling to hold Patch in focus. He began to mutter to himself, the same words Howlett had heard time and again, that had always been punctuated by slashes from jagged glass.

But the prisoner had heard more than enough of *"Mein Wille"* over the past couple of days. He now told the commandant, in words often heard in Royal Canadian Army barracks, exactly where he could put his *Wille*.

Baumann blinked at him as if Patch were a pet that had unexpectedly performed a new trick. *"Du kannst sprechen,"* he said.

"I can do more than *sprechen,"* Patch said. He flexed his forearms and, for the first time in weeks, his claws tore themselves free of his flesh.

The SS officer, secure in his drunken arrogance, did not blanch as many others had done at the sight of Patch's armament. He gripped the bottle by its neck and struck it against the table's edge so that wine and glass sprayed in all directions. *"Komme,"* he said softly, the jagged remnant of the bottle in his hand, *"komme, kleine üntermensch."*

"Oh, I'm coming," Howlett said. He moved forward and Baumann took a drunken swing at him with the broken glass. The Canadian met the weapon with the claws of his right hand, then twisted his wrist to tear the bottle neck from the commandant's hand and send it clattering into a corner. "Now," Patch said, "let's see how your precious *Wille* stands up to a little of your own medicine."

He flicked one set of claws across the Nazi's chest, shredding cloth and scoring the flesh beneath. Baumann looked down at the welling blood and said something Patch figured was a curse. The pry bar was still on the table and the commandant snatched it up and came at him, the heavy steel raised two-handed above his head.

But Patch easily dodged the drunk's clumsy swing, responding with another flick of a claw to lay open Baumann's left cheek. The officer took one hand from the pry bar to touch fingertips to the wound, but even as he was looking at the red dripping from his hand, a claw ripped the skin on the other side of his face.

"There," said Patch, standing back like a portrait painter considering a work in progress, "now you look like a real Hun. Dueling scars and all."

His remark earned him only more German curse words, delivered in a shriek, as Baumann swung the heavy bar one-handed. The Canadian stepped lightly out of the Nazi's reach, then his claws swept downward to tear the sleeve from the arm that held the weapon, slicing the skin and muscle beneath.

Baumann gave a scream of mingled pain and rage, staggering sideways as he swung the bar backhanded. Again, he missed his target, but this time he connected with the oil lamp on the table, smashing its reservoir and splashing kerosene on the walls and floor. The lamp's burning wick fell into the spreading liquid and, with a *whump* the fuel ignited.

Flames ran across the floor and simultaneously climbed to the ceiling. A few burning drops landed on Baumann's tunic and he dropped the pry bar as he frantically beat them out. Then he looked with horror at the expanding inferno and made for the door.

"Not a big fan of fire?" Patch said, putting himself between the Nazi and the room's only exit. He flexed his arms and the claws withdrew as the other man tried to push past him. Then he put both palms on Baumann's chest and shoved him back toward the flames. "That's a funny attitude for a man who keeps his ovens going day and night."

The SS man babbled something, then began to scream and beat at himself as droplets of kerosene that had landed on his boots when the lamp shattered caught fire and set the cloth of his breeches alight. He staggered away from the worst of the blaze, slapping at his legs, his screams becoming animal-like yelps of pain and panic.

The heat in the small closed room was now so intense that Patch felt his skin beginning to scorch and his eyes drying out. The pain was bad, but he had stood worse. Baumann rushed at him again, desperate to get at the door. Howlett threw the man back at the pool of fire rising from the floor, and now the gray cloth on the Nazi's back smoldered and burst into spontaneous flame. A second later, Baumann's hair was ablaze.

"Maybe that will of yours can put it out," Patch said.

With a sound that was pure terrified, agonized beast, the burning SS Obersturmbannführer threw himself at the door and the man who blocked it. Howlett thought the man looked like a human torch as he caught the shrieking, charring mass of panicked flesh and hurled it back once more into the inferno.

"You're not quite done yet," he said.

Now Baumann was fully ablaze, his body wreathed in flames of yellow and red, and a black greasy smoke already rising from him as he sank screaming to the burning floor. Patch knew the smell of that smoke. It had been clogging his nose for all the weeks he had spent in this place. But this time, it didn't smell so bad.

He turned his back on Baumann's last moans and opened the door. The rush of fresh air into the fiery space was like a draft into a blast furnace. Patch's ragged clothes caught fire and fell from him. He walked out into the hallway, the fire coming along beside him like a faithful, boisterous dog. By the time he reached the front door, it was already playing with the commandant's trophies—the volumes of Goethe, Schiller, and Heine scattered about the office—sending burning pages floating up into the superheated air.

Outside, the cold wind felt good on Patch's heat-tortured skin. Flames shooting from the burst windows of the burning *kommandantur* lit the immediate area of the darkened camp. He could hear screams and shouts and sustained bursts of automatic fire from the direction of the SS barracks. For a moment, he considered going there to help, but the voices raised in panic all carried German accents, while the cries of vengeance and triumph came in other tongues. He decided to find the man with the red skull.

Sprawled in the dirty snow not far from the *kommandantur* he found the body of the short, pink-skinned man, most of his brains spewed out the back of his head. The farther he got from the burning building, the more the icy wind bit, and Howlett knelt to quickly strip the corpse of its gray SS garb. The dead man had been about the same height and build, though the boots pinched a little. The rim of the cap needed cleaning at the back, but a handful of snow did a pretty good job.

His weeks in the camp had taught him the layout. SS officers' country was close by the *kommandantur.* Howlett figured he'd be able to find the Red Skull who'd experimented on him. The man had an unusual smell about him: an odor of chemicals and the harsh soap that doctors used to scrub their hands. When he found him, the Nazi might already be dead from the revolt. But if not, that was an oversight that Patch Howlett could soon set to rights.

The moment the lights went out, von Strucker put the flask into his valise, snapped it shut, and went to the door. He eased it open a little and put one eye to the crack. He could see nothing but he heard the crunch of on-coming footsteps on the crusted snow.

He stepped clear of the door, leaving it ajar, and a moment later it swung silently inward. The baron pressed himself against the wall, shielded from view by the door. A beam of light from a penlight briefly swept across the room, then winked out. A moment later, the footsteps sounded again, moving away in the direction of the SS barracks.

The Prussian waited until the night was still again. Then he put on his cap and greatcoat and headed for the main gate. The two-man guard detail that should have been posted there was not to be seen, but when he got close enough he saw two lumps lying in the shadows along the fence. Their throats had been cut and their weapons were missing.

The main gates had a small man-size portal built into them. The baron quietly opened this and slipped out. The car he had acquired at the Luftwaffe station was parked not far from the fence. In moments he was behind the wheel and pressing the starter. The well-maintained engine caught instantly and von Strucker turned the wheel toward the gray strip in the darkness that was the road out of here. A half mile on, he turned on the headlights and accelerated.

The Luftwaffe station was manned around the clock, but at this time of night the duty section consisted of a leutnant and a couple of enlisted men. They kept themselves warm in a small hut that had a coal stove, the leutnant conscientiously going out once an hour to check the guard posts, though Polish partisans had not operated in the area for some time. Sometimes, as the hours of the night dragged on and the conversation with his subordinates grew stale and repetitious, he wished he'd joined another branch of the services—one where he might have seen more action.

When the guard at the station's front gate telephoned to advise the leutnant that the high-ranking SS officer from Berlin who had come through that morning was back and looking for his plane and pilot, the duty officer sent one of the airmen to wake up the flying officer. He sent the other airman to the hangar to tell the flight sergeant to get the plane ready to fly.

He was standing at attention when the Red Skull came into the hut. He saluted and reported his actions, but the Oberführer merely grunted. The officer's attention had gone to the other man in the hut, the plump and jowly SS Hauptsturmführer from the nearby concentration camp who had shown up some hours before with an urgent message to go out on the morning's mail plane to Berlin.

"Schenkel, isn't it?" the Red Skull said, his brows contracting above eyes of blue ice. "What are you doing here?"

The other officer had seemed nervous before, disdaining to chat with the Luftwaffe leutnant and his men. Now he rose to his feet, mouth opening and closing as if he couldn't get the words past a paralyzed tongue.

"He is waiting for the morning mail plane," the Luftwaffe officer said helpfully.

"Ah," the Red Skull said, studying the now plainly terrified Hauptsturmführer. The cold eyes turned to the Luftwaffe officer and their owner said, "Herr Leutnant, pass me your sidearm."

"Herr Oberführer?"

"Your pistol. Now. I have come away without mine."

"At your order," said the leutnant, unbuttoning the flap of his holster and producing the weapon. The Oberführer put down his valise, accepted the pistol, and racked back the slide to chamber a round.

Then he raised his arm and shot the Hauptsturmführer through the head. Even as the sound of the shot reverberated in the small space and the dead man slumped to the floor, the SS officer handed the pistol back and said, "This swine deserted his post. You will contact the local head of the SD and inform him that there has been a revolt at Höllenfeuer. The prisoners have killed the guards and are escaping."

The Luftwaffe officer's eyes went from the Oberführer to the corpse and back again. "Herr Oberführer—" he began.

"Now, Herr Leutnant," said the Red Skull, "or you can join him wherever he has gone to."

From outside came the sound of an aircraft engine sputtering into life, then rising to a roar. The SS officer's modified Heinkel was warming up on the apron.

"At your order," the leutnant said, and rang the crank on his field telephone. As he made contact with the local office, he saw the Oberführer kneel beside the corpse and slip a hand into the man's tunic. It came out holding an envelope.

The Red Skull made a *tsk*-ing sound as he slipped the envelope into his own pocket. Then he scooped up the valise and departed without another word.

The phone to his ear, the leutnant watched from the hut's single window as the SS officer strode across the concrete apron to where his plane waited. Beyond were the runways and a screen of tall trees, and above those, in the direction of the concentration camp, the sky was lit an angry red.

A voice spoke in his ear. "SD. Who is calling?"

The Luftwaffe leutnant said what the SS man had told him to say, then he added, "and I've got a dead Hauptsturmführer here."

When he finally hung up, he decided that he had seen all the action he needed.

The scent trail of the man with the scalpel faded under the smell of fresh exhaust fumes outside the camp gates. The SS officer had gotten away. For a moment, Patch considered running after him; perhaps he'd catch him at a crossroads, lost and studying a map. But the cold-eyed man hadn't looked the type to get himself lost, and Howlett decided it was time to go back where he belonged.

The Russians were in the east and the only Allied armies in Europe were in the south. There was always talk about a new front in France sometime, maybe in the spring. Patch decided he'd work his way west, until he found an invading Allied army coming to meet him. Perhaps he would fight a private war along the way, targeting the SS wherever he found them.

He'd keep the uniform. From what the man with the scalpel had said, Patch had figured out that the officer was part of some special SS unit that hunted for people like him—mutants, the Canadian divisional staff officer at the Ortona field hospital had called them. If he now made his way west across the Reich, wearing the Red Skull insignia and ripping up Nazis as he went, Patch might be taken for some rogue monster that had emerged from the SS's own laboratories to stalk and haunt them.

He struck out west, into the Polish forest. It felt good to be running through the trees again.


Von Strucker landed at Templehof as dawn was breaking. He commandeered a car and driver and was at the Prinz Albrechtstrasse headquarters demanding to see Heinrich Himmler as the offices were just opening.

"The Reichsführer has a full schedule," said a stiff-necked Standartenführer in Himmler's outer office.

"He'll want to cancel it when he hears of the opportunity I bring him," the baron said. "And he'll want to see you digging latrines in Russia if he finds that you prevented me from doing so."

Minutes later, the Prussian said to the Reichsführer-SS, "Kaltenbrunner is going to have a bad day. I thought you might like to know why before he does."

As he left the building, he was telling himself that this morning's gift to the little man behind the big desk would at least buy him some leeway to continue his research. But what he needed most of all was to find the little Canadian mute.

Find him, not for the Reich, but for the only cause on earth that truly mattered to Wolfgang Freiherr von Strucker: to live, healthy and whole, forever.

## Berlin, Germany, the present

"REMEMBER ME?"

Logan heard the voice before he saw the face. His eyes were closed and he realized that he must have been dozing—drifting in a half-conscious state, somewhere between true dreaming and true wakefulness. He didn't want to leave this twilight zone. There were images here—faces, scenes, buildings—and he was sure that they were not conjured just from dreams, but from recalled reality. Something had happened to shake loose some of his memories, and they were passing before his mind's inner eye like leaves blown from a tree in autumn.

"I said, 'Remember me?' " Despite himself, Logan opened his eyes and the images fled. He looked up at the lean face that hovered over him. Then his eyes flicked around to take in the rest of the scene: the roof of the van in which he was lying on his back, the swarthy young men squatting on bench seats along the inner sides of the vehicle, the concrete parking garage glimpsed through the gap between the van's rear doors before they closed. He heard the vehicle's motor come to life, followed by the rattle of a segmented steel door as it opened, then they began to move. In a moment they had exchanged artificial light for the cold glow of a winter morning.

His gaze came back to the man who had spoken. He took in the prominent cheekbones, the taut skin along the jawline, the frigid blue eyes, the close-cropped blond hair, and the bloodless lips set in a self-satisfied smile. "No," he said, "and yes. I remember your face, but not where I know you fron. Though I think I ought to."

The smile disappeared; his eyebrows arched in curiosity. "Are you trying to play a game with me?" the man said in German-accented English. "You must have remembered Höllenfeuer—or else why would you have gone there? And if you remember the camp, you surely remember me."

Hearing the voice as well as seeing the face was indeed triggering some response in Logan, deep sediments were stirring in the bottom of his mind. He sniffed. There was an odor about the man, different from the miasma of sweat and spice that hung around the others in the van—a smell of soap and chemicals, almost medical. "Are you a doctor?" he said.

"Is that memory," the German said, "or something else? You sniffed at me, didn't you? Is your sense of smell mutated, too?"

"I don't know what you mean," Logan said.

That won him a little laugh from his captor. "Come now, let there be no games between us. It will go easier on you. I am not a sadist, but I will do what I have to do to get what I need."

"Wouldn't we all?" Logan said, playing for time. He could feel memories floating below the surface, insubstantial as layers of cigarette smoke in the air of a closed room. Yet if he tried to make them appear, the effort would just blow them back to nothingness. He sought to keep his mind still, to let the fragile ghosts rise into his consciousness. But it was hard to force tranquility on himself, because he had found someone who knew him—who knew secrets about him.

"The Pole with the fancy camera," he said, "he was working for you."

"Say he works for a man who works for me," said the German. "Which leads me to ask: For whom do you work?"

"I don't know."

"I find that hard to believe."

It was hard for Logan to shrug while chained to a dolly, but he did the best he could. "Lately I've been having to believe a lot of things that are hard to swallow. Like the idea that I'm old enough to have been in a Nazi concentration camp. Or, come to think of it, that so are you."

The German hunched forward on the bench seat, put his fingertips together, and touched the ends of his index fingers to his lips. He studied Logan's face for a moment, then said, "Are you telling me you don't know what you are?"

"Something has happened to my memory."

The man above him cocked his head to one side and pulled at his chin. "How far back does it go?"

"A few weeks. A couple of months. I'm not sure. Behind that it's all fog."

"Then why Höllenfeuer? That was more than sixty years ago."

"I found a clue and followed. That was where it led."

"Then it led you to me."

"Yes. And you remember me. So tell me, who am I?"

The man above him shrugged. "I wish I knew," he said.

•  •  •

"Where are you taking me?"

"A place where we won't be disturbed. We have a lot to do."

The van had stopped in an airplane hangar and Logan had been hauled into the passenger compartment of an oversize private jet. The plane immediately taxied out and rolled toward a runway. A couple of minutes later they were airborne.

"Are you going to keep me like this?" Logan said.

"It seems prudent," said the German.

"Perhaps we are on the same side."

"Doubtful. My side is essentially limited to me."

"Still, we could be allies."

His captor made no reply, but the lean face showed an amused skepticism.

"At least tell me your name," Logan said.

"Wolfgang, Freiherr von Strucker. 'Freiherr' is a title. The English equivalent is 'baron.' And you are?"

"Logan."

"Is that a first or last name?"

"I don't know. It's the only one I've got."

One of the cockpit crew came from up front and said something to von Strucker in what Logan assumed was Arabic. The German said to Logan, "We will have plenty of time for conversation later. Right now I must attend to something else." He went forward, out of Logan's sight.

Logan was a little surprised by how he was reacting

to being taken prisoner by these men. Chained and carried off in a private jet to who knew where, he thought he ought to be feeling fear, or at least apprehension, but he didn't. His captors, except for the baron, were obviously of Middle Eastern origin. They gave a clear impression of being highly trained, like Special Forces or security service officers. When they had seized him in the dark, they had seemed to move with superhuman speed.

He had no idea what they meant to do with him. Logic said he ought to be worried. Yet, curiously, Logan felt entirely at ease. *Like a tiger surrounded by bobcats,* said a voice from the back of his head, *a wolverine among foxes.* But it was not his voice, just a snatch of unconnected memory drifting through his damaged mind. He found that he was flexing his back, shoulder, and arm muscles against the chains that held him, reflexively testing them.

But when he bunched his forearms, he again felt a flash of anxiety—and again wondered where it had come from. The fear clashed with the confidence he had just been feeling and now he wondered which of those conflicting emotions was the right one for the situation. And which one had been planted in him by the mysterious somebodies who lurked in his shuttered past.

*Enough thinking. I'll lie back, learn what I can. And when the time comes for action, I'll do whatever comes naturally.* With that thought, another wave of confidence came washing through him. *A wolverine among foxes,* he thought, this time in his own voice. He liked the image it put in his mind.

There was a private compartment with four seats between the cockpit and the main cabin. Von Strucker put his head out the folding door that separated the two and beckoned to Al Borak.

"I've had a call from home base," the baron said when they were alone. "Our Yemeni friend is waiting for us."

"He was not expected?" the Pashtun said.

"They have been getting anxious about Operation Severed Head."

"So have I. We don't have a plan that can work, even allowing for maximum losses."

The baron smiled his wintry smile. "We do now."

Al Borak cocked his head toward the main cabin. "Because of him?"

"Yes."

"I am your second in command. When will you tell me how he fits in?"

"I am still working it out," von Strucker said. "But he may have more uses than just the one I originally intended for him."

"Why is that?"

The Prussian's icy eyes looked off into the middle distance. "Because he's a man who needs someone who can tell him who he is."

"And you can?"

"Oh, no. I only know what he is." The smile grew even colder. "But I am sure I can think of something to tell him."

The plane had stopped somewhere and refueled along the way, again taxiing into a closed hangar for the purpose. The men had disembarked to stretch their legs. By the sounds of the hand clapping and chanting, Logan thought they had indulged in some kind of folk dance. They looked happy enough when they came back onboard the plane, stepping over him but otherwise ignoring his presence. He returned the favor, letting the thrum of the jet's engines lull him into sleep.

He dreamed of cold, of a place where men huddled together, shivering, trying to keep warm, a place where it always seemed to be dark even when the sun was in the sky. He dreamed of screams and fists and boots, of muzzles of gray steel spitting flame. The face of a madman kept coming into the dream, shouting at him in slurred German. There was pain and blood and shattering glass, then it all dissolved in fire.

He awoke to the sensation of changing air pressure in his ears. A few minutes later, he heard the plane's landing gear lock into place, then the bump of tires hitting a runway and the thrust reversal of the engines. The aircraft slowed then taxied, finally passing out of daylight.

The baron appeared above him again, giving instructions in Arabic. Logan was tilted up on his dolly, wheeled to the plane's door, and handed down to the ground. He was in a sizable hangar, its only natural light coming from windows in the main door that was now rattling shut.

The German said something to the men from the plane that caused them to form a double line and march off. He then called over the tall, gray-eyed man and gave him instructions. Logan heard the click of a lock behind him, then the grip of the bonds that held him to the dolly slackened. He flexed his muscles and the chains fell to the ground. He stepped free.

"If you will come with me, I will show you something," von Strucker said, gesturing toward the hangar door.

"All right," Logan said.

The German led him to a man-size portal set into the segmented steel of the main door. He opened it and stepped outside. Logan followed and immediately the heat of the desert afternoon struck him like a gust from a furnace. Sweat broke out on his face and chest, and he could already feel trickles of moisture running down his sides under the winter-weight clothing he had worn in Berlin.

Without a word, the baron walked along the front of the hangar, then around the back. Logan followed again and soon found himself climbing a gentle slope that was the disguised roof of the building. At its top, von Strucker waited.

"What did you want to show me?" Logan said when he reached him.

"Nothing," the German said. He swept his hands to indicate the horizon in all directions. "Nothing as far as the eye can see."

Logan realized he had just learned something more about himself: he didn't like people who played cute. "Meaning?" he said.

"Meaning that I have decided that you are not a prisoner here. But, if you decide to leave, I don't think that even your peculiar abilities will keep you alive."

"What peculiar abilities?"

The blue eyes studied him. "You truly do not know what you are?"

" 'Who,' " said Logan, "the word is 'who.' "

" 'Who' is only part of it," von Strucker said. "Let us go in before we suffer heatstroke. We have a lot to talk about. But first I have to meet with a client."

Logan followed him back down the slope. "What is this place? Who are you and what do you do here?"

"All in good time. You have stepped into a complicated situation, but I am increasingly sure that it will deliver to you what you are looking for."

The man seemed to enjoy wrapping himself in an air of mystery. Logan fought down his irritation. If this "complicated situation" could work for him, he could be patient. "I am looking," he told the German, "for myself. And for whoever stole my life from me. Can you deliver that?"

"Yes, I think so," von Strucker said. "Give me a little time to make some inquiries. It may turn out that you were right when you said we could be allies."

The baron met the Yemeni in the planning room. The visitor was studying the tabletop model, one slippered foot tapping impatiently. "Well," the client said, "what have you to tell me? And it had better be good news."

"It is very good news," von Strucker said. "We can carry out the operation."

"And the odds of success?"

"Virtually certain."

"God willing," the Yemeni added.

"Of course," said the baron.

The visitor narrowed his eyes in suspicion. "What has changed? Last week, you were not at all confident."

The Prussian smiled. "Last week, I did not have the perfect weapon. Please return to your superiors and tell them that I will need a local staging area for the operation. A large house, walled and secure, at a reasonable traveling distance from the target."

"There are many such in the Mansour district," the Yemeni said. "Those who grew rich under the Beast of Tikrit have fled to other countries now that the Armies of God are reclaiming Iraq for the true faith. Their mansions stand empty."

"Then let us have one readied." The Prussian

clicked his heels and inclined his head. "Now, if you will excuse me, I must tend to our new weapon."

When the German asked him what he remembered of Höllenfeuer, Logan said, "Nothing. Flashes of disconnected images. Faces, voices, flames, screams, a bad stink."

"Hmm," von Strucker said, nodding as if Logan's words had confirmed his expectations. "And what do you recall of your more recent life?"

"It's as if it only started a few months ago."

"Tell me about that."

They were seated in what looked to Logan like a well-equipped infirmary. The place had an X-ray machine and full-body scanners, lab benches with computerized equipment he couldn't even begin to identify. Through the glass panels in two swinging doors on the far side of the big room he had glimpsed an operating room.

The sights and smells of the place put him a little on edge. But, as always, when he reached for a reason why they should have this effect on him, he found himself grasping at fog. He concentrated on what he knew for sure, telling the German of his life in the condo in Ottawa, of the monthly delivery of funds and whiskey.

The baron stopped him. "The whiskey comes to you? You do not buy your own?"

"There's no need."

"And you never feel an urge to drink something different? Another brand."

"No," Logan said, and even as he said it he felt a twinge of anxiety.

The German was watching him closely. "The idea of drinking another kind of whiskey disturbs you, *ja*?"

"Yes. I never realized that until now. How come?"

But the other man just pulled at his chin and said, "Hmm."

Anger flashed through Logan and his forearm muscles tensed. But he fought it down. "What does it mean?" he said.

"It probably means," von Strucker said, "that your mind has been attacked by powerful psychoactive drugs. Whoever has done this has chemically carved out a small part of your psyche. It's the part that you know of as 'just Logan,' the part that's talking to me now. The rest of you is shielded, as if they've built a dungeon inside your own brain and locked most of you inside it. All your memories. Your true identity."

"Why?" Logan wanted to know. Then he said, "No, more important is who?"

The baron held out his palms like a barrier. "Let us come to that in a moment. The important part right now is not why or who, but how." He leaned toward Logan. "They have to keep administering a steady maintenance dose of the memory suppressant. They do so by putting it in the whiskey. Then they condition you to want to drink nothing else."

The moment he said it, it was obvious to Logan—as if it were something he had been seeing constantly from the corner of his eye but somehow at which he had never turned to look directly. "That makes sense," he said.

"We can probably reverse the effects," von Strucker said, "though first we have to identify exactly which drugs, and in what combination and strengths, have been applied to you."

"You can do that?"

"Probably," said the baron. Then, in a self-chiding tone, he added, "No, I am too cautious, always the scientist. I will say, almost certainly."

Logan felt a fierce elation go through him, but it was followed immediately by a sense of caution. He noted the reaction and thought, *So I'm not a guy who believes in the tooth fairy.* Aloud, he said, "And what's in it for you?"

The German turned his cold hard eyes toward him and said, "The same as for you. Revenge."

"Against who?"

But the other man backed off. "You said on the plane that we might be allies. I do not know if that is so. But it is possible that we have the same enemy."

"Who?" Logan had wanted to hear more, but the German held him off. "Premature," von Strucker said, "until we know exactly what has been done to you and how."

Logan could feel the anger building in him. "Don't play games with me. Why is it premature?"

"Because you might be just what you seem. Or you might be a weapon sent against me."

"What kind of weapon?"

"The kind that's programmed to go off at a preset time, or if someone says the right word."

Logan did not think there was any truth in von Strucker's supposition, and yet he couldn't say for sure that the man's concern was groundless. "So what do we do?" he said.

The baron rose and opened a white-doored cupboard, taking out sterile equipment wrapped in cellophane. "We start by taking some blood and seeing what it contains," he said. "I'm afraid I'll need a lot of blood. The drugs we're looking for come in nano-doses."

Logan rolled up a sleeve and bared the crook of an elbow. "All right," he said, "but tell me about Höllenfeuer."

Von Strucker had worked out what he meant to tell the strange little man about the camp. It was a nice mixture of fact and fancy, with a good twist that would deliver to the mutant what he wanted to hear.

"Höllenfeuer was no ordinary concentration camp. It was a real camp, but it was set up to disguise an ultrasecret operation under the personal direction of Heinrich Himmler's Office of Special Projects—the group they called the Red Skull SS. Its goal was to find human mutations that could be developed into super-soldiers."

"Mutations?" the small man said. "You mean freaks?"

"No, I do not mean freaks," said the baron, wrapping a rubber tourniquet around Logan's bicep and tapping the vein in the elbow to make it stand out. He positioned a needle-sharp canula and slid it into the blood vessel. "I mean people who have useful genetic anomalies. People like you. And people like me."

He saw the other man's pupils contract, a micromovement that would have been imperceptible to most observers, but was plain to the Prussian's trained perceptions. "You don't believe me?" he said.

"I'm not a freak," Logan said.

"Then how do you explain this?" von Strucker said. He withdrew the heavy needle from the man's vein. Immediately the puncture closed. In a moment there was no sign of a wound.

"What did you do?"

"I did nothing," the baron said. "Watch." He took a scalpel from a sealed package and made to set its point to the back of Logan's forearm.

"Hold it!" Logan said, drawing back his arm.

"It will be no more than a scratch," von Strucker said, "and it will heal within moments."

Logan extended his arm again. The scalpel's tip drew a red line, beaded with blood, through the dark hairs. The scratch disappeared almost as quickly as it had formed.

"Now watch this," von Strucker said. He bared one arm and performed the same operation on his own flesh. His wound also disappeared, though not quite as quickly as the other man's.

"Some kind of trick," Logan said. "That scalpel is a movie prop."

"No trick." The baron handed him the scalpel. "Try it yourself."

The man did so, and von Strucker saw his consternation as the wound healed instantly. "This is why they have interfered with your mind, kept you in storage in Ottawa," the Prussian said. "The people who use you as a weapon do not want you to know what you are. They have probably sent you to do terrible things, things you would find it difficult to live with if you remembered them."

He watched the subject's pupils expand and contract, a tiny flicker of movement, and knew that such was at least a subconscious fear of this man.

"It was the same sixty-three years ago in Höllenfeuer," the baron said, then paused for effect before adding, "except for the one big difference between you and me."

The man looked up. "What's that?"

"I escaped from the camp, to become my own weapon. Apparently, you stayed on to continue being theirs."

• • •

It was a lot to take in. Logan lay on his bunk in the room the baron had assigned him and thought about it. Some of it made instant sense—the idea of drugs in the whiskey, for example. He was sure his mind had been interfered with. His amnesia was not natural. Now he understood the little rush of anxiety that went through him when he thought about drinking any other liquor than Seven Crown. Or the stronger surge he felt when he made a fist.

*I'm a killer,* he thought, *an assassin.* He said the words to himself in the privacy of his mind and waited for a reaction. Nothing much happened. He imagined killing some stranger, doing it with a knife or with his bare hands. Again, nothing much stirred inside him. *How many must I have killed,* he wondered, *to be able to contemplate murder as if it were no more than a trip to the corner store?*

He could even accept that he was a mutant. The way he instantly healed was proof that he was seriously different from the rest of humanity. He doubted it was an ability that could be instilled as the result of drugs or mind control. The German had shown him the same ability.

"Mutants are rare," von Strucker had said, "but they do occur. In the camp, there was a boy who could make himself invisible and a girl who could send her mind traveling back through time."

He had described the one they called Al Borak as

another mutant, though different from him and Logan. The Pashtun's nervous system contained powerful natural capacitors that could generate intense electrical shocks discharged from his hands. It was how they had subdued Logan in Berlin.

But what about the rest of the baron's story? That, after the war, the Nazi experimenters had built a shadowy international organization, offering mutant intelligence agents and assassins to any government or corporation that paid their exorbitant fees? That Logan was one of those operatives, but had somehow broken through his conditioning, at least enough to set out on a quest for his true identity?

It almost rang true. Yet when Logan thought about Nazis, thought about doing their bidding, killing for them, something deep inside him snarled a refusal. He had said as much to the baron, only to be met with another shrug.

"Of course you hate them," von Strucker had said. "Of course you wouldn't work for the swine. So they edit your thoughts for you, make you think that you're on the side of truth and justice."

They had been struggling to get blood out of Logan's veins. Even with the largest canula, the blood tended to clot in the tube almost as soon as it began to flow. The baron had had to inject Logan with large quantities of an anticoagulant to keep the red liquid flowing.

"You know already that your memories have been

stolen," von Strucker had continued. "You suspect that some of your thoughts are not your own. What kind of people would do that to you?"

"Maybe you're right," Logan had answered. "Whoever I've been working for, it hasn't been the Boy Scouts. But Nazis?" He made a sound of disgust.

Again, the shrug. "Well, they're not Nazis anymore, are they? Now they're just businessmen, selling your services for whatever the market will bear."

Anger swelled in Logan, and he knew it was coming out of his true core. "Then putting me back in the warehouse until another customer comes through the door," he said.

"Except now you've broken out of the warehouse. Now you're in business for yourself."

"And you know who these people are? The ones who have been using me?"

"I think so," said the German. "As I say, I need to make some inquiries. I would not want to point you at some innocent parties."

"Are there any innocent parties anymore?" Logan asked.

Again, von Strucker had only shrugged.

Alone in his secure room, von Strucker poured the mutant's blood from its clear plastic collecting bag into several test tubes and arranged them in the slots of the centrifuge. He activated the machine and waited as it whirred. When it was finished he drained off the unneeded blood components, storing them in a graduated cylinder for later study, then decanted the precious remainder into a sterile flask. He lifted the vessel and examined the cloudy fluid within. It held five times as much as his monthly injection.

"And now," he said to the empty room, "it requires a test." Moments later he was striding through the concrete hallways toward the section where the lowest-ranking members of the facility's staff had their barracks. From the doorway of the open dormitories he saw several off-duty porters, janitors, and kitchen workers sprawled on their bunks reading magazines or seated at tables, hunched over their perpetual games of backgammon. When he stepped unannounced into their midst, they sprang to their feet, scattering their diversions in all directions.

The baron pointed to a pop-eyed man whose face was disfigured by acne, and said, "Come." Then he spun on his heel and led the way to the main laboratory.

"Sit there," he said, indicating a stool, "and roll up your sleeve."

Trembling, the man did as he was told. The baron tied off the underling's upper arm with a rubber hose. When he produced a hypodermic, the man made a bleating noise.

"This will not harm you," von Strucker, filling the syringe from the tube of elixir.

The man rolled his protruding eyeballs and looked

as if he wanted to do nothing so much as run, but the
baron could see that fear of punishment would keep
him seated on the stool. He swabbed off the subject's
inner elbow and inserted the needle's tip into the
prominent vein. Then he depressed the plunger, removed the spike—and waited.

He did not have to wait long. The bead of blood
that had leaked out the moment he removed the hypodermic grew no larger. The baron wiped it away
with a swab. The skin beneath showed no sign of a
puncture.

"Give me your hand," he said, and when the man
did as he was told von Strucker gripped his hand, took
up a scalpel, and sliced into one fingertip. Blood
spurted and the man cried out in pain, but in moments
the bleeding stopped. Even as the Prussian watched,
the wound healed, leaving only the thinnest scar.

The baron let the hand go. The man brought his
finger before his eyes, rubbing away the blood with
his thumb and staring in wonder at the undamaged
flesh.

The Prussian brought a small-caliber pistol from
the side pocket of his breeches. The man on the stool
had only enough time to shriek in terror before von
Strucker fired a bullet into his chest. The impact
knocked the subject sprawling on the tiled floor. His
eyes blinked once, then his gaze lost cohesion. His
chest heaved, then was still.

The baron leaned over the dead man. He tore open the shirt, sending buttons flying, to see the hole where the round had penetrated his flesh. The wound bled sluggishly, as always happened once the heart stopped beating and gravity began to rule the circulation system. As von Strucker watched, the bleeding suddenly freshened. The chest filled again with air and the man breathed once more. Now he saw that the wound was filling itself in. A few seconds later, the healing flesh actually forced the slug out of the man's body.

The Prussian caught the bullet as it came clear of the man's recovered body. He looked at the smooth metal object and smiled. The man was sitting up, poking at his chest in wonder, joy and relief plain in his eyes.

"What is your name?" von Strucker said.

"Achmed, master," was the answer.

"Well, Achmed," said the baron, "I have good news and bad news for you. The good news is that your acne is clearing up. The bad news is that you have lost your job."

He stepped outside the lab and summoned a security detail. "Arrest the man inside," he said. "Bind and gag him. Drive him a hundred kilometers out into the desert, dig a hole—a deep hole, mind you—and bury him alive." As the guards set to work, he added, "Do not speak of this to anyone, or you will join him."

Then, as the guards dragged the squirming Achmed

away, he called after them. "Mark the spot." It would be interesting to see if the man was still alive in a couple of weeks.

In the meantime, he refilled the syringe with elixir, though half the amount that he had given Achmed. That time the recovery had been too fast. When the needle was filled, he left it on the lab bench and went in search of a second test subject.

The gray-eyed Pashtun they called Al Borak had begun life as the child of peasant farmers in a hill-country village in southern Afghanistan's remote Helmand province during the war against Soviet occupation. While he was still an infant, his parents and most of the rest of his village had died in an attack by the Red Army. The Russians had learned that a party of mujahideen were sheltering in the community overnight, after going over the border into Pakistan to collect arms and ammunition from the American CIA.

In the hours before dawn, when all were sleeping, a squadron of Hind assault helicopters had swept in out of the darkness, their rockets and cannons ripping apart the mud-brick houses. As the gunships came back around for a second pass, a missile struck a box of antitank mines. The resulting explosion leveled most of the village, but a corner of Al Borak's house remained standing, and in that corner rescuers later found him in his cradle, sheltered from the collapsing roof by a heavy pole that had fallen against the still-standing piece of wall.

His name then had been Batoor, the Pashto word for "brave," and he would have needed all the courage he could have summoned to survive as an orphan growing up in a country mostly destroyed by military invasion, civil war, and religious revolution. It helped that, as a toddler, he began to demonstrate the peculiar things he could do with his hands—like shocking senseless an older boy who tried to steal his rice cake.

From that day, the other orphans—and their keepers—stepped carefully around the strange little boy with the light-colored eyes. There were whispers about him—that he was possessed by a demon, that his mother had lain with a devil. He was sent to sleep alone in an outbuilding that had a leaky roof. But Batoor was hardy. And he was lucky. When he was eight, a European had come through the town where the orphanage was, a blue-eyed man who said he was a doctor. The man was looking for unusual children, those who did not easily fit within deeply conservative cultures, where the strange were feared and unwanted. Orphanages were a good place to find them.

The orphanage director gladly produced Batoor. Money swiftly changed hands, a document was signed, and the child departed in the infidel's Land Rover. Life immediately got much better for Batoor—good food, a warm place to sleep, medical care when he needed it. He exchanged his Pashto name for an

Arabic nickname, Al Borak—the Lightning. Now, fifteen years later, he had grown to become his deliverer's most faithful follower. He had done all that had been asked of him, and more. He was willing to do all that might be asked of him in the future.

But Al Borak was worried. In the days that followed their return from Germany, von Strucker had spent much of his time closeted with the small man. Medical technicians had pulled extra duty running batteries of tests and conducting scans. When Al Borak had sought out the baron to report on the progress of training for Operation Severed Head, the Prussian had brushed him off, eager to get back to his new fascination.

Perhaps von Strucker had found a new favorite. Batoor had seen times when the man would return from one of his mutant-hunting trips with some new prospect. A flurry of tests would follow, high hopes leading to dashed expectations, and the newcomer would be assigned to menial duties or, more often, would quietly disappear.

But this new prospect was no oddball child or teenager from a third-world orphanage. This was a grown man and it was clear to the leader of the Green Fist that there was a history between him and the baron—a history that von Strucker was keeping to himself.

Though preparations for Operation Severed Head continued, to Al Borak's eyes, the problem with the planned assault had not changed. The mission was still suicide and its chances of success were still effectively zero. Yet von Strucker seemed well content with the progress of the training drills, when he bothered to listen to Al Borak's reports.

Lying in his bunk in his private room, staring at the posters and photographs of Bollywood film stars that decorated the walls, the man who had once been the despised orphan Batoor worried and wondered. Had von Strucker found what he had been seeking all these years? Had the Green Fist and all its predecessors been merely steps toward a goal that the baron now saw as within his grasp?

Did that mean that Al Borak and his men were about to be thrown away in a pointless death charge against an impregnable position? A convenient way of wiping the board clean so that the Prussian could begin a whole new game, with all new pieces?

Al Borak stared unseeing at the image of a smiling plump Indian actress in a flowered sari while blue sparks rippled across the backs of his fingers.

Wolfgang Freiherr von Strucker had a decision to make. The medical examination of Logan had brought a shock. The routine bloodwork was under way and the man's DNA was being sequenced—von Strucker was sure there would be something interesting in the X chromosome. They had come to the stage in the series of tests when a full scan by the magnetic resonance imager would have been appropriate. But the moment the subject was broached, the Prussian had seen an almost instinctive alarm register in the man's eyes.

"You have a problem with the MRI?" he said.

"I think so," Logan said. "I don't know why, but something in me says that's a bad idea."

A cold wave of fear rose in the baron. The man had been cooperative up until now. Suddenly, he seemed to have something to hide. The Prussian wondered, had someone slipped a living bomb past his defenses? Von Strucker had made enemies, some of them as intelligent as they were ruthless. Could one of them have put together the right clues from his decades-long search for the man from Höllenfeuer, then manufactured a cunning replica with a few kilos of explosives tucked away in its chest cavity? Is that why the man was so surprisingly heavy?

*Paranoia,* he told himself. *This is the same man I knew in 1944. The speed with which he heals is proof enough.* But then another thought came. Someone else had clearly found this Logan and put him to work, erasing his memories to make him more manageable. Perhaps his handlers had hired him out to some enemy of the baron's, his job to take out von Strucker.

For decades, the Prussian had sought the man he had once had nailed to a table. His desire to find Logan was a vulnerability, and he would be most vulnerable at the moment he achieved his desire. He was reminded of the old wisdom about being careful what you wished for, because you just might get it. *Or it just might get you,* he thought.

But he rejected the idea. If Logan had been sent to kill him, he had already had plenty of time to do it. His reluctance to enter the MRI chamber must come from some other cause.

"Let us take an X-ray," von Strucker said. Minutes later, in the X-ray suite's control center, as the first plate came out of the chemical bath, he said, "*Grösse Gott,* what have they done to his bones?"

"They are sheathed in metal," the technician said. Even the tiny hyoid bone in his throat was coated in a dense metallic substance that bounced X-rays like steel.

"No wonder he weighs so much," the baron said. "He must be carrying an extra thirty kilos."

"Look at this," the technician said, securing a new image to the light board. "There's a great deal more of the stuff in his forearms. It's as if they've inserted a bundle of rods in there, like reinforcing concrete."

"What is it, steel?"

"Something harder, judging from the X-ray reflection. We'd have to drill into it to get a sample for analysis. But it's a good thing we didn't put him in the MRI. It could have torn him apart."

The baron studied the image. "Obviously, he has been rebuilt for unarmed combat. With those arms he could defend himself from any kind of blow," he said. "And he could probably batter down a brick wall."

He rubbed his chin. One thing was clear: his original plan—to get more marrow out of the subject and culture it for permanent production of elixir—had just struck a formidable obstacle.

On the other hand, someone had gone to a great deal of trouble to turn the little man from Höllenfeuer into a devastating weapon. The baron had uses for such an unstoppable killing machine. The question was: Could he control it?

Whoever had been working with the subject had access to first-level psychoactive drugs and biotechnology that could permanently graft metal to bone throughout an entire skeleton. The baron was no slouch at biotech, but he could only vaguely imagine how the metal—*could it be adamantium?* he thought—had been seamlessly attached to living bone. He also had a good grasp of the kinds of drugs that could separate a man from his memories without rendering him insane or incompetent. He suspected that Logan's handlers had mixed a delicate blend of neurochemicals into a precisely targeted cocktail. *Probably arriving at the right formula only after extensive trial and error,* he thought.

Yet however expert those mysterious psychopharmacists might be, their creation had clearly slipped their chemical leash. If he ever found out who had been using him, von Strucker had no doubt that nothing would deter Logan from getting at them. He was like an unstoppable vengeance-seeking missile that was quite capable of curving in flight and arrowing back to the people who had launched it. And his impact would bring them annihilation.

That brought him back to the question that must be decided: How to play the mutant to gain what the baron wanted—then how to dispose of him.

The intercom on the wall buzzed and von Strucker slapped its control. "I said I was not to be disturbed."

"It is Al Borak," said his second in command's voice. "I would like to talk to you."

"Some other time," the baron said, and pushed the button that broke the connection.

Logan had free range of the facility, except for the operational planning room. "That is on a need-to-know basis," von Strucker had told him. "I must run a secure establishment or see my clients desert me."

"Just who are your clients?"

"If we end up working together, you will be told. At this point, I can only give you categories. I offer my services to corporations, national governments, and some nongovernmental organizations."

"And the nature of those services?"

"High-end security contracting. Let us say I specialize in threat assessment and threat reduction."

"You're a mercenary," Logan said. He noticed that the thought caused him no concern. Apparently, he inhabited a world in which soldiers of fortune were part of the scenery.

"But a choosy one," von Strucker said. "I do not work for just anyone."

And that was as much as the German would divulge. "But feel free to look around," he said. "We do research, training, and operational planning. I believe you will find a clean, well-run facility. No dungeons, no torture chambers, no mass graves."

Logan had been given a plastic visitor's badge with a data strip programmed to open doors as he approached them. He hung it on a lanyard around his neck and went everywhere. *Know your operating environment,* said a voice from the back of his mind. *Surprises can be deadly.*

The place was big, the equivalent of a spacious ten-story building set underground, with self-contained water and waste systems drawing from deep aquifers left over from the end of the last ice age, twelve thousand years ago, when this arid land had been rich in lakes and rivers. It was also self-sufficient for power, drawing electricity from geothermal heat exchangers spread out over miles of desert. The differential between the baking days and freezing nights at the surface, contrasted with the permanent temperature in the mid-fifties Fahrenheit just ten feet below ground, provided ample generating capacity.

One level down from the barracks and the well-stocked armory he found the training area. In an immense room big enough to contain a mocked-up residential street, he watched a squad of fatigue-clad men practice urban warfare. While weapons teams laid down suppressing fire from two well-placed machine guns, four pairs of riflemen went down an alley using the time-honored "shoot and scoot" tactic—one man firing, while his partner went forward to the next opportunity for cover, then fired as his partner leap-frogged forward.

It was professionally done, Logan thought, and realized that he could make the judgment because he knew the difference between real soldiering and amateurism. As he heard the crackle of weapons fire and the impact of live rounds hitting targets that popped up in windows and doorways, the smell of cordite biting into his sinuses, images came to the inner screen of his mind: racing across rocky terrain, the flash from a machine gun muzzle aimed his way; chips flying from whitewashed brick and the whine of steel-jacket rounds ricocheting away; a bayonet point lancing toward his eyes, behind it a face under a helmet, teeth bared.

*I've been a soldier,* he said. *I've fought in wars.* He was coming to accept that he was an old man who had somehow never aged. He must have had twice or three times the experiences of normal men—for all he knew, he might be not just decades, but centuries old—and all of that had been stolen from him. The anger came up in him again and he clenched his fists and forearms. With the reflex came again the anxiety, as if he had come in darkness to the edge of a great precipice and dared not take another step lest he fall into . . . *into what?* he thought. *Why have they made me afraid of my own rage? What is the secret they are keeping from me?*

The training exercise was wrapping up, the men returning to the starting point. They seemed to be preparing to conduct the alley assault again, though to Logan's eyes the first run had looked flawless. But now he saw that the squad leader was distributing a pair of pills to each man. They washed them down with water from their canteens, then resumed their jump-off positions.

The leader's whistle blew, the machine guns opened up, and the two-man teams went down the alley again. This time, however, an assault that had taken almost two minutes the first time was over in less than thirty seconds. The men moved with limb-blurring speed, but their bullets went to the targets with no loss of accuracy. To Logan, it looked like a speeded-up film. He remembered the struggle in the darkened room in Berlin, how his captors had seemed to come at him with superhuman speed. Now he understood.

When it was over, the men formed up and marched off, singing in Arabic. They looked happy in their work, Logan thought, then checked himself as he realized there was an exception—their leader, the tall light-eyed one, sent him a parting look that left no doubt of the man's hostility.

• • •

Von Strucker wanted to sing, wanted to dance, maybe throw his hat in the air like a schoolboy. But he had learned early the value of maintaining an image of dignity, even when he was alone. So he simply removed his monocle, polished it on a handkerchief, and reset it before his eye. Then he once more read through the results of the DNA analysis while the joy bubbled up in him again.

The mutation was definitely confined to the X chromosome. More important, it was not a particularly complex change—just a different arrangement of the four component nucleotides, like scrambling the letters of a word to produce an anagram. The best part was that the immortality gene was a prime candidate for being extracted and spliced onto a different biological platform. In a matter of months, von Strucker could have a barn full of transgenetic pigs or rats whose marrow would produce Logan's blood indefinitely.

That meant he did not need Logan. Or at least he would not need him once Operation Severed Head had been successfully carried out, as now it surely would be. All he needed was a few more pints of blood from which to filter the cells that would allow the men of the Green Fist to share temporarily the mutant's ability to recover from wounds that should have been fatal.

With Operation Severed Head safely behind him, he could ease out of the assassination business. He would command the funds to build a new facility, in some more livable region of the world, dedicated to producing the elixir in substantial amounts. The planet was increasingly populated by multibillionaires, all of whom would pay whatever it cost to enjoy their wealth through eternity. Other customers might lack wealth but could pay von Strucker in the equally valuable coin called power. And when he had acquired enough of both, the baron would quietly and discreetly rule the world.

He locked the analysis away in the safe in his hidden room. No one but von Strucker had had access to the gene-sequencing lab during the time it had taken to conduct the analysis. No one else knew the secret of Logan's blood, and he meant to keep it that way.

To calm himself, he filled his lungs, then permitted himself one long and shivery exhalation. Then he went to the intercom and called Al Borak. "Meet me in the planning room immediately," he said. "It is time to finalize Operation Severed Head."

"I'll be there," his second in command said.

Logan had almost made up his mind about von Strucker. He was certain the German had never been his friend, and he wasn't entirely sure that they hadn't been enemies, back in the long ago. The man's tale about their both having been inmates of a secret Nazi camp for mutants rang both true and false—like hearing an almost familiar song played on a piano that had a couple of notes that were out of tune.

Besides, the more time he spent in the man's vicinity, the more something stirred down deep in the blocked-off parts of his mind. Maybe it was something as primal as the way the baron smelled—Logan had heard somewhere that odor could be the most powerful trigger for forgotten memories. And the German's odor of carbolic soap and laboratory chemicals was making some buried part of Logan cock its ears and bare its fangs.

He had seen all there was to see of the facility. It looked to be what von Strucker had said, a research and training operation for a high-end mercenary outfit. Some of its clients were "nongovernmental organizations," the German had said—that could be anything from the Red Cross to the Old Man of the Mountain. Logan wasn't sure if he himself was the kind of assassin who drew moral lines—if he worked for ex-Nazis, he probably didn't. If von Strucker had fled rather than work for those same Nazis, he might even turn out to be more ethically choosy than Logan.

*But somehow that doesn't smell right, does it?* Logan doubted that he himself was any kind of Boy Scout. Yet there was a whiff of something about the baron that told him the German was the kind of man who could give nightmares to the world's hard-asses.

He was in the base's main cafeteria, seated at a table by himself. The menu leaned heavily toward Middle Eastern cuisine—rice, lentils, couscous, beef, and lamb, all served with fiery and pungent sauces—but none of it seemed completely foreign to Logan. *If I'm an assassin, I probably travel a lot,* he thought. *Got to go where the work is.*

The men he had watched at the assault exercise were eating at a table on the far side of the big room. He couldn't understand the Arabic, but the way they talked and laughed among themselves said that they were a well-knit unit. *Buddies,* he thought, *guys who know they can trust each other.*

The thought called up an echo of a memory. He reached for it, and this time it did not immediately disappear. He remembered squatting with his back against a wall, eating from a mess tin. A face swam up from below, laughing. Red hair and green eyes, tough but good-humored. *Rob Roy,* Logan thought. *My friend.* And then the image was fading.

But it was good, he told himself. That had been genuine recall. Whatever had been done to him—the baron's talk about psychoactive chemicals rang true— it was wearing off. At least a little.

Suddenly Logan needed more. He needed to see more faces he recognized, places he had been, moments that had been his before he had been robbed of them. The German had been taking regular supplies of blood—*he must have three quarts by now*—while telling him that the business of isolating the combination of drugs in trace amounts was delicate and time-consuming.

But someone had consumed all of Logan's time, everything except the last few weeks of his life, and he wanted to know who and why. And as the German had said, the first question that had to be answered was "how?" Logan decided he had waited long enough for that answer.

He got up, the food forgotten, and made for the door.

Al Borak walked the corridor to the operations planning center and tapped the entry code into the pad beside the heavy metal door. As it slid open with a sound like compressed air being released, a voice from behind him called, "Hey!" He turned to see the baron's new fascination coming his way from the direction of the elevator bank.

"Your security people told me that von Strucker is down here," the small man said, heading for the open door.

"Not for you," Al Borak said. He knew his English was poor, so he reinforced the message by putting a hand against the man's chest.

"That's not a good idea," Logan said. His own hand came up and took a grip on Al Borak's thumb, then he twisted. Suddenly the bones of the Pashtun's wrist were strained almost to the breaking point.

Al Borak let loose a string of Pashto words that touched upon the man's parentage, personal hygiene, and the least valuable types of goats. At the same time, he reflexively sent a jolt of electricity from his palm into Logan's hand.

Now it was the small man's turn to swear inventively, as his grip involuntarily loosened. He took a step back, shaking his shocked arm and giving the Pashtun a thoughtful look through narrowed eyes. Then he said, "Okay, let's see how this works out," and took a step forward.

"Yes," Al Borak said, "we see." Even as he spoke, he was setting his feet and summoning the strange feeling that since boyhood he had called "the spirit of the clouds." He felt the energy rising and crackling through his whole body. He raised his hands and blue plasma wreathed his palms and fingers.

"Stop this!" shouted von Strucker, stepping through the door and putting himself between them. The Pashtun had to lower his hands and step back to avoid an accidental discharge into the baron.

"What is the meaning of this?" the Prussian said, first in English to Logan, then in Arabic to the tall man.

"I need to talk to you," the Canadian said. At the same time, Al Borak was saying in Arabic, "This offspring of a incontinent dog and a diseased she-goat tried to force his way where he is not wanted."

Logan couldn't have known what the Pashtun was saying, yet he had clearly gotten the gist of it. His small, glittering eyes locked onto Al Borak's and he growled—to the tall man, it sounded like a real animal's snarl—and said, "Anytime, pal."

The baron was still between them, his hands raised to keep them apart. "I said, stop this!" he said. "Why are you fighting?"

The question was addressed to both of them. The small man just shrugged. Al Borak began to speak, but then the other man raised his voice to drown him out. He was saying something in English to the baron, something about needing to know, being tired of waiting.

Al Borak spoke softly into the Prussian's ear, "You should let me take care of this one. He is a danger to us. A disruption."

"No," von Strucker snapped, in Arabic. "He is essential to my plans."

Al Borak subsided and said no more, but he had caught the difference between the words he had used and the baron's answer. The Pashtun had spoken of "us," but von Strucker had said "my plans"—and to the man who used to be Batoor, that small distinction revealed the existence of a great chasm, with him on one side and the man who had taken him from the orphanage on the other.

*This is all I need,* von Strucker was thinking as he stood between the two mutants and sought to calm the situation. But then he told himself, *My need for these two is only temporary.* The thought brought an ironic smile that he made sure did not reach his lips. The truth was, he would not need either of these two volatile genetic freaks for more than another couple of days—only long enough to complete Operation Severed Head. After that, he would have no further requirements for mutants of any kind. He would surround himself only with normal human beings, and the only genetic qualities he would select for would be that the women would be beautiful and the men would know how to take orders and carry them out.

This vision of his future, soon to be achieved, gave von Strucker the tranquility of mind needed to pitch his voice calmly. "This is no time for emotional outbursts—" he began.

Logan cut him off. "You got the operative words—'no time.' I'm tired of spinning my wheels. You've had plenty of my blood. What's the verdict on the drugs? And what about an antidote?"

"We are almost there," von Strucker assured him. "It takes time for the active ingredients to precipitate out of the blood. They have to form as tiny crystals on an inert medium. Do you understand?"

He saw the mutant frown. Of course the man didn't understand, because there was nothing to be understood. The whole business about identifying the psychoactive drugs had been just a tale to keep him tranquil while the Prussian got enough blood to treat the assault squad for Operation Severed Head, and while he decided what to do with Logan afterward. Von Strucker had enough blood now, and the elixir had been distilled, but he thought it wouldn't hurt to take just a little more. Better to have a back-up he didn't need than to lack one when he needed it.

"As a matter of fact," he told Logan. "I'd like to take one more sample then put the results in front of a colleague of mine. He's more knowledgeable about neurochemistry than I am, and I think he could give us the definitive answer."

He saw Logan studying him from under frowning brows. Even in his good mood, the baron found the man's gaze to be unsettling. It was like locking eyes with a wild beast in a zoo, except that here no bars separated them. The mutant was dangerous, becoming more so as the memory suppressants apparently lost effect. Von Strucker would be glad to be rid of Logan, as soon as he had served his purpose.

"Okay," Logan said. "One more. But that's it. When does this expert get here?"

"He doesn't," the baron said. "We'll have to go and see him."

The man's too smooth, Logan was thinking. There was nothing he could put his finger on, but he was becoming increasingly sure that he and the German were not destined to be allies. *He smells wrong.*

As he stared into the man's eyes, smelling his pervasive odor of harsh soap, something was stirring again in the sealed rooms of his mind, where his memories lay hidden. He resisted the urge to grab at the trace. Instead, he let a long, slow intake of breath filter through his nose, allowing that distinctive chemically smell to dominate his senses, to call up whatever it was linked to in the fog that he could not penetrate.

An image came: the German's face looming over him, looking down at him with clinical detachment. There were emotions attached to the image—rage, frustration, hate—and a sense-memory of being pinned down, like a laboratory animal on a dissecting table. Logan felt the echo of a deep ache in his wrists and elbows, his ankles and knees.

By a mental effort, he held his mind back from lunging at these faint wisps of substance in the general fog. He let them swirl past him while, mentally, he stood still and watched.

"What is going on with you?" the German asked. "Are you recovering memories?"

Logan did not answer. He closed his eyes and paid no attention to the distraction of the man's voice, willing his mind to think of nothing, to stand passively while his memories came stealing toward him like timid ghosts.

Here was the German's face again, looking down at him, light flashing from his monocle. Another man peered over his shoulder, fleshy faced, his skin a scrubbed pink. *These are real memories,* Logan thought. He let the image solidify, saw that the other man wore a military cap with a badge on its front: a stylized eagle, wings spread and claws grasping a circled swastika. And below that emblem was another, a skull against crossed bones. And the skull was enameled in red.

So some of what the German had said was true, Logan now knew. He had been a captive of the Red Skull SS. But now the scope of the mental image expanded a little more. He saw, on the pink-skinned man's gray tunic, square black collar tabs with SS runes on one side; on the other, four diamonds were worked in silver thread. It was then that he noticed that around von Strucker's neck was the same kind of collar, the same runes, but with a double oak leaf instead of diamonds.

"Logan!" von Strucker's voice was harsh, insistent. "What is happening to you?"

Logan's eyes had been closed no more than a few seconds. Now he opened them and saw the baron staring at him with exactly the same expression as in the memory, like a scientist examining an interesting specimen. And over his shoulder, the face of the tall Pashtun was filled with anger and suspicion.

"I'm fine," he told von Strucker. "A little dizziness, probably from the shock your friend gave me." He turned his gaze to the gray-eyed man. "We should try each other out some time. Could be interesting."

The Pashtun met his eyes and said something back that Logan understood even though he knew none of the words. The tall man's hostility didn't bother him, he noticed. That told him something else about the kind of man he was: *I don't have a crying need to be liked by everybody I meet.*

He turned his attention back to the German. "When do we leave?"

Al Borak spent a busy hour making sure that the men of the Green Fist were properly outfitted for the first stage of the operation. Again, they would be pretending to be a soccer team owned by the son of one of the emirs whose principalities were combined in the United Arab Emirates. This time they would fly from Abu Dhabi across the Persian Gulf to Basra in Iraq. From there they would transfer to a convoy of ground vehicles that would take them north to the Mansour district of Baghdad, where everything needed for Operation Severed Head would be waiting.

The twenty mujahideen were happy to be making the trip. As they changed into the designer clothes and put on the personal jewelry that fitted their disguise as pampered playthings of a Middle Eastern potentate, their eyes shone and they kept flashing quick smiles at each other. "Paradise," Gassim whispered to Yussuf as he stuffed his travel bag with bright-colored shirts he would never wear.

"*Inshalla,*" breathed Yussuf. If God wills it.

"You chatter like women on a shopping trip," Al Borak snapped. "*Imshi!*" Move it!

Two minutes later, the mujahideen were at attention in their barracks, their travel bags at their feet, open for inspection. Al Borak went methodically from one man to the next, distributing the forged passports and checking each detail. When they landed in Basra, they might be looked over by British security forces, and the British had no reputation for being lackadaisical.

But as he did his job, the Pashtun's mind was on other matters. Within him, a great sadness fought with an even greater anger. The baron had been like a second father to him. He had always thought that he and von Strucker would go on together, building an ever more powerful instrument until, in the fullness of time, he would inherit this business. Now he knew that would never be his future. All these years, the man he had looked up to had been looking for someone else. Now he had found him. And Batoor was, once again, to be orphaned.

A tear of mingled rage and sorrow came to his eye and he knuckled it away before any of the mujahideen might notice. Of course, they, too, were about to be thrown away, once their purpose was served. But, as von Strucker had said, that was what they were for. He had not realized that, to the cold-eyed Prussian, he was just as expendable.

He shook off the emotion. *Time to be practical,* he told himself. He had spent all of these years watching von Strucker, learning from him, modeling himself on his second father. So what would the baron do? The answer, when Al Borak thought about it, was obvious: von Strucker would betray those who trusted him in order to get what he wanted. Batoor, known as Al Borak, could do the same.

He swept his eyes over the Green Fist one final time, saw nothing out of place. He ordered them to make for the elevators that would carry them up to the hidden building's rooftop hangar. As he followed them out of the barracks, the plan leaped fully formed into his mind.

They were bound for Baghdad, where they would meet the man who represented their client. In Baghdad, Al Borak would find an opportunity to have a private word with the Yemeni fanatic. He knew how to speak the language of the faithful, knew how to plant a doubt about a blue-eyed infidel. The Yemeni's master, hidden away in his mountain fastness, was a man who prized certainty. Faced with a doubt, he would act swiftly and ruthlessly to remove it.

The baron carefully packed the vials of elixir into a small carrying case lined with cushioning foam rubber. He had taken a final pint of blood from the mutant, brought it to his secret room, and spun out the white blood cells that carried the immortality factor. Although it was days yet before he would require a new injection, he prepared a hypodermic and shot a dose of the fluid into his veins.

As the stuff entered his system, he felt a rush of vitality. *Purely psychosomatic,* he told himself. The elixir did not act as a direct stimulant to the central nervous system and the body's adrenal and paradrenal glands, like the formula he had created to speed up the Green Fist mujahideen. Still, after all these years, he had found the grail of endless life—who could blame him if the discovery filled him with joy?

He went into his sleeping chamber and changed into a sedate suit of lightweight gray cotton, with a white shirt and understated tie appropriate to the team doctor of an emir's soccer squad. His false passport and other documents were in the pockets, but he checked each thoroughly. Now was no time to be tripped up by some petty detail, when his life's ambition was within his grasp.

He went to the elevators and tapped the button for the floor that housed the communications center. As the car rose, he was surprised to find himself humming a tune he hadn't heard since his student days. *I must be careful,* he told himself. *The time to enjoy the feast is when the cooking's done.*

In the communications center, he dismissed the duty officer and his assistant. When they were gone, he activated the encryption logarithm that shielded his exchanges with the client, then typed and transmitted an urgent request through the satellite uplink.

The reply came moments later:

```
Confirm receipt of message. Will have
the materials waiting at destination.
What is their purpose?
```

The baron smiled and typed a response:

```
To confound our enemies.
```

*Never tell a lie when the truth will serve just as well,* he told himself and broke the uplink connection. He returned control of the communications center to its staff and went up to where the aircraft waited.

They hadn't told Logan where they were going. "Need to know" was all the German would say. When Logan pressed for more information, von Strucker said, "I can tell you this much: I've been training a group of special forces troops for the government of a Middle Eastern country. Now I am going to deliver them.

"As it happens, the man I want to consult with about you is also in the region. We will meet him. He will look at your test results. It is very likely that he will be able to pinpoint the precise mix of drugs that have been used to hide your memories. If so, he can provide an antidote."

"And then what?" Logan said.

"Why, then we will know who you are and who has done this to you. We may even know why. Then you and I can have a talk about joining forces."

"Suppose I'm not interested?"

The baron spread his hands, palms up. "Then you will go on your way. But you will remember that I have helped you. You will owe me a favor. A great deal of what gets done in the world is on the basis of favors granted and repaid."

It all sounded plausible to Logan. He nodded and said, "Okay. We'll see how it goes."

But he had noticed that the German had a habit of watching him closely during their conversations. *Maybe that's part of his mutation,* he thought, *he can read people through their eyes, the way I seem to be able to smell stuff.* So he kept his eyes down.

Back in his room, he changed into the clothes they had laid out for him. His bogus passport was back in his room at the Mercure Hotel in Berlin, but they'd made him up a new one, along with other documents that identified him as a Canadian who worked for a soccer team in the United Arab Emirates. Apparently, that was part of the special forces outfit's cover story. They'd also put credit cards and a few hundred in U.S. currency in his wallet. He didn't put much stock in the generosity, though—what was given could always be taken away.

When he was ready to go, he paused a moment before leaving the room. His hand and arm still tingled a little from Al Borak's shock. He looked again at his fists, saw the tiny lines of scars between his knuckles. He accepted now that he healed completely. The scratch he had cut into his arm with von Strucker's scalpel was completely invisible, without even a hairline of scar tissue. *So why the scars on my hands?* he thought. *Have I done so much damage to them that they can't heal without marks?*

Something shifted in the deep sediments at the bottom of his mind. Immediately, he felt a jolt of anxiety. But now he had no doubt that somebody had planted that reaction in his mind, and he didn't give in to it right away. He continued to stare at his knotted fists, bunching the muscles of his forearms. It felt good, even though the artificially induced anxiety sent his heart rate pounding. It felt like something was going to happen, something real, something decisive.

*The electric shocks help:* the realization came to him all at once. They'd shocked him in Berlin to subdue him. Then, while he was coming to, he had seen a whirlwind of images shaken loose from behind the chemical barrier that divided his mind. And just a few minutes ago, when Al Borak had sent a jolt through him, the fog had cleared enough to give him a true image of von Strucker at Höllenfeuer.

The realization opened up a new option. If this mysterious expert that the German was taking him to see turned out to be a lie, Logan had found another way to crack the wall that separated him from his own life. *All I need to do is give El Zappo a backhander,* he thought, *to get him going.* He filed the thought away for future reference.

They took the Gulfstream V again. To disguise their point of origin, they skimmed the desert into Yemen's air space, then rose with the mountains that divided that small country from Saudi Arabia. Soon they were headed north along the Arabian Peninsula's east coast, angling down to a private airstrip at Abu Dhabi. They refueled and took off again for Basra.

Von Strucker and Logan traveled in the plane's private compartment. Al Borak and the Green Fist were in the main cabin, the mujahideen singing songs and clapping their hands, the Pashtun sitting by himself in a rear seat, glowering at everything. The baron had noted the man's change in attitude. Clearly, Logan's arrival had upset Al Borak's picture of the world. He supposed he should deal with it, but he was ready to admit to himself that he had had enough of dealing with temperamental mutants. Perhaps when he gave the men the injections that were crucial to the success of Operation Severed Head, he would give the Pashtun a placebo. It would be one less loose end to tie up.

As he mulled his options, his hands absently stroked the carrying case that contained the elixir. He would not let it out of his sight until Operation Severed Head was behind him. Now he cast an occasional glance across the plane's center aisle to where the small Canadian reclined in his seat. Logan slept, or appeared to sleep, with his arms folded across his chest. Occasionally, the overdeveloped muscles of his forearms bulged as he unconsciously flexed them. The baron found the motion distasteful. It looked to him to be not like a human action, but more like the autonomic movements of a python digesting a baby pig.

*No more mutants,* von Strucker thought. He smiled. It would be a good life, living forever and ruling the world. And after all these years of hiding in a hole in the ground a thousand miles from anywhere, it was no less than he deserved.

Logan kept his eyes closed but did not sleep. He was finding it increasingly easier to just let the memories come to him. They arrived in a flood now, though they made no coherent sense. He saw faces, streets, forests, and jungles, empty rooms and ferocious battlefields, square-bodied old cars and sleek modern automobiles, all jumbled together. It was as if everything were shaking loose, but coming at him in random order, with no system to organize the information.

But he wasn't worried. He'd decided he wasn't the kind who worried. *If you can do something about a problem, do it,* that familiar voice said from the back of his head. *If you can't do anything, wait until you can. Either way, worrying about it doesn't get anything done.*

From time to time he flexed the muscles of his forearms and noted how it always brought that same flash of fear. But he was now certain that the fear was not his, that it was a reaction that had somehow been planted in him. If he pushed it, it would break and he would step through to the other side. Only one thing kept him from doing so: the possibility that the mysterious "they" might have implanted something worse on that "other side"—maybe some self-destruct mechanism, built around a pound or two of plastic explosive wedged up against his backbone. Or maybe he would be launched into a preprogrammed berserker mode and mindlessly kill everyone around him. Whatever the outcome, the fear had been put there for a reason. He decided to walk carefully around it until he knew why.

Across the aisle, the German was humming a song to himself. It sounded to Logan like something you'd hear in a *bierkeller,* played by a band that would have to include a tuba. He wondered what was in von Strucker's head. Then he thought, *Not too long from now, I'm going to find out. Even if I have to crack it open to take a look.*

## Basra, Iraq, the present

THINGS WENT SMOOTHLY AFTER THE GULF-stream touched down just after dark in a section of the city's airport that was under the control of a militia whose senior officers had been bribed to let slide the formalities of entering the country. The passengers transferred to a canvas-topped truck that made its way north through the city, convoyed with a pair of armored SUVs with tinted windows. The cars carried several rifle-toting militiamen whose fashion sense largely centered on wearing as much black as possible. They crossed the city on secondary roads, then when the outskirts gave way to desert, the vehicles swung away from the main highway onto a dirt road that wound through scattered villages.

The road had not been repaired in many years and the men sitting on the bench seats that ran along the inner sides of the truck were constantly bounced up and down by the endless ruts and potholes. Al Borak soon got tired of having his buttocks battered and stood up beside the raised rear gate, holding on to the steel frame that supported the canvas cover and letting his bent knees cushion the relentless jolts and impacts.

The baron was riding in the truck's cab along with the militia officer who would talk them through any Iraqi checkpoints—their route would avoid any U.S. or British forces, most of whom stayed buttoned up in their bases at night. The small infidel had climbed in with the Green Fist, though he had made no attempts to make friends. He ignored them as they ignored him, and sat on the end of one of the benches at the rear of the truck, leaning forward with his thick forearms on his knees.

But when Batoor rose and stood in the half-open back of the truck, gazing out at the desert night, Logan also got up and stood beside him. They were lit by the headlights of the SUV following them, and Al Borak could see that the man's face bore a look of condescension. After a moment, he said something to the

Pashtun in English. Al Borak caught only a couple of words—"little trick"—but from the way the man gestured at his hands, he knew that the reference was to his power to summon the lightning for which he was named.

"If you want a demonstration," he said in his native Pashto, "I can give you one."

And even as he said the words, the idea came to him. They were both holding on to the same steel bar that arched overhead. Al Borak had but to call down the spirit of the clouds and discharge it into the roof support and the power would shoot through the small man. Then, while he was twitching helplessly, the Pashtun need give him only the gentlest push on the shoulder and the man would tumble over the gate and onto the road. If the shock and fall didn't kill him, he would be crushed under the wheels of the heavy car following close behind them. And whatever plans von Strucker might have had for this interloper would become a thing of the past.

Al Borak set his mind to the summoning. In a moment he experienced the sharp metallic taste in his saliva that told him that he was charging. He looked down into the face of the infidel and smiled, then let a full charge surge from his palms. He held the discharge steady while Logan's face twitched into a rictus of spasming muscle and his heels beat a tattoo on the floorboards of the truck. Wisps of smoke wreathed around the places where the man's hands touched the steel. The Pashtun could smell burning flesh. Then he reined in the lightning and put his hand at the back of his victim's neck. The small man was already slumping forward and it took only the slightest push to send him toppling over the gate and into the road.

They were moving fast and the chase car was not far behind. The body bounced hard and the SUV driver had no time to touch the brakes before the vehicle's reinforced bumper struck the fallen man and threw him forward. Logan rolled along the dusty road in a tangle of limbs, the impact knocking him out of his borrowed shoes. The chase car's driver strove valiantly to stop the hurtling vehicle, but he couldn't prevent the front wheels from smashing into the tumbling body. The front end bumped over Logan, then the rear wheels completed the job.

The truck continued to move down the road at full speed, its driver ignorant of what had happened behind him. Then Al Borak saw a black-clad man get out of the passenger side of the SUV, a hand-held radio to his mouth. The Pashtun had to tighten his grip on the steel rib as the truck slammed to a skidding halt. Its gears ground as the driver found reverse and they began to back up toward the spot where the SUV waited.

Al Borak put on the face of sorrow he wanted the baron to see when he explained how Logan had lost his balance and fallen from the truck. He tried out the words in his mind: *I reached for him, but it was too late.*

He would offer to help bury the body beside the road and they would all move on. It was no great loss. The man was, after all, nothing but an infidel.

The truck backed up all the way to where the tragic scene awaited, and Al Borak jumped down to express his sorrow as von Strucker, carrying case in hand, came hurrying back from the cab to see what had happened. But they were met by a grinning little figure brushing dust from his clothing and shaking it out of his hair. He thanked the astonished militiaman who brought him his shoes and sat on the extended bumper of the SUV to slip them back on.

Then he looked up at von Strucker and said, "Guess I slipped. No harm done."

The baron went back to the front of the truck while Logan climbed agilely into the back. Once aboard, he turned and extended a hand to Al Borak. The Pashtun took the offered hand. It felt normal—no blisters, no ridges of charred flesh—and he saw again the same look of condescension as Logan pulled him into vehicle. "Yeah," the small man said, "a good little trick."

Logan settled back onto the bench seat, folded his arms, and closed his eyes. He had learned a couple of things from the experiment. One was that, surprisingly, his bones didn't break. The impact of the SUV's bumper smashing into him had been like hitting a brick wall at fifty miles an hour. It had hurt like hell, had torn his flesh, yet nothing had snapped, not even his smallest finger. Nor had his chest been crushed when both sets of wheels had thumped over his body.

That was a bonus. He'd been willing to put up with the pain of fractured bones, at least until the amazingly rapid healing process did its work. Now he found that it was only his flesh that could be damaged, and it repaired itself so quickly that he was practically indestructible. The realization brought no surprise. Although it was news to the part of his mind that thought of itself as Logan, the rest of him took being shocked, smashed, and run over, then bouncing right back up, as no big deal. *No wonder I have this basic self-confidence,* he thought. A wolverine among foxes didn't have all that much to worry about.

He'd also tested Al Borak's power. He was sure that the tall man had meant to deliver a killing shock. But the surge of electricity hadn't even knocked Logan out, although for a long moment as he'd tumbled and rolled he'd felt dazed, even a little drunk. They'd shocked him into unconsciousness in Berlin, but that was after they'd already pumped his system full of some powerful sedative, and that time Al Borak had administered the jolt directly to Logan's head. So even though one of the foxes had a little extra kick, he wasn't that much of a threat.

As he rolled these thoughts through his mind, a new set of images were flickering out of his inner darkness. The electric jolt had worked its accidental magic again, as he'd hoped it would. *I should keep Sparky around for a while,* he thought. *He comes in handy.* Again, the pictures were random, but many of them involved violence. He saw bodies with gaping wounds, bellies and chests ripped open, severed limbs, pools of gore.

Often he saw the faces of people who were on the receiving end of catastrophic bodily harm, saw time and again the knowledge that could fill a man's eyes as he took the wound that would soon kill him. He knew he had seen that look many times, and at close range. The faces he was seeing belonged to people he had killed. Some of them were women. He knew their blood must have drenched him, their guts must have spilled at his feet, their dying screams and moans must have filled his ears.

*And how do I feel about that?* he asked himself. *Do I really want to know who I am, if it means knowing everything I've done?*

Despite all the damage he had sustained, he went through the world scarcely showing a scar. But maybe all the damage he had done to others had put scars on him where they didn't show. For a moment he even entertained the thought that maybe he had asked to have his memories wiped. But almost as soon as he asked himself the question, something inside said, *Nah, you're not the kind of guy who can't carry your own load.*

He watched the pictures come and go. There were a lot of them. After a while he opened his eyes and turned to look out the opening above the truck's rear gate. The overcast that had blocked the light of the stars was glowing gray. Some of it was the approaching dawn. Some was the reflected glow of lights on the ground, the lights of a city. They were coming to their destination, wherever it might be.

*Good,* he thought. *Time to get some things settled.*

## Outskirts of Baghdad, the present

As the small convoy entered Mahmudiya, the southern suburb of Baghdad, they were met by a guide on a lightweight Kawasaki motorcycle. The commander of the militiamen brought him to talk with von Strucker.

"Iraqi Police commandos have sealed off the roads leading into the Mansour district," the guide said. "Something has them stirred up."

The baron knew what that "something" was, but these men had no need to know. "Can we not make an arrangement with them?" he said.

"They are not of our faction," the commander said.

Von Strucker found a map of the city and had the guide show him where the checkpoints were. He chose the most useful one and said, "Take us to within two blocks of here."

The vehicles rolled on through the predawn silence of the city, past burned-out buildings and houses whose windows were shuttered by metal grilles, the doors protected by steel bars. The man on the motorcycle waved them to a stop just before a corner, next to a deserted public market whose ornate façade had been scarred by a recent car bomb. The baron got out of the truck and went to the rear gate.

He spoke to Al Borak. "I want four men with knives."

There was a rustle and a muted *clank* as the chosen four clambered out of the back of the truck and their leader took four fighting knives from one of the equipment lockers. He passed them to the men, then began to climb out after them.

"No," said the Prussian, "they will go on their own."

He brought the four mujahideen to the front of the truck. There he gave them a set of instructions, brief and direct. The men grinned, and the baron knew that there would be no need to augment their performance with drugs from the carrying case. "Go," he said, and watched them disappear around the corner.

He went back to the rear of the truck. Al Borak was plainly unhappy at not being allowed to lead the attack. The Prussian waved away his truculent protest and said, "I have a more important task for you. When we move forward again, keep the stranger distracted. He does not need to see what happens next."

The Pashtun said he would do as he was bid, but von Strucker sensed a lingering resentment. He reminded himself that his days of humoring moody mutants and catering to the wishes of various fanatics would soon come to an end. Cherishing that thought, he went and sat in the cab of the truck with the valise back on his lap, and waited for the men to return.

The second time the convoy halted, the German came back to the rear of the truck and spoke in hushed Arabic to the Pashtun. The latter tapped four of the men on the benches, sending them over the tailgate, then rummaged in a crate at the front of the compartment, coming up with four knives that he passed to the men outside. Then came another whispered exchange and Logan knew, from the way the tall man's eyes flicked toward him, that he was the subject of the conversation.

The German went away and they all sat in silence for a few minutes. Then came a rush of footsteps and the four men were clambering back over the tailgate, handing back the knives to Al Borak. They resumed their places on the benches, and immediately there was a subdued hubbub of conversation that the Pashtun cut off with a snapped order. The truck started up and rolled around the corner.

*So much for von Strucker's cover story about training special forces for an unnamed government,* Logan was thinking. To his heightened sense of smell, the stench of fresh blood was unmistakable. He could see that none of the four was wounded, so it was clear that they had been out cutting other people's throats, probably to clear a checkpoint of some kind. Legitimate special forces units rarely found it necessary to sneak about the back streets and eliminate sentries in their own countries. Whatever the German had been training these troops for, it wasn't to hand them over to the government of Iraq. He was also pretty sure that Iraq was the country where they had now ended up, though the baron had not volunteered the information. But not too many big cities in the Middle East looked like a war zone. He didn't recognize the streets they were passing, but he had a pretty good sense, as he had had in Berlin, that he had been in this place before.

Less than a minute after they got rolling again, Al Borak was suddenly hovering over Logan, delivering some kind of diatribe in Arabic. The Canadian obliged him by looking up at him and smiling, which seemed to send the tall man into fresh paroxysms of anger.

*He's keeping me busy so I don't look out and see what I'm not supposed to see.* It didn't matter. Logan could smell the blood and the loosened bowels of dead men as the truck rumbled past the killing ground. He looked away, toward the men on the benches. They were becoming edgy, seeing their leader so worked up. The four who had done the killing were still powered up, their eyes flicking bright in the darkness of the truck. Logan wondered how it would be to fight them, even when they were juiced up—Berlin didn't count; it had been a lot of flailing around in the dark—and decided he wouldn't mind finding out.

That told him something else about what kind of man he was. *Guess I'm not big on speculation. I'm a guy who prefers to get hold of things, give them a good shake, and see what falls out.* Not everything he was learning about himself was good news. He had to accept that he had killed a lot of people, probably including quite a few who might not have deserved it. *Collateral damage,* he thought. But on the whole, he was coming to think that he'd be able to live with himself.

Al Borak wound down after a while and went to sit farther forward. Logan watched the streets of Baghdad fill with the thin light of dawn and looked forward to getting some answers.

## Mansour district of Baghdad, the present

THE SUN WAS JUST CLEAR OF THE HORIZON when the convoy reached the high-walled compound that had formerly belonged to the owner of Iraq's most successful candy manufacturer whose factory had been stripped to the walls by looters during the chaos of 2003. A year later, after his eldest daughter had narrowly escaped kidnapping by a gang that targeted private schools, the man moved his family to Jordan and put the mansion up for sale. He had hoped that one of the countries seeking to open an embassy in the capital of the new Iraq might buy it— the luxurious Mansour district being a favorite for foreign missions—but there were no offers. It was leased for a while to an international security contracting firm (the newly preferred term for mercenaries). But as the city became a hunting ground for Islamist fanatics, Shiite death squads and unaligned but enterprising criminals, even these hardened ex-South African paratroops and former Russian *spetsnaz,* eventually decided that it was safer to operate from the ultrasecure Green Zone.

The commander of the militiamen had a key that opened the tall steel gates. The SUVs and the truck followed a circular driveway made of crushed white quartz and parked with all three vehicles facing the gate.

The carrying case never left the baron's grasp as he made a quick inspection of the grounds while the militiamen and the Green Fist were led across the house's pillared portico and through the main doors. The client's men providing security all had the gleam of jihad in their eyes, but they appeared to know their jobs. As he returned to the front of the mansion, he was met by Al Borak.

"Everything we require has been provided," his second in command said. "Nonetheless, I will have the men field strip the weapons as soon as they have completed morning prayers."

"Good," said von Strucker. He told the Pashtun to carry on, and made to mount the broad front steps. But Al Borak put a hand on his arm to detain him. The baron saw that the man was agitated. "What is it?" he said.

Al Borak cocked his head over his shoulder. "Him," he said.

The Prussian turned to look. Logan was standing beside the fountain, hands in his pockets, gazing about the courtyard with interest. Then his eyes came around to von Strucker and stayed on him.

"I have told you, he is not your concern," von Strucker said. He turned to enter the house, but again felt the restraining hand on his arm

"What is he doing here?" Al Borak said.

The Prussian stiffened. "You have no need to know that."

The man's grip tightened. "You said he was essential to your plans. Not ours, just yours. Am I no longer a part of your plans?"

"Do you not trust me?"

"Should I?"

The Pashtun was growing more agitated. Von Strucker felt a warning tingle cause the hairs on his arm to stand erect. "Listen," he said, "Logan is not for you to worry about. When we leave Baghdad he will not be going with us. He will remain here, as a decoy. He will lead the enemy astray while we cover our tracks."

"But he knows far too much."

The baron smiled. "In a little while, he will not even know how to tie his shoes."

The tingling stopped. Al Borak took his hand from the Prussian's arm.

"Come," von Strucker said. "It is time for you to learn what Operation Severed Head entails. Then we will deal with Logan."

He waved and smiled at the small man standing by the fountain. Logan did not wave back, but stood with his hands in his pockets, shoulders hunched forward, watching as they went inside.

"What about the schedule?" von Strucker asked the Yemeni. "Have there been any changes?"

They were in the family dining room where the candy maker's family used to gather around the rosewood table for the nightly feast in the month of Ramadan. But instead of sweetmeats and fiery sauces, the polished board now supported only a detailed map of central Baghdad.

"None that make any difference," the client said. "God willing, he will arrive at the airport in a little while. Within the hour, we may begin."

"Excellent," said the baron. He turned to Al Borak. "Have the men assemble in the large banquet room, armed and ready for the jump-off. You may have the honor of telling them the target of this great mission."

Al Borak said, "Who is the target?"

And then von Strucker told the Pashtun the name of the man they had come to Baghdad to kill.

Logan watched the German and the gray-eyed man pause on the steps into the house. He couldn't hear what they were saying, but when the tall one cocked his head in his direction, he knew that he was the subject of the conversation. Something about the scene tickled the back of his mind. It was the sight of the German, his back mostly turned to Logan, speaking quietly to another man. *I've seen this before.*

He didn't strive for the recollection. That was not how it worked. He simply stared at the two figures on the step, saw the baron glance his way and return to his discussion. And all at once another scene superimposed itself: a brightly lit room, von Strucker in a field gray SS uniform, officer's epaulets of silver braid on his shoulders, talking with another officer who was round-faced and pink of skin.

Now Logan closed his eyes, letting the memory come. And, out of the past, he heard the sound of their voices, speaking in German. *"Meine erste Neigung soll das Blut studieren,"* von Strucker was saying.

*"Eine einzigartige Blutzelle?"* the other man asked.

The words meant nothing to Logan. Except, as he listened, he kept hearing the same word repeated, a word that sounded like "bloot."

Now it came again, the pink-skinned man saying,

*"Wenn es das Blut ist, dann sollten wir das Mark studieren."*

*Bloot.* Logan rolled the word over in his mind. A lot of German words sounded like their English equivalent. And then the memory unwound a little further. He saw von Strucker picking up a mallet and chisel, and the other man putting a scalpel to his thigh.

He felt the ghost of that long-ago moment's agony. His fist clenched in his pockets and the muscles of his forearms strained. The motion conjured up the automatic anxiety again and he forced himself to relax.

He opened his eyes. Al Borak and von Strucker had gone into the mansion. *Das bloot,* Logan said to himself. *The blood.*

The candy maker's banquet room had tall windows and a long mahogany table overhung by a vast chandelier imported from Austria. It also had sixteen mujahideen dressed for battle in Iraqi Army camouflage fatigues, their boots, helmets, and M-16 rifles identical to the U.S. Army's standard issue. They stood at ease in two ranks as Al Borak inspected them.

When von Strucker came into the room, carrying the case that had not left his possession since they had departed Saudi Arabia, the Pashtun called the men to attention. The Prussian nodded to him and Al Borak raised his voice and spoke to the sixteen.

"Mujahideen of the Green Fist," he said, "God is great! He will give us today a great victory. A thousand years from now, the faithful will still speak with wonder of the deeds we will do this day, here in the city of the Caliphs.

"God willing, we will strike the infidel and the apostates who serve them, in the place that is the heart of their power. We will strike a great blow, and all the world will know that God is great!"

As one, the sixteen raised their fists and chanted, "*Allahu akbar! Allahu akbar!*" God is great! God is great! As they did so, von Strucker placed the carrying case on the table, opened it, and spread it wide. Inside, nestled in foam, were the tubes that contained the distillation of Logan's unique blood cells.

"Men of the Green Fist," he said, "I know that you are ready to lay down your lives as holy warriors. I honor you for your courage and dedication. But I am able to tell you that today you will triumph over your enemies *without* making the martyr's sacrifice. For God has granted us a miracle."

He turned to Al Borak and said, "You are their leader. Yours is the honor of preparing them. I must return to our client." He filled a hypodermic syringe from one of the tubes, handed it to the Pashtun, and said, "Carry on."

# Baghdad International Airport,
the present

THERE WERE NO LONGER ANY GENTLE, GRADUAL descents into Baghdad Airport. Whether civilian or military, incoming flights stayed high until the last moment, then made a steep, spiraling dive down to the runway, to provide the least inviting target to anyone on the ground who might have one of many heavy machine guns or even an antiaircraft gun that had gone missing from Iraqi armories in the systematic looting that followed the sudden dissolution of Saddam's army. Some flights also fired flares to confuse any shoulder-fired, heat-seeking missiles—quite a few of those had also gone missing in the spring of 2003.

U.S. Air Force Colonel Arlen McKittrick employed both defensive techniques as he brought the white-and-powder blue–painted Boeing 747 spiraling swiftly down from the overcast skies that were typical of Mesopotamia in late December. He jammed on the brakes a second after his wheels scorched the runway. As soon as the aircraft's ground speed could be matched, it was flanked by armored Humvees and fighting vehicles that came racing along the tarmac on either side, guns aimed outward. The escorts accompanied the plane to a spot less than halfway to the end of the main runway, where more armored vehicles and a half battalion of special forces troops surrounded two

Nighthawk and six Apache helicopters, their rotors already turning.

McKittrick remained at his post in the cockpit, ready to slam forward the throttles and put the jet into an emergency takeoff if necessary. Then he heard the *thump* of the plane's lower rear door opening, the exit usually used by journalists who accompanied the single passenger for whose use this customized 747 was always reserved. But this morning, the reporters and cameramen had to stand aside as a fit and compact man in a dark suit descended the rolling staircase that had been brought to the door. Surrounded by sharp-eyed men with earpieces and automatic weapons, he strode to the waiting Nighthawks, followed by the four pool reporters who were to accompany him on the six-minute flight to the Green Zone. The rest of the press corps would follow in an armored convoy.

As he stepped up to the door of the lead Nighthawk, the man in the suit looked back at the 747's cockpit and snapped off a salute in McKittrick's direction. The colonel returned the salute. Then, as the helicopters powered up and lifted into the sky, heading east into the Iraqi dawn, he reached for his radio mike, depressed the button, and said, "Baghdad tower, this is Air Force One. We require immediate refueling and clearance for takeoff as and when necessary."

"Air Force One," came the reply, "fuel is on the way and the runway is yours for as long as you need it."

## Mansour district of Baghdad, the present

LOGAN BELIEVED HE HAD IT FIGURED OUT. HE had stayed by the fountain, working it through while the Pashtun and the men who had come up with them from the baron's desert headquarters piled back into the truck and went out the front gate. The SUVs and the handful of black-clad men who had come in them remained behind. The militiamen took up defensive positions around the mansion and the grounds. One or two of them gave Logan looks that told him they were not interested in making friends. That didn't bother him. Neither was he.

The blood was the key. Von Strucker had focused on it all those years ago. He must have figured it contained the secret of Logan's phenomenal ability to heal. That secret was what the German wanted out of him, why he had set up the Höllenfeuer Remembrance Society to find him again. All the talk about helping him, the "I'm a mutant, just like you" and "your enemy is my enemy" was all a smokescreen to keep Logan around and quiet while he got a good quantity of the precious stuff. And now he had gotten plenty.

The German had taken bone marrow from Logan in 1944. He hadn't aged a day since. Those two facts had to be connected. Now he had brought the walking container of the miraculous blood to Baghdad, and

Logan had no doubt the German had something in mind. Maybe the idea was to sell Logan to someone else. Maybe to put him on ice and bleed him indefinitely.

Whatever the baron's plan might be, it was not meant to feature a happy ending for one memory-impaired Canadian. *They use you, then they throw you away.* He paused as a growing racket broke into his thoughts. He looked up and saw a flying convoy of eight helicopters passing overhead from the southwest, moving at top speed. Every few seconds, flares fired from the copters. Tiny door gunners looked out and down, the muzzles of their machine guns constantly traversing left and right. On the grounds of the mansion, the men in black shirts and turbans shielded their eyes and watched the machines pass. One of them said something and the others laughed.

The aircraft passed out of sight and Logan returned to his thoughts. It was not an ideal situation to be surrounded by armed guards who were under the orders of a cold-eyed man who meant him no good. But, faulty as his powers of recollection undeniably were, he was now certain he had been in exactly that same position sixty-odd years ago. And he had come out of it all right.

So it was time to deal with von Strucker. His forearms clenched again, and again the same flash of dread filled him. The unwanted emotion angered him. It didn't come from him. It had been implanted. It was like an insidious parasite that lived in his body, and it needed to be dealt with. *But first the German,* he thought. *Time for the truth.*

He turned toward the mansion.

Just off the family dining room was a cozy den with leather chairs and couches and a wide-screen plasma television connected to a satellite dish on the roof. The set was showing the raw feed from the Baghdad bureau of CNN. The hawk-nosed Yemeni, dressed in traditional Arab robes, sat in the butter-soft leather embrace of a tan-colored armchair, his hooded eyes fixed on the images.

The baron was in the dining room, rolling up the map and preparing for their departure that would come as soon as the client had seen what he was waiting to see. The foam-lined carrying case stood upright on the floor by his feet, closed and locked. The noise of a scuffle caught his attention and he looked up to see one of the black-clad militiamen attempting to prevent Logan from entering the room from the foyer. The guard was bigger, and he was using his rifle like a baton held in both hands, but the small Canadian had hold of the weapon and was steadily pushing the larger man back. Then he twisted it from the other's grasp with an effortless display of strength.

"Stop!" von Strucker cried, then repeated himself in Arabic, adding, "there is no need for this. The man is a guest. He may enter."

To Logan, he said, "I was just about to come and look for you."

"Uh-huh," the Canadian said. He handed the guard's rifle back with a casualness that von Strucker noted and came into the room, shutting the door to the foyer behind him. The baron saw his eyes take in the rolled map and pay attention to the case on the floor, and he thought to himself, *Not a moment too soon.* Whatever Logan had been in 1944, whatever he was now, with or without his memories, he was a dangerous man.

Von Strucker put on a smile and rubbed his hands, saying, "I have had a chance to show your blood work to my esteemed colleague—" he gestured toward the den, "—and he confirms my supposition."

"Is that so?" Logan said. "Just what did he confirm?"

"You have been attacked by a complex of drugs that are collectively known as mnemophages—'memory eaters' is a rough translation of the medical term. Of course, they do not actually devour your memories. They inhibit the electrochemical action of the regions at the ends of your brain's neuron cells. Signals cannot pass from one cell to another. The memories are still there, but they cannot be accessed."

"Uh-huh," Logan said.

"Do you understand what I am saying?" von Strucker said. "Having identified the precise mix of chemicals, we can offer you a countereffective substance that will unlock your mind."

"Hmm," the mutant said. "And did your colleague happen to bring any of that substance with him?"

"He did," said the baron. "He has already prepared an injection for you."

"Well," said Logan, "let's get on with it."

"Indeed," said von Strucker. He went to the door into the den and spoke to the Yemeni in Arabic. "Will you please bring the materials I asked for? This man speaks no Arabic. He thinks you are a doctor who has a cure for his problem."

The Yemeni did not rise, but gestured to the television. "I wish to see the event," he said.

"This will take but a moment. Besides, it is important to the 'event.' This man will lead the enemy astray. They will not know who has struck them."

"But we want them to know who has struck them," the client said. "That is the point of the exercise."

The baron held his irritation in check. Soon he would be beyond fanatics, as well as mutants. "We want them to know that you have struck them, certainly. There is nothing to be gained from revealing my part in the matter."

The dark-eyed man grunted and levered himself out of the embrace of the chair. The baron had the impression, not for the first time, that the client was of that desert-bred type who would ban all of life's comforts and force the entire world to sit on goat-hair rugs. Again, he was glad he would soon be leaving this life behind.

The man felt in the pocket of his robe and brought out two flat plastic cases, each longer than his hand. "Here is what you asked for."

"Which contains the memory eater?"

"This," said the Yemeni, offering one of the cases.

"Good," said von Strucker. "We will not need the other."

The Arab put the other case on a side table next to the chair he had been sitting in. The baron said, "Now, if you would just play along for a few more moments, we will be finished."

The Yemeni snorted. But he put down the remote, leaving the set showing the CNN raw feed. A man in shirtsleeves and wearing a combination headphone and mike was sitting at a desk, talking to the cable station's Atlanta headquarters, giving a rundown on the main stories that would be fed through the satellite that morning, and scheduling a live go-to for the news summary at the top of the hour. Then he broke off as a young woman came to bend over him and say something in his ear. The man listened, then said, "Wait a minute, Wolf. I've got to check something." He pushed the phone away from his mouth and began to talk with the woman.

The Yemeni came into the dining room and made an effort to look not quite so disdainful of the infidels.

Von Strucker took the case from him, laid it on the table, and opened it. Inside was a large-bore hypodermic syringe, filled with a green substance.

The baron picked up the needle and smiled at Logan. "If you would roll up your sleeve," he said. As he spoke, he depressed the plunger slightly to remove air from the spike. As a thin jet of the green liquid arced into the air, von Strucker was surprised to see the mutant put out a hand so that the tiny squirt of the drug landed on his palm.

Logan brought his hand to his face. The Prussian saw his nostrils flare as he took a long, slow sniff of the smear of moisture on his palm. Then the hard, dark eyes locked on his and a voice in von Strucker's head said, *Ach, scheiss.*

### Green Zone, Baghdad, the present

JAN VISSER, BORN AND RAISED IN PRETORIA, HAD joined the Fourth Reconnaissance Commando regiment of the South African Defense Forces—later renamed the 451 Parachute Battalion—straight out of high school. Twenty years later, having risen from raw recruit to the rank of captain, he took his pension, resigned his commission, and went to a meeting in a Pretoria hotel room with a former colonel of the British SAS. It was a brief meeting, from which ex-Captain Visser emerged with the rank of major and a salary several times greater than what the Republic of South Africa offered its field-grade officers. His new employer was Strategic Outcomes Corp., headquartered in the Cayman Islands, and one of the fastest-growing security consulting firms in the immensely less predictable world that came unexpectedly into being after the collapse of the Soviet Union.

Since joining SOC, Visser had seen service in West Africa, guarding diamond exporters; in Central Asia, guarding oil drillers; in South America, guarding people who didn't discuss their business interests with the hired help. In 2003, he became one of tens of thousands of "security consultants" who found high-paying work in the chaos of Iraq, guarding everything from pipelines and power plants to foreign embassies and bases full of regular soldiers.

This morning, Major Jan Visser was in charge of the SOC security team that operated one of the main entry points into Baghdad's heavily fortified Green Zone. The actual gate was a heavy steel pipe with a counterweight at one end that could be lifted to allow vehicles in. But that wouldn't happen until Visser's team had checked identification documents, thoroughly searched the trunk, passenger compartment, and under the hood, run a mirror on a wheeled pole underneath the body, and let a bomb-sniffing dog give everything and everybody the once-over.

To either side of the entry point, as well as just a few feet behind it, stood tall blast walls of reinforced concrete topped by razor wire. A vehicle passing through the gate would have to slowly wend its way around these barriers, then pass through a narrow channel, also lined with blast-proof concrete and guarded by machine guns, before emerging onto the wide streets that ran between the Iraqi parliament buildings, the headquarters of key ministries like oil and defense, and Saddam Hussein's sprawling, domed Republican Palace, which now housed the United States Embassy.

The closest a car bomb would get to the softer targets inside the zone would be the first barrier. If a suicide bomber blew himself up there, he might take out Visser, his car-searching soldiers, and their dog. An assault team could get farther, though not much; if they were good, they could shoot their way in, but those who made it past the blast wall and into the channel would be cut to pieces.

Visser had warned his men to be extravigilant today. It was supposed to be a secret that the Green Zone would be receiving a UIP—Ultra-Important Visitor— and certainly no one had officially passed the word down to those who guarded the perimeter. But the South African had seen security "flaps" before in the zone, and the heightened preparations always turned out to be in anticipation of at least a cabinet-level official, if not higher. When the helicopter convoy came sliding down from the gray sky not long after his team started their shift, he nodded to his men in confirmation.

"Okay," he said, "extra tight until we see those copters heading back to the airport."

It was still well before office hours in the zone, and incoming traffic was light. The broad street outside the high walls—still named 14th of July to commemorate the Baathist revolution that overthrew the old monarchy—was empty. Then a canvas-topped truck, the kind commonly used by the Iraqi Army, came at a moderate speed from the direction of Saddam's Tomb of the Unknown Soldier, with its two pairs of giant concrete hands holding crossed sabers.

"Sharpen up," the major told his men. Around him he heard the click of rifle bolts as each man chambered a round.

The truck stopped directly across from the gate. The driver, helmeted and wearing Iraqi Army camouflage, leisurely opened his door and got out. He ambled to the rear of the vehicle, where he unlatched and lowered the tailgate. Now more soldiers got out, with M-16s—one of them handed a weapon to the driver—and stood around the back of the truck like recruits in need of a brass-tongued sergeant who would snap them into formation.

"You there!" Visser called to them. He had acquired enough Arabic to say, "Don't move!"

But the men did move. They unslung their rifles, holding them loosely but with the muzzles aimed in the general direction of the SOC team. And they began to drift across the street.

Visser was thinking, *A bunch of idiot farmboys who've gotten lost,* but he had not survived three tours of duty in Baghdad by taking chances. He brought his own weapon to his shoulder and aimed at the closest man. Around him, his team were doing the same.

"Stop!" he shouted. "Put down your weapons!"

Yet they didn't. Instead, the man the major was looking at over the sights of his rifle fired a shot. It was just one round and Visser heard it *whuff* past him, a foot or more over his head.

"Fire!" he shouted, squeezing the trigger of his M-16 and sending a three-round burst through the chest of the Iraqi soldier. His men opened up and cut down the men who were still coming toward them, one or two of them getting off unaimed shots from hip level.

"Cease firing!" Visser said. "Get the dog and check the truck!"

The truck was empty. No explosives were stacked within or packed in the chassis. Sixteen dead men lay sprawled in the middle of the street. Visser's top sergeant, a red-faced Australian, gingerly examined the bodies for explosives.

"Nothing," he reported, "no ID tags, no paybooks."

Jan Visser pushed his helmet back from his sweating brow and said, "Well, what the hell do you think that was all about?"

The Australian had no answer, except that he reckoned they had just met "the most incompetent bunch of drongos in the whole bleedin' insurgency."

## Mansour district, Baghdad, the present

FOR LOGAN, THE SMELL FROM THE SMEAR OF green liquid on his palm was almost enough. It didn't trigger any precise memories, but it rang a warning bell somewhere in the back corridors of his mind. But just to be sure, he said to von Strucker, "How does he know this is the right dosage? He's never even seen me before."

The German was quick with an answer. "I sent him all your information. This is his area of expertise, after all. Now roll up your sleeve."

Logan looked at the Arab. He couldn't have told from the man's appearance if he was a world-class neurochemist or just a particularly successful goatherd. Whichever he was, his attention was being pulled back toward the TV in the other room, where someone was talking in an excited voice.

"He doesn't look like he's all that interested," Logan said. "Is he missing his favorite show?"

Von Strucker said something to the other man in Arabic. The hawk-faced man snapped back at him and his sun-darkened hand made a brusque gesture. "He is not used to having his medical judgments questioned," the German said.

The Arab was half-turned away now, clearly wanting to get back to the TV, where somebody was definitely excited about something, though the sound was too low for Logan to make out the words.

None of this smelled right to Logan. Instinct told him to push the situation. "If he's the expert," he said "I'd like him to give me the injection."

The baron spoke to the Arab again, and this time the man spewed a stream of what was surely invective at both the German and Logan. He turned his back and made for the other room.

"Tell you what," said Logan, moving forward and plucking the hypodermic from von Strucker's fingers, then catching the Arab's arm in a grip that stopped him short, "how about I inject *you*?"

And he stuck the needle through the sleeve of the man's robe and into the shoulder muscle, depressing the plunger. The German let out a surprised squawk and grabbed for the syringe, but Logan had already stepped back to observe the effects.

The Arab had turned toward him at the jab of the hypodermic, his harsh face forming a mask of outrage. But in less than a second, the man's expression softened. His pupils dilated until scarcely the thinnest rim of their dark irises showed and his grim mouth went slack. He blinked and looked around the room as if he had just woken from a deep dream and hadn't yet shaken its grasp. He said something that Logan would have bet was the Arabic equivalent of "Where am I?"

"Uh-huh," the mutant said. "So that clears that up."

Von Strucker was making for the door to the foyer. Logan caught him by the collar and yanked him back. As the German came backpedaling on his heels, trying to keep his balance, the Canadian cocked the fist of his free hand and delivered a short, sharp punch to the side of von Strucker's jaw. The baron went limp in his grip and Logan lowered him to sit on one of the dining room chairs. The Arab watched, eyes wide and mouth open, like a surprised infant. Then his knees buckled and he sank to the floor.

Logan first went to the case that von Strucker had guarded so jealously. He cracked it open and saw the rows of test tubes nestled inside. Most of them were empty. That was obviously part of the puzzle. He next went to the map on the table and unrolled it. It was marked in Arabic, so he couldn't read it, but he recognized it as a map of Baghdad. Marked with arrows and dark lines was an area of land confined by a bend in the river. *Another piece of the puzzle,* he thought.

He found the third piece in the small room where the voice from the TV was now speaking excitedly. It belonged to a man in shirtsleeves sitting at a desk and scanning a piece of paper in his hand while saying, ". . . confirm that the president arrived this morning on Air Force One under ultratight security. He flew by helicopter to the Green Zone where he is scheduled to meet the new Iraqi national unity government this afternoon.

"But first he's going to enjoy a Christmas Day

breakfast with thirty servicemen and women from all branches of the military. And, Wolf, I'm told he's brought each one of them a Christmas present from their families. This has been in the works for weeks, with all the families sworn to secrecy. It's amazing they managed to keep it under wraps.

"The breakfast is at the U.S. embassy in the Green Zone. Right after that the president's going to visit a hospital that's only a couple of hundred yards away. He will award Purple Hearts to several wounded soldiers and marines—we're getting their names and hometowns now."

The man checked another piece of paper that someone handed him from off-camera. "So, Wolf, this is going to be the major story of the day—well, probably the whole holiday season. We'll need to change the line-up for the top of the hour, and I'm going to reassign Christianne from the go-to so she can interview the troops at the breakfast and in the field hospital. She's on her way to the embassy right now."

The feed didn't carry the audio of the reply the man was receiving from Atlanta, but Logan could see him nodding an affirmative, then he said, "Right, no problem, we were already set up at the embassy press room, so I'll just pull—"

He broke off as a young woman rushed into the shot and leaned over to speak to him. Logan saw alarm appear on the newsman's face. He said to the woman, "This is confirmed? Get a crew there! Right now! I

want eye-witness interviews from the security consultants before some PR flack comes and throws a
blanket over it."

As the woman left, he turned to the camera and
said, "Wolf, we have a confirmed report of some kind
of insurgents' attack on a gate leading into the Green
Zone. I've got a crew heading there now."

The young woman was back. He listened to her,
then said, "No casualties among the guards at the gate.
Sixteen insurgents killed by rifle fire. No car bombs.
No follow-up attacks. Doesn't seem to have been a di-
version."

He listened to the reply from Atlanta, then said,
"No, the bodies are being taken to a morgue where
army intelligence will take photographs, fingerprints,
and DNA samples in case the attackers can be identified. I'm told the insurgents had M-16 rifles, so they'll
get their serial numbers. The information might point
to which element of the insurgency had sent them on
this apparent suicide mission."

He listened again, then said, "I'll have Christianne
talk to the intelligence people on the scene. The
morgue where they're taking the bodies is in the same
field hospital where the president is giving out the
Purple Hearts."

And now, for Logan, the pieces all fell into place.
He looked back through the door to the other room,
where the Arab was sitting dazed at the table and von
Strucker was beginning to stir.

He would have liked to have stayed right there in the house. He had a lot of questions to put to the German. But he couldn't.

The TV was connected to large remote speakers in the corners of the room. Logan pulled the wires free and used them to tie von Strucker firmly to the sturdy wooden chair in the dining room. Then he gagged him with strips of cloth torn from the Arab's robe. The Arab had sunk into what looked like a catatonic state. He was lying on his side on the floor, staring at nothing.

Before he left, Logan took another look inside the German's carrying case. Then he went quietly to the door to the foyer and eased it open. The black-clad militiaman was still standing outside when Logan silently opened the door to the foyer. This time, the mutant dealt less gently with him. Before the guard could turn, Logan put one hand on the man's chin and the other on the crown of his turbanned head. A sharp, hard twist and he heard the neck bones snap. He lowered the man to the floor and took his rifle.

He looked back at the baron struggling against the bonds that secured him to the chair. The image tickled his memory with a faint sense of irony, but he didn't have time to let the full picture come. *Later,* he told himself. *There'll be plenty of time later.*

As he closed the door to the small room and crossed the foyer to the main entrance, a voice in his head kept saying, *My blood. My responsibility.*

• • •

Batoor the orphan learned early on not to trust what people said to him. He also learned how to read faces and voices and body language. Even with his power to summon the spirit of the clouds, he would not have survived long enough to be rescued by von Strucker if he could not tell a lie from truth.

The Prussian had told him about the miracle of the elixir drawn from the veins of the man they had brought back from Germany. He had cut his own flesh and let Al Borak watch as the wound healed itself in seconds. So that much the Pashtun knew was true. But the rest of it? That the mujahideen could die and rise to fight again?

Maybe it was true. Maybe it was not. Maybe what he had shot into their arms was the true elixir that von Strucker gave to himself. Maybe it was not. Or maybe the dose was not enough. And maybe the stuff von Strucker had shot into Batoor's vein was not the real thing, if indeed any of this was real.

Al Borak did not know. But what he did know, with the sensitivity of a third-world orphan to those who held him in their power, was that von Strucker was done with him. Something had changed since the small man had come. Now the baron looked through Batoor, his eyes focused on some future that beckoned the Prussian the way paradise beckoned the sixteen fools who believed in the tales of perfumed gardens and willing maidens.

Whatever the future von Strucker saw gleaming on his horizon, there was no place in it for a Pashtun orphan with a peculiar power in his hands. Al Borak knew that for sure.

And would the baron casually dispose of him, to clear the board for his new game? Of that, Al Borak had no doubt. When they had been training the original thirty men from whom the final sixteen had come, he had helped bury the failures.

So after von Strucker had delivered his little speech in the banquet room, after he had given Al Borak the first injection, then left him to do the others, the Pashtun had done as he was ordered, putting the needle into each grinning man of the Green Fist. But he had not climbed into the truck. Instead he had told the men that he would meet them in the hospital morgue and lead them in the glorious last phase of Operation Severed Head.

"If I am delayed," he said, "Khan will take charge. And you will proceed without me."

Then he had led them in a shout of "God is great!" three times and the men had filed out to board the truck. Al Borak had closed the door of the banquet room, except for a crack through which he spied across the foyer of the mansion at the small room behind whose closed door the baron and his new favorite were now cooking up some kind of plan.

*We will see about that,* the Pashtun thought. If Operation Severed Head succeeded after all, Al Borak would appear, having survived and escaped, to share in the glory. If it did not succeed, he would still appear—to point the finger at the blue-eyed infidel who had sabotaged the mujahideen. Either way, Al Borak meant to secure his place with the Yemeni and the man in the faraway mountains who was his master.

He had learned long ago in the orphanage how to wait patiently and he stood and watched as Logan came in from outside, forced his way into the small room, and disarmed the guard. While von Strucker was calming the situation, Al Borak was replaying in his mind the ease with which the small man had taken the rifle away from the militiaman, and the casual contempt with which he had handed it back. He also thought about how the Canadian had survived the shock and fall from the truck on the road to Baghdad.

He was still thinking about it when the door to the small room opened silently and Logan efficiently broke the guard's neck, scooped up his rifle before it could hit the floor, and headed outside.

Al Borak watched him go, then went and opened the door of the small room. When the baron saw him, he began to make noises around the gag in his mouth. But the Pashtun ignored him. Instead he knelt and examined the Yemeni, finding him apparently unharmed, although he had clearly been the recipient of whatever had been in the empty hypodermic that lay near him on the floor.

Von Strucker made noises at him as he rose. Al

Borak looked down at him and was tempted to raise the spirit of the clouds. He started to let the warmth grow in his palms. Then came the sound of rifle fire from outside. He turned and ran for the door.

Seven militiamen had accompanied them from Basra. The group's commander had gone in the truck, to guide the Green Fist mujahideen to a point near the Green Zone. Logan had killed the one in the house. That left five, three of whom were guarding the compound's gate, their attention on the street outside. The Canadian had shot all three without warning, firing the dead guard's M-16 with the efficiency of a veteran combat soldier. When the Pashtun came out the front door, Logan was dragging one of the bodies out of the way so he could open the gate.

Al Borak stepped into concealment behind one of the portico's pillars. When the gate stood wide, Logan went to the remaining SUV parked near the fountain and opened its driver's door. He was just getting into the car when the two remaining militiamen, who had been stationed at the rear of the compound where a gate opened onto a service lane, came running around the corner of the house. One of them charged, screaming, at the small man, firing his weapon as he came. The other knelt, put his rifle to his shoulder, and aimed. The shot went true, and the Pashtun saw Logan's head jerk back and blood fly as the bullet struck his forehead.

Then, as if the bullet had been no more than a

thrown pebble, Logan snapped up his own weapon and shot the kneeling man through the head. As rounds from the charging man scarred the SUV's bulletproof windows, he calmly fired twice into the militiaman's chest.

*So it is true,* Al Borak said to himself as the mutant threw the rifle onto the front seat of the SUV and climbed behind the wheel. His mind raced. *Perhaps the mujahideen will truly awaken from death in the enemy hospital and strike their great blow. But who will get the credit?*

Even as these thoughts were crowding Al Borak's mind, Logan was starting the vehicle and the Pashtun was sprinting from the porch to the SUV, summoning the lightning as he ran. As the Canadian put the car into gear, the Pashtun slapped his palms to its metal body and released a full charge. The paint beneath his hands smoked and bubbled as the jolt of electricity shot through the SUV, frying every silicon chip that controlled its state-of-the-art systems. The engine died as Al Borak lifted his hands from the vehicle and he had the satisfaction of seeing the small man jerk and spasm as the electricity went through him.

The tall man rushed to the driver's door and yanked it open, meanwhile summoning a new charge. This time he wanted the Canadian grounded, not insulated from the earth by rubber tires as he had been on the truck. He would see if the mutant's healing powers could cope with flesh that had been cooked to carbon from within.

Logan found it all worked fine if he didn't think
about it. Or if he just thought about what needed to
be done, but left the actual doing of it to instinct. *Or
habit,* he thought as he lowered the dead guard to the
floor of the mansion's foyer and picked up his rifle.
Some part of him was highly trained, extremely competent at the business of killing. The fact that he
couldn't remember the training didn't seem to matter. When it was needed, it was there.

He went out the front door, spotted the three men
at the gate, and put them down with three three-
round bursts from the M-16. The weapon felt right in
his hands. He had done this all before.

He had cleared the gate and got it open and was
getting into the SUV when the other two arrived. The
bullet to his head rang his bell—it actually made a
metallic clanging sound inside his head—and he mar-
veled again at the strength of his bones. He shot the
men and got into the vehicle.

But then as he started its engine, his muscles locked
up as a heavy jolt of electricity surged through him.
When the electricity stopped, the vehicle was dead and
Logan himself was dazed by the shock. His muscles
twitched and jumped and he felt as if someone had
stuffed foam rubber into his cranial cavity.

As he shook his head to clear it, the driver's door
flew open and he was pulled out onto the crushed
white stone of the driveway. But even as he rolled, his

physical and mental equilibrium was coming back on line. He got his feet underneath him, feeling the muscles bunch in his forearms—and again feeling that sudden alien anxiety. It angered him. He growled, the sound deep in his chest, while his mind was telling him, *Enough of this!* and he knew he didn't give a damn about whatever would happen next.

He started to rise, his hands forming fists as they came clear of the gravel. Then he felt two hard palms slap the sides of his head and a fresh jolt of electricity shot through him like white fire. The soles of his boots smoked, his blood boiled in his veins, and every muscle spasmed as the grounded current raced through him and down into the earth.

His vision darkened around the edges, so that it was as if he were looking down a tunnel. He had been raising his fisted hands in front of him and now he saw them centered in his field of vision. Then, as the flesh of his forearms rippled and jerked, he was astonished to see three foot-long knives of gleaming metal shoot from between his knuckles—astonished, and then suddenly he was not surprised at all. *Of course,* he thought.

He was able to think because the blades had not shot out into empty air, but straight into the flesh of the tall man who had bent to clap his hands to Logan's head. Their points had pierced the Pashtun's pectoral muscles just in from the shoulder joints, ripping through the corded fibers as if they were tissue paper.

The man had staggered back, his arms gone slack and his hands falling away from Logan, taking their lightning with them.

In moments, the small man's own tissues had repaired the tears and burns that the jolt had caused and his head had cleared. He rose and looked at Al Borak, standing there with blood pouring from six deep gashes in his chest, his gray eyes full of the long-sighted gaze of a man in shock. Logan raised his right hand, turned it to examine the three deadly claws.

*Of course,* he thought again. The implanted panic reaction—the alien parasite someone had slipped into his mind—had lost its power, was gone, null and void. Logan still didn't know how he came to have metal sheathed claws, didn't know whether they were part of his mutation or something that had been grafted onto him by whoever had stolen his memories. But his body knew that he had had them a long time. And it knew how to use them.

He drew back his fist to send its claws through Al Borak's chest, but at that moment the man's clouded eyes closed and he toppled to the ground. Logan made a sound that dismissed the Pashtun with contempt and turned his mind back to what he had to do. He resheathed his claws and left the crumpled form in a spreading pool of blood. He went to the second SUV, parked behind the first. Its engine roared and he spewed gravel as he steered the heavy vehicle toward the open gate.

## Green Zone, Baghdad, the present

JORGE CARDERO'S LIEUTENANT WOULD NOT have enjoyed hearing the things that the specialist was muttering as he dug the ink pad and fingerprint forms from his army-issue briefcase in the morgue of the field hospital. The lieu himself should have been supervising the taking of prints from the sixteen dead hajjis, laid out side by side on the concrete floor. Instead, the officer had watched as the specialist had recorded the serial numbers of the M-16s, then he had made some excuse about taking the rifles to storage, scooped them up, and disappeared. Cardero knew that the lieutenant had really just dumped the weapons somewhere, then sloped off to get a peek at the UIP who was scheduled to come through the hospital's front door in just a few minutes. The enlisted man would have liked to have seen the commander in chief—hell, he'd voted for the man, which he suspected the lieutenant had not.

"But rank has its freaking privileges," he said, adding a detailed and inventive comment about what the lieutenant could do with his rank and his privileges. Then he sighed and knelt beside the first of the dead men, taking the corpse's wrist and reaching for the ink pad.

*Hey,* he thought, *this guy's awful warm for a—*

It was Jorge Cardero's last thought and it was never

finished. The hand that belonged to the wrist had formed itself into a stiff-fingered spike that jabbed straight into the specialist's Adam's apple. While he was struggling to get air through his shattered trachea and the swelling tissues of his throat, the hand came back again. This time the heel of the palm struck the base of the soldier's nose, snapping off the nasal bone and driving it straight into the frontal lobes of Cardero's brain. The body would twitch for a while, but the person that had inhabited it was gone forever.

Ismail Khan came fluidly to his feet and crouched as he scanned the morgue. The place was empty. He ran his hands over his bloodstained fatigue shirt, felt bullets shake loose from the cloth. He turned to the man lying beside him and shook him. "Wake up," he said. "Our moment is come."

## Mansour district, Baghdad, the present

LOGAN DROVE HARD, SWINGING THE SUV around corners on two screeching wheels, accelerating down the wide, straight avenues of the upscale Mansour district. Occasionally he took one hand off the wheel and flexed its arm, causing the gleaming claws to shoot from his hand, then retract, over and over. Each time he brought them out, they caused a little pain like fire in his knuckles, like being touched by a lit cigarette. But the flesh healed and the pain went away. Then he'd pull them in and flex them out again, and the arrival of the little pain was always like meeting an old forgotten friend. And the reflexive anxiety? That had been reduced to a tiny, squeaking pygmy mouse way off on the edge of his mind. *How did I ever let them take this from me?* he thought. *And just wait until I find the bastards.*

He was coming down a long straight stretch. Ahead at an intersection a white Toyota pickup was angled half across the road, and half a dozen rifle-toting men in Iraqi uniforms were in and around the vehicle. An officer raised his hand at the SUV's approach.

"No time," Logan said to the windshield. His foot pressed the gas pedal down and he hit three solid blasts on the horn.

The officer screamed an order and the rifles came up. Logan saw the muzzle flashes, then the tinted windshield suddenly showed a galaxy of small, white stars as the steel-jacketed rounds chipped the armored glass. Other rounds rang off the hood and reinforced bumper, but none penetrated to the engine compartment.

The Iraqis scattered as the SUV struck the corner of the pickup's front bumper and spun the Toyota out of the way. Logan fought the wheel as the heavy vehicle fishtailed from the impact. Then he got it settled down and hit the gas again.

• • •

Von Strucker struggled against the wire that bound him to the chair, but the mutant had done too good a job. The Yemeni lying on the floor at his feet, a pool of spittle forming beneath his slack mouth, could be no help. By now the mnemophage would have so blocked his mental pathways that he was effectively an infant and would not remember how to talk, let alone untie knots.

The original plan had been for Al Borak to send the Green Fist into the zone, then return to the mansion. Von Strucker had amended that plan, without telling the Pashtun about it, and had injected his second in command with a placebo. Now the baron regretted that decision. He should have kept the mutant to sell to someone who could use him. Although that was assuming that the Pashtun would have ever returned from the mission. The baron had no doubt that Logan would make every effort to foil his plan. As he had been tying the baron to the chair, he had muttered through clenched teeth, "My blood, you bastard! My blood!"

Over the course of his extended career, the Prussian had often left men tied to chairs, waiting for him to come and deliver their fate. He had never wondered how it felt to be in that position—he'd always had more important things to think about. Now he knew what those men had known, but he didn't feel that he was profiting from the knowledge.

He heard a noise from the other side of the closed door that led to the foyer. The gold-plated lever that worked the latch was jiggling. Then it rotated down and the door opened inward. Al Borak lay facedown in the doorway, his upraised hand falling from the handle as the door swung in. Behind him, the floor of the foyer was smeared by a trail of blood from the front entrance.

Now the Pashtun levered himself up onto his forearms, like a soldier crawling belly-down under enemy fire. Laboriously, he pulled himself into the small room, and von Strucker could see that the front of his shirt was soaked in red and that his face was ashen pale from loss of blood.

Weak, panting, Al Borak came forward, his legs and belly sliding on his own gore. The baron grunted around the gag in his mouth, but the Pashtun did not look up. He came steadily, slowly on, forcing his way past the comatose Yemeni, his dull eyes fixed on only one thing: the baron's carrying case, on the floor beside his chair.

He made it, weakly pulled apart the hinged case, his bloodless hands fumbling for one of the tubes of elixir, then for a hypodermic. His breath came in shallow gasps as he filled the syringe's barrel, then lay down on his side. With trembling fingers he brought the needle toward the crook of his elbow. But before he could insert the spike, his eyes rolled up in his head and he fainted.

The baron roared in rage and frustration behind the gag. Thrusting his body against his bonds, he tried to scoot the chair across the short distance to where Al Borak lay unconscious in a spreading pool of blood. There could not be much more left inside him, von Strucker knew. Soon it would be too little and then it would be too late for the baron.

The Pashtun's eyelids fluttered. Weakly he raised his head, focused dull eyes on the syringe in his failing hand, and brought its spike to his pale flesh. He pressed the plunger and the cloudy fluid was forced out of the barrel. Then his head slumped again, the needle fell from his nerveless fingers, and again the baron raged against his impotence.

Time ticked by. Al Borak did not move, but he continued to breathe. It seemed to von Strucker that the bleeding had at least slowed, perhaps stopped. More time passed and now the man's color seemed to have deepened. A minute later, the Pashtun took in a harsh, gasping breath. His eyes opened and the lackluster gaze quickly sharpened.

He levered himself half up, then pushed against the smeared floor until he was kneeling. His hands tore away the blood-soaked shirt, touched the wounds that were now closing rapidly. He looked at von Strucker and it was a hard look. Then his eyes went briefly to the Arab on the floor and he said, "What of him?"

The Prussian grunted. Al Borak got to his feet. He seemed to have recovered his full strength. He worked the gag free and the baron said, "Quick, untie me."

"What of him?" Al Borak said again.

"He got the memory wipe that should have been Logan's."

"Can it be undone?"

"There is an antidote," von Strucker said. "Now untie me. We must get away from here."

But the Pashtun's hard fingers came to pinch in the baron's cheeks, forcing his mouth open. The spit-soaked gag was crammed into his mouth again.

"First things first," Al Borak said. He gave himself another injection of the elixir. Then he was gone.

## Green Zone, Baghdad, the present

THE THREE-STORY HOSPITAL HAD BEEN BUILT for Saddam, his family, and favorites. Its administration, imaging, laboratory, and emergency departments were on the main floor; surgery, postop, and ICUs were on the second; and longer-term care wards and rehab were on the top floor. The morgue was in the basement, along with the laundry and storage areas.

Ismail Khan's orders were clear: they were to find their rifles, then remain undetected in the morgue until they heard the hubbub that would accompany the arrival of the target. They were then to wait long enough for the UIPs to take the elevators to the top floor, to make it more difficult for the target to escape.

Then they were to swarm up the fire stairs to the third floor and carry out the mission. Any of them who survived should scatter and try to find hiding places, though it was expected that the infidel would hunt them down.

Khan did not care about the consequences. Nor did the others. "Paradise," they whispered to each other as they waited behind the morgue's swinging double doors. They were not worried when they revived to find their rifles missing. In the autopsy suite next to the morgue they found heavy scalpels, knives, and a couple of big cleavers. They tested the edges, found them keen, and smiled at each other, whispering about the glorious rewards to come.

A steel-and-glass door across the hallway led to the fire stairs. Khan had sent a man halfway up the stairs to listen for the sounds that would tell him when to order the strike.

He put a finger to his lips to tell the men to be quiet. It would not be long now.

Major Jan Visser saw the SUV take the corner onto 14th of July Street on two wheels. When it thumped down onto all four wheels and rocketed toward his gate, he did not hesitate to yell "fire!" even as he brought his own rifle to his shoulder and sent a stream of 7.62-millimeter bullets at the vehicle. But the rounds bounced off the scarred paintwork and darkened glass.

"Come on!" the South African shouted to one of his men, who sat behind the wheel of an armored Humvee. The vehicle lurched forward in an attempt to block the gate, but the move came too late. The SUV did not decelerate as it swerved off the broad avenue and slammed directly into the heavy steel pipe, tearing it from its mounts before continuing into the gap between the blast walls, then crashing into the high concrete barrier that blocked the route beyond.

"Down!" Visser screamed to his men, who had scattered at the SUV's approach. They threw themselves face-first onto the sidewalk and pavement, or dove for cover behind anything that could shelter them from the blast they knew must come. Nobody drove a vehicle into a Green Zone checkpoint unless it was packed with explosives. The last time this had happened, a second vehicle—a cement truck whose huge rotating reservoir was loaded with the contents of looted artillery shells—had crashed through the gap made by the first blast, then blew itself up inside the zone.

Face pressed against the concrete, Visser waited for the blast he was sure would kill him. For some reason, he found himself counting the seconds. But when no explosion ripped apart the day, he looked up. The SUV was against the gate's rear blast wall, its front squashed in like an accordion and its windshield popped out and lying on the bent hood.

"Up!" the major ordered. He told the Australian

sergeant to check the wreck and set the rest of the men to watching the street for a follow-up.

"Nothing," the sergeant said. The nervous dog was sniffing at the vehicle's open door, but not excitedly wagging its tail as it always did when it smelled what it was trained to find.

"The driver?"

"The car's empty, Major," the Aussie said.

"Remote control?"

"Maybe. It's too messed up to tell." The sergeant passed his hand across his brow, wiping away sweat. "Hell of a day, isn't it, sir?"

Before Visser could answer, they heard the automatically aimed machine guns beyond the blast wall open up. "Check that!" the South African said.

But when the sergeant reported back moments later, he said there were no bodies in the killing ground. "Might have been some drops of blood on one wall," he said, "but if the crash buggered up the electronics and started those machine guns firing independently, I don't reckon on going in there to find out."

Visser weighed it up. First the sixteen idiots offering themselves as targets, now somebody crashes an unmanned vehicle into the gate. "Maybe somebody's just practicing," he said. "Call the techs and get the machine guns checked. And intelligence will want to look at the car."

The president and his Secret Service security detail, accompanied by embassy staff, military brass, and the media pool, filled all three elevators that came up to the top floor of the hospital. As they emerged from the three cars, an army doctor stepped forward to be their guide to the wards where the commander in chief would present the Purple Hearts. But as he opened his mouth to say "Welcome, Mr. President," they all heard a rattle of distant rifle fire, followed by a heavy crash.

The Secret Service men had left their machine pistols at the embassy. The president's media handlers didn't think it looked good for him to be surrounded by heavily armed bodyguards when he was visiting wounded soldiers and marines. Now they drew their nine-millimeter Glock pistols and positioned themselves around the president. The senior agent, the one the president had called Frank, spoke into the microphone on the inside of his left wrist, "Bluepoint, this is Eagle One. I want the nearest helicopter sent to the hospital roof, right now." Then he turned to the three-star general whose command included the Green Zone and said, "Are there armed troops in this building?"

"Just that Marine Corps guard of honor that saluted in the lobby," the general said. "But they'll only have one clip apiece."

"Get them up here. Tell them to come by the fire stairs."

The three-star looked as if he didn't enjoy being

ordered around by a civilian, but then the moment passed and he began issuing orders.

The senior Secret Service man turned to the president and said, "Sir, I think we should go up on the roof. I have a helicopter coming."

But the man in the blue suit said, "Frank, that ruckus sounds like it's pretty far off, and I came to see the men and women on this floor." He turned to the doctor and said, "Doctor, would you like to lead the way?"

The mujahideen in the stairwell heard the commotion above when the target and his party arrived. He reported back to Ismail Khan in the morgue.

"God is great," the Pakistani said.

He crept out into the corridor and put his ear to the concrete wall that ran down toward the elevator well at the center of the structure. He heard the heavy hum of all three electric motors and the sounds that the cars made as they rose in the shafts.

He returned to the morgue and said, "He is here. Make ready."

Each man of the Green Fist reached to the small of his back to tear free a small patch of surgical tape. Beneath were two gray pills. One of them fetched water from a sink and they solemnly took the stimulants. They waited a moment for the drugs to take hold, then, eyes glittering with excitement, they took up their weapons.

"Come," Khan said and led them out into the corridor. He opened the door to the fire stairs and listened. He was about to begin climbing when he heard the sound of distant gunfire, followed by a heavy impact that might have been an explosion.

Then came silence. He paused to think, although the stimulants now coursing through his blood argued for action. But he reminded himself that this mission must not fail. He would take the time to make sure. He listened, but when he heard no more weapons fire, Khan decided that nothing had happened to change his orders. Then he heard boots in the stairwell above him, climbing fast. And then came the *whup-whup* of a helicopter approaching.

"Now!" he whispered to the mujahideen. "God willing, we strike!"

The men of the Green Fist charged up the stairs.

The hospital had two wings extending from a central core. It was only luck that the first ward the president was to visit was at the end of the wing that stood three stories above the laundry instead of the morgue. But it was also only luck that made the marine honor guard choose the fire stairs that were at the end of the wing that contained the morgue. They were between the second and third floors when they heard boots coming up the concrete stairs behind them—coming fast.

The veteran gunnery sergeant in charge of the detail didn't wait to find out if whoever was coming up after him was friend or foe. Friendly fire was a risk a soldier had to take. He turned and fired a three-round burst at an angle down into the stairwell so that the rounds ricocheted off the concrete walls.

The seven other marines in the honor guard turned and leveled their weapons down the stairs while their gunney waited to hear what would come next. If it was "hold your fire!" he would wait to see who came around the corner.

If it was anything else, they would give them hell.

He didn't have long to wait. A shout of *"Allahu akbar!"* came from below, then the rapid clatter of bootsteps.

"Fire!" The marines opened up, filling the narrow well with the blasts of riflery and the whining of ricochets. "Keep firing! Back your way up the stairs!" the gunney said.

The honor guard wasn't geared for real combat, none of them slung around with extra clips of ammunition. The noncom wanted them up and behind a steel fire door they could barricade, before they had nothing left to throw at whoever was coming up the stairs.

Three of the Green Fist had died in the withering fire from up the stairs. Four had been wounded, though their wounds might heal if they lived long enough. The baron had warned them that the elixir would probably allow them to rise from the dead only once.

He'd said he had had to balance the dosage—giving them enough to recover from the first death, but keeping that recovery slow enough that they would already be in the morgue before they revived.

Ismail Khan did not care whether he lived or died. Paradise awaited. He cared only that he fulfill the mission. "Gassim, Ahmed, " he said, "pick up one of the martyrs. Hafiz and Yussuf, pick up another. Hold them before us as barriers. Now, God willing, let us fight!"

"God is great!" the mujahideen cried as the bullets from above thudded into their comrade's dead flesh. They went up the stairs.

"Fix bayonets!" shouted the gunnery sergeant as he fired the last round from the single clip in his M-16. A couple of his men squeezed off final shots, then reached for the brilliantly polished blades that were part of any honor guard's gear.

The fight had been too fast. They would not make it through the third-floor door in time. So they would fight and hold them on this side.

"Here they come!" said one of the marines. He spat to one side and set himself.

Below them, two dead men came around the last corner of the stairwell, moving fast. Then, as the men holding them realized that there would be no more rifle fire, the corpses were flung aside and the mujahideen, knives and cleavers flashing, charged.

*No guns,* was the gunney's thought. *We'll stop 'em.*
Then he had time only for, *My God, they're—* before
the attackers were upon them, like a ninja movie on
fast-forward, flicking aside the out-thrust bayonets
and stabbing, slicing, hacking so fast that the gunney's
throat was cut and he was falling forward down the
steps even as the word "quick!" was forming in his
mind.

The three-star general hadn't fired a shot in anger
since he'd been a young field officer in Vietnam's Ia
Drang Valley, but Baghdad was a war zone and he carried a loaded sidearm. He'd ordered the doctors and
nurses to barricade the doors to the wards, then he'd
gathered his effectives—three Secret Service agents,
one of them a woman, a Marine Corps colonel, and
the army captain who was his own aide-de-camp—in
the wide space in front of the elevators at the near end
of the corridor from which the firing had come.

It was a long, straight hallway with nothing in it but
closed doors. Whoever came out of the fire stairs at the
far end would have no cover for as long as it took
them to run the hundred and twenty feet to the elevators. The general took up a position at one end of the
wall, standing and aiming his pistol toward the distant
stairwell. The marine colonel placed himself on the
other side of the gap and drew his own sidearm, a
pearl-handled Colt .45 that was no longer service
issue.

The colonel saw the general looking at the weapon. "It was my old man's," he said.

"Good enough for me," said the three-star.

Two of the Secret Service agents knelt beneath the military men, while the third lay on his belly to fire directly down the middle of the hallway.

The captain stood behind his boss. He was unarmed. "One of us goes down, Charley," the general said. "You get the weapon."

"Yes, sir."

And then they waited.

But not for long. The firing from the fire stairs stopped. Moments later, the faraway door to the stairwell eased open and a face peeked out, then rapidly withdrew.

"Ready now," the general said. "Make them count."

The door was yanked open from within. For a moment, the general's heart leaped up as two marines from the honor guard came through the opening. Then he swore as the reality of what he was seeing struck home and he heard the cries of "*Allahu akbar!*"

"Open fire!"

The reek of cordite and the pop of pistols, punctuated by the harsher sound of the colonel's .45, filled the space before the elevators. But the enemy came on so fast, crouching behind the bodies of the American dead held up on the points of their own bayonets. The Secret Service agents could shoot, and the colonel had lost none of his skill, but a charge that should have taken at least thirty seconds, under fire and burdened by corpses, was over before any of those with pistols could squeeze off three aimed shots.

Some of the attackers went down, tumbling and sprawling on the tiles. But the others came on, at impossible speed, to toss aside the shielding corpses at the last moment and fling themselves upon the defenders. And suddenly the general's world was a blur of limbs and blades, of blood and screams, of white teeth grinning in cruel faces. And he was sinking to the floor, holding his ripped belly, and seeing at least four of the killers racing away down the other corridor.

"Move!" yelled the head of the president's security detail as he and one other Secret Service man pushed their charge up the flight of fire stairs that led to the roof. The man he was raising his voice to was the commander in chief, but that wasn't going to stop him from doing what the job required.

The stairs ended at a trapdoor that damn well better not be locked, Frank was thinking. Below and behind him, down in the long third-floor hallway that ran the length of the hospital wing, he could hear firing—single shots from nine-millimeter Glock pistols—and the screams of men dying. But he could also hear cries of "*Allahu akbar!*" And they were getting closer.

Above him, he could hear the sound of the military chopper he had called for. If it was a gunship with a door gunner, they would be fine. If it was a medivac, this situation could still be too close to call. The Secret Service man in front reached the trapdoor to the roof. It was secured only by a sliding bolt. The man threw the bolt and pushed—and the door opened.

*So far so good,* Frank thought. The chopper sounded comfortingly louder as he pushed the president of the United States out into the open air.

The helicopter was coming in, and, *dammit, it's unarmed,* the head of the security detail was thinking. *And only the pilot aboard.* He signaled the other agent to be ready to bundle the president through its open hatch the moment it was low enough. Meanwhile, he kept his eye on the trapdoor through which they had come, his pistol ready in his hand.

"Frank!" came the other agent's voice.

The chief risked a quick look in the direction of the incoming chopper. It all looked okay. Then he saw what had alarmed the other man. Someone was clinging to the underside of the aircraft, arms and legs wrapped around one of the skids. As the copter swung over the building, still twenty feet above the roof, the figure let go—legs first, then hands—to plummet straight down to the tarred surface.

The man landed on his feet with a *thump* that Frank felt as a vibration through the soles of his shoes. The impact should have broken both of the man's short legs, but he simply rolled hard and came up blowing air out of his cheeks, as if he'd stubbed his toe and was waiting for the pain to go away. His clothes were full of holes, as if he had been used for target practice by a squad of machine gunners. Smears of blood surrounded many of the holes, but he seemed unscathed.

Then, his hands held in front of him in a gesture that said he was not looking for trouble, the newcomer took a step toward Frank. But that meant he was taking a step toward the president of the United States under conditions that didn't allow anybody to take such a step. So whatever he was or wasn't looking for, what he got was what the training manuals called for: a pistol round in the center of the visible mass.

The slug struck the man's breastbone—Frank was rated expert as a marksman—but it didn't put him down. Instead, he plucked the metal out of his chest and tossed it down. Then he said, "Don't do that. It hurts."

Frank wasn't taking advice right now on how to do his job. He sighted the pistol on point of the widow's peak that descended into the man's forehead and put calculated pressure on the trigger. Behind him he could hear the chopper racketing louder than ever and feel its wind throwing him forward. *I'll have to adjust for that,* he was thinking.

The small man was taking something from a pants pocket and swallowing it. *Enjoy your last meal,* Frank thought.

Then behind the target, the trapdoor sprang open and four men in bloodstained Iraqi Army fatigues swarmed onto the roof and raced screaming toward him—*No, toward the chopper,* Frank thought as he swung the pistol toward them and fired.

He got one, the man went down, but the other three had already closed the distance between the trapdoor and the man who had leapt from the helicopter.

But that was as far as they got.

Ismail Khan recognized Logan right away. For a moment he wondered if the baron had sent him here to help, then he saw that that was not the case. As the target's bodyguard turned, so slowly, and fired his pistol at the mujahideen, the small man turned to face the four of them and the look in his eyes left no doubt as to what he intended to do.

*But God will not let you,* Khan was thinking even as he registered Gassim's taking of a bullet in the chest from the bodyguard's gun. The death did not matter. What mattered was the bloodstained bayonet that the Pakistani had taken from one of the marines in the stairwell. He would use it on the man with the gun, leaving Logan to be disposed of by his two comrades who still survived.

Khan saw it all, knew just how it would happen. He would rip open the one who had just shot Gassim, then he would run to where the helicopter—its blades rotating lazily—was just about to kiss the surface of the roof. He would kill the second bodyguard who was even now, but far too slowly, squatting to boost his master into the aircraft.

Then with a shout of "God is great!" Khan would seize the enemy, throw him down, and thrust the bayonet into his heart. Then he would slice off the infidel's head. He would carry it to the edge of the building where its rear overlooked the Tigris River. Holding it by the hair he would cry out in a voice to carry across the city of the Caliphs, "There is no god but God, and Muhammad is his Prophet!"

Then he would fling the head of the Great Satan into the eternal waters. After that he would sit down and await his martyrdom and then the perfumed gardens of paradise.

His heart bursting with the sacred joy of holy war, Ismail Khan brandished the bayonet and rushed forward.

Logan would have gone for the one with the bayonet, except that when he moved to do so, he saw that the two coming right behind the Pakistani were now rushing straight at him.

When they had come out of the trapdoor they had been moving quickly, just as he remembered from watching the training exercise. But the baron's pills were also fast-acting. No sooner did they hit his stomach than he felt the effects—a cold ripple seemed to pass through his skeletal muscles and suddenly everything was slowing, the *whup-whup* of the landing helicopter behind him suddenly sounded like half speed, then quarter speed, then as slow as the leaky tap back in his condo in Ottawa that dripped lazily into the bathroom sink all night.

The two Arabs were coming at him, one with a cleaver, the other with some kind of big autopsy knife. Their faces showed a happy expectation of an easy job, soon to be out of the way.

But Logan flexed his forearms, felt the thin pain tear his hands, then fade as soon as it appeared. And when the men came at him, one slashing with the cleaver, the other stabbing upward with the knife, he made no move to block the blows.

Instead, he swept his hands forward and up, palms raised, so that his claws entered their bellies and sliced upward through flesh and gristle and even bone. He cut through them as if they were made of nothing more substantial than Jell-O.

*I thought so,* he said to himself, even as he was turning to go after Khan. He didn't know what the metal was that came from his hands, but he was getting comfortable with the idea that he could cut his way into and out of anything.

The Secret Service man who had shot him was down on the tarred surface, the hand that had held the pistol slashed to uselessness and his chest laid open by a second wound. Still he was reaching with his other hand for the fallen Glock.

Khan was already at the helicopter, hacking at the other agent. Logan could see a red furrow along the side of the Pakistani's face and half his ear was gone—the Secret Service agent must have got off a shot that had almost done the job.

But now the agent was dead and the Pakistani was dragging the man in the blue suit out of the helicopter's open bay. His face was alive with cruel glee as he threw the victim down and raised the bayonet above his head.

"*Allahu*—" he cried, but the "*akbar*" never came. Logan's claws flashed, sending both hand and weapon spinning off while blood fountained from the stump.

"My regards to the virgins," the mutant said, then he thrust three blades through the side of the Pakistani's neck and sawed sideways. *Like a hot knife through butter,* he thought as the mujahideen's head toppled from the severed neck and rolled to land nose-down on the tar.

Logan flexed and the claws disappeared, the torn flesh instantly restoring itself. He reached down to help the president of the United States to rise. At least he assumed it was the president. He wasn't sure he recognized the face. *But people always look different on TV,* he thought.

The man in the suit was staring at him. Then his eyes flicked down to Logan's hands. "You better get on the chopper," the Canadian shouted over the noise of the rotors. "This might not be over."

He put a hand on the man's arm and lifted him into the copter.

"I know who you are," the president said. "Code name Wolverine."

Then the chopper was lifting and pulling away, too late for Logan to jump aboard, too late for him to do anything but yell into the wind, "What? What does that mean?"

But the aircraft was going, going, gone. He watched it dwindle in size as it banked and headed toward the big domed building that flew the Stars and Stripes. Behind him, the wounded Secret Service man was saying something.

"What?" Logan said, turning. But suddenly he was convulsing as a lightning bolt surged through his body, the energy bringing a fiery pain that passed from his head down to his heels. Its heat melted the tar beneath his soles.

Two hard hands had gripped the sides of his head. The power continued to pour agony throughout his body. He could smell his hair burning beneath Al Borak's palms. He could feel the saliva boiling in his mouth. Again the darkness was creeping in from the sides of his vision, the light narrowing to a circle that kept getting smaller.

And still the energy kept pouring through him, till he wondered, *How much more of this can I take?* His mind didn't know. And for all the confidence that his body seemed to have in its own power, he had a feeling that he'd never been subjected to sustained electrical shock of this magnitude for this long.

Then he heard, as if from far away, a small *pop* and the hands left him, taking the pain away. He staggered, his eyes not yet able to tell him where the edge of the roof was, so that he almost toppled over into the water below. Then his vision recovered, along with his strength, and he looked to see what had caused Al Borak to release him.

The tall man was reaching over his own shoulder, down the back of his shirt, to pluck something from his flesh. His hand came back with a nine-millimeter round between his thumb and forefinger. He looked at it, then tossed it aside. He glanced at the wounded Secret Service man, but the agent had done all he could do, squeezing off one shot before fainting from shock and blood loss.

Al Borak turned his attention back to Logan.

"It's all over," the smaller man said. He gestured with his thumb to the distant helicopter. "He's out of reach."

The taller man shrugged. "You say, that time, we should try, each one and the other. Could be interesting."

"I remember that."

"How about now?"

It was Logan's turn to shrug. "I got other things to do. People to see."

"After today," said the man who used to be Batoor

the orphan, "I got nothing." He spread his hands, and blue sparks danced between them. "Except this, and you."

He crouched, his hands extended before him like a wrestler's, and came forward.

The now familiar little pain lanced momentarily through Logan's hands. He circled warily, then flicked a clawed hand at the Pashtun. Two things happened: he got a solid shock down one arm; and the wound he opened up in Al Borak's forearm closed almost as soon as it began to bleed.

"You've been taking our friend's special medicine," Logan said.

The other man smiled. "I want it to be like you say—'interesting.' "

"Well, then," Logan said, "this ought to interest the hell out of you." He lunged forward, arms straight, claws point first. The six blades tore into the Pashtun's chest and sprang out of his back, slicing flesh and piercing bone as if it were balsa wood. Al Borak screamed in pain and rage, but his arms reflexively closed on the smaller man's neck and the spirit of the clouds burst from him as never before.

Logan's teeth ground against each other and his eyeballs felt as if they might be forced from their sockets as the force of the discharge boiled the tissues of his brain. He had lost control of his limbs but that no longer mattered because the momentum of his rush carried both of them back over the edge of the roof.

They tumbled as they fell, Logan's greater weight putting him on the bottom, so that his back struck the narrow strip of riverbank below. But his claws were wedged deep into Al Borak's torso, and the Pashtun continued to pour his energy into the Canadian, as they bounced, then rolled, then toppled over the top of the stone wall that confined the Tigris.

The water was silty and deep, and the Tigris could get cold in a Baghdad December. But the important thing, Logan thought as they sank into its murky depths, was that this river was no friend to the man who was impaled on his claws. He felt the tall man convulse as he himself had convulsed when Al Borak's lightning had gone through him.

Then the current was bumping them along the bottom, plowing them through silt and waterlogged wood, and occasionally smashing them against blocks of stone that had probably lain there long enough to interest an archaeologist. After a while, the rigidity went out of the other man and he hung limp in Logan's grip.

The Canadian kicked against the river bottom and sent them both rising toward the surface. As the light brightened, he could see that the Pashtun's gray eyes were open, that he was even conscious. Enough of the elixir stolen from Logan's blood was in his veins to have kept him from drowning or from shocking himself to death.

Logan's head broke into the air. He filled his lungs

and dove deep into the river, taking the Pashtun with him. He felt with his feet along the bottom until he found a place where there were plenty of stones. Then he freed Al Borak from the spikes that held him. The man tried to swim upward, but he wasn't fast enough.

Logan used his greater weight to hold Al Borak down. He pressed him into the cold ooze of the Tigris, then piled stones on top of the Pashtun until he had made a good-size underwater cairn. A couple of times, he broke off to rise to the surface and fill his lungs, then dove down to continue the work. As he heaped the stones up, a voice from the back of his mind said, *If a job's worth doing, it's worth doing well.*

Logan wondered whose voice it was. Then he got back to work.

## Mansour district, Baghdad, the present

WOLFGANG FREIHERR VON STRUCKER HAD fallen asleep in the chair, worn-out from the effort of trying to scoot it across the little dining room and out into the foyer. He had hoped that the front doors might have been open and that he might somehow attract the attention of a passerby. But when he finally got beyond the small room he found the outer doors locked.

He awoke when the gag was pulled from his mouth. But his moment of hope ended when he saw the face of Logan looking down at him. The mutant's eyes were hard and dark as volcanic glass.

"We need to talk," he said.

"I only wanted to help you," von Strucker said.

"Good," said Logan. "You can start by telling me who I am."

"I don't know."

"Wrong answer."

"I never did."

"For both our sakes," Logan said. "I hope that's not true. Because, if it isn't, I'm going to be unhappy. But by the time we establish to my satisfaction that it's not true, you're going to be downright miserable."

The baron swore to him that he could not tell Logan what he wanted to hear. But he promised to drop all other concerns and use all his resources to find out. While he was making these statements, the mutant brought over an end table and set it down near the chair. Then he went into the dining room and returned with the carrying case. There were still several tubes containing the elixir and he filled the hypodermic from one of them.

"The thing about being me," he said as he squirted a jet of cloudy fluid from the needle's tip and bent over the baron's arm, "is that you have to know how to suffer. Being able to recover fast doesn't do anything to stop the pain. You heal, all right—but first you hurt."

He shot the stuff into von Strucker's vein.

"I figure we've got a lot of time before anybody comes to check on the house," he said. "But I'm anxious to get started."

The baron watched in horror as the small man flexed his arms and three gleaming claws sheathed in adamantium sprang from each hand.

As he moved toward von Strucker, he said, "Now, you just won't believe the things I can do with these."

"Please," said the baron.

Logan laid the tip of one claw against the corner of von Strucker's left eye. "What does 'Code name: Wolverine' mean?"

A great wave of relief washed through the Prussian. Even buried in the Empty Quarter, one heard things. He would be able to answer the mutant's first question. "Wolverine," he said, "is a member of a group of mutants known as the X-Men."

The name rang an echo somewhere deep in Logan's being. He withdrew the claw from beside the German's eye, and saw the man's gaze follow the movement of the gleaming length of razor-edged adamantium.

"I've heard he has claws," von Strucker said.

"So I could be this Wolverine?"

"You could," von Strucker said. "You very definitely could."

"And these X-Men, what do they do?"

"They help other mutants, especially young ones.

There's some kind of school, run by a man named Charles Xavier."

That name almost called up an image of a face, but the features would not come into focus. Still, an almost animal sense of familiarity welled up from the bottom of Logan's mind. He felt he knew a man called Charles Xavier. And the man was not his enemy, might even be a friend.

Regardless, he now had a new lead to follow.

"Where is this school?" he asked the man in the chair.

"Somewhere in the United States," von Strucker said. "They don't advertise the location."

Logan set the claw back against the corner of the German's eye and said, "You're not being a big help."

Then he saw the man swallow nervously and watched an expression of indecision flicker across von Strucker's face. "Looks to me like you're trying to decide whether or not to tell me something. My advice is to spill whatever you've got before I have to dig for it."

He pressed with the point of the claw, following as the man tried to move his head away from the needle tip.

"All right, all right!" von Strucker said. "I'll tell you!"

The small man eased up on the pressure but kept the claw against the German's face. "I'm listening."

"When we came here," von Strucker said, speaking fast, "I still wasn't completely sure what I wanted to do with you. I asked the Arab to bring the mnemophage that would wipe your memory. But I also asked him to bring the antidote." He swallowed again. "It's in the television room."

Logan stepped back and studied the man. "You expect me to shoot myself up with another one of your concoctions?" He trailed the tip of one claw down the baron's chest, slicing through clothing to score the flesh beneath.

The German twitched and gasped. "Even if it was a massive dose of poison it wouldn't do me any good! Five minutes later you'd be back to normal and I'd still be strapped into this chair!"

Logan thought about it and conceded the point. "But what if it's a superdose of memory eater? What if I lose what few memories I've managed to recover?"

He saw the German thinking hard. Then von Strucker looked up and said, "Write yourself a note and pin it to my chest. Let it say, 'If you don't know who you are, kill this man.' "

The mutant examined the proposition from every angle he could think of. "There's still some risk," he said.

"For me, too," said von Strucker. "You'll remember what passed between us at Höllenfeuer."

"I already do," Logan said, and saw the German's Adam's apple go up and down again. But a voice from the back of his head was telling him, *No risk, no reward.* He sheathed his claws and went into the TV room, found a small flat case on a side table, and opened it to reveal a hypodermic full of a blue liquid.

There was paper and a pen in the family dining room. He wrote himself a note, using the exact words that the German had suggested—except to the phrase "kill this man" he added the word "slowly." He showed it to von Strucker and received only a shrug in reply.

He pinned the paper to the man's chest, then took up the hypodermic, squirting some out of the needle to remove any air bubbles. Then he set the tip against the vein in the crook of his elbow and put his thumb on the plunger.

For a moment he paused. The thought came again that he might have done terrible things. He had no doubt he had killed men and women. For all he knew, behind him lay a bloody trail of slaughter, of the guilty and the innocent both, a heap of torn bodies that were his doing.

Did he want to know? he asked himself. And from deep inside came the answer: *Yes. A man does what he has to and lives with the consequences.*

He pushed the spike into the vein and squeezed the blue liquid into his body. The stuff burned as it surged through his system. He could feel it climbing his arm to his shoulder, now into his neck and now hitting his brain.

And all at once, there it was. All of it. Faces and names, places and events, the dead and the living, the good he had managed to do and the evil that he had been part of. The blood. The pain.

Charles Xavier. Jean Grey. Mariko. Roanoke. Weapon X. Alpha Flight.

It did not come back to him. It had always been there, and now he came back to it.

He dropped the hypodermic on the table and looked at von Strucker. The bound man said, "I told you the truth. Now you know who you are."

"Yes," said Logan, "I do."

"Then will you let me go? This will not be a good place for me in a little while."

Logan remembered the little room in the *kommandantur* at Höllenfeuer, remembered being left nailed to a table.

"No," he said. He headed for the door.

As he left, he was thinking, *I know who I am, and I know what I can do.* He also knew who had stolen his memories and why. And he knew exactly what he was going to do about it.

## About the Author

Hugh Matthews is a pen name of the fantasy and science fiction author Matthew Hughes. His web page is at www.archonate.com.